D0330394

THE LAST SECRET

ALSO BY LYNN SHOLES & JOE MOORE

The Grail Conspiracy

FORTHCOMING BY LYNN SHOLES & JOE MOORE

Indigo Ruby

A COTTEN STONE MYSTERY

THE LAST SECRET

LYNN SHOLES & JOE MOORE

FIRST EDITION
First Printing, 2006

Book design by Donna Burch
Cover design by Kevin R. Brown

Midnight Ink, an imprint of Llewellyn Publications

Library of Congress Cataloging-in-Publication Data

Sholes, Lynn, 1945–
The last secret: a Cotten Stone mystery / Lynn Sholes & Joe Moore.
p. cm. — (Cotten Stone mysteries series; bk. #2)
ISBN-13: 978-0-7387-0931-4
ISBN-10: 0-7387-0931-X
1. Women journalists—Fiction. 2. Good and evil—Fiction. I. Moore, Joe, 1948–
II. Title. III. Series.

PS3619.H646L37 2006
813'.6—dc22 2006046244

Midnight Ink
Llewellyn Publications
2143 Wooddale Drive, Dept. 0-7387-0931-X
Woodbury, MN 55125-2989, U.S.A.
www.midnightinkbooks.com

Printed in the United States of America

The authors wish to thank the following for their assistance in adding a sense of realism to this work of fiction.

Capt. Jennifer Faubert
Public Affairs
North American Aerospace Defense Command

Dr. Wayne D. Pennington, PhD.
Professor of Geophysical Engineering
Michigan Technological University

Serafin M. Coronel-Molina
Department of Spanish & Portuguese Languages & Cultures
Princeton University

Deanna Wesolowski
Classics Department
Marquette University

A special thanks to:
Harriet Cooper
Lee Jackson

Satan; so call him now, his former name
is heard no more in heaven.

—JOHN MILTON
PARADISE LOST, BOOK V, LINE 658

PROLOGUE

SINCE THE DAWN OF time, there have been mysteries, unexplained phenomena, and strange occurrences that have haunted mankind. Some could be attributed to nature or the sciences. But a few myths—those passed down through generations—continue to persist even to the present. A few have never been explained.

One comes from Genesis in the Old Testament and deals with a race of giants called the Nephilim—the Fallen Ones. Cast out by God for siding with Lucifer in the Great Battle for Heaven, the Nephilim were condemned to walk the earth in eternal damnation—able neither to die nor ever to enter Heaven again. Down through the ages, the Fallen Ones adapted to the ways of man in appearance and behavior until their presence was all but forgotten.

Led by Satan, the Nephilim meticulously planned for the day they would strike back at God and take away the one thing he treasured most, his prized creation: man.

The time for the final conflict was approaching. The gathering Dark Army of the Nephilim prepared. But one thing stood in their way. The only human ever to share their legacy and their blood. Cotten Stone had stopped them once before. The Fallen Ones would not make the same mistake again.

SHOOTDOWN

00:20:15

THE PASSENGER IN SEAT 2K in the business-class section of the Virgin Atlantic Airbus A340 stared through thick eyeglasses at the cockpit door. Only ten seconds before, his head had shot up from his copy of *Newsweek* at the sound of a loud bang coming from the cockpit.

Now, along with those around him, he sat stunned as the pilot's words blared from the intercom.

"This is Captain Krull. We are experiencing technical difficulties. Everyone remain seated."

The captain had made other announcements during the flight from London to New York. But this time his voice sounded stressed, edgy.

A flight attendant moved cautiously from the galley that separated first class and the cockpit. She stood silently in front of the heavily reinforced flight deck, still holding a towel that she had been using to clean a stain from her apron. The passenger in 2K followed her gaze to the lettering on the middle of the cockpit door, which read: *Restricted area. No admittance during flight.*

As he watched, the flight attendant pulled a handset from the wall and pushed a button that he assumed connected her to the cockpit. She spoke into the receiver and waited for a reply. He saw her facial expression change as she listened. Then, slowly, she hung up the handset and covered her mouth with her palm. Her face paled as she turned toward the passengers.

The man nudged his glasses up the bridge of his nose and started to stand.

"Please stay in your seat, sir," she said.

"What's going on?" a woman called out.

"What the hell was that noise?" another passenger asked.

Despite her order, passenger 2K rose. "Is there something wrong with the plane?" he asked.

"No, the aircraft is fine," she answered, still seemingly trying to digest what she had just heard.

"Are we being hijacked?" he asked.

She bit her bottom lip. "Captain Krull says he shot the copilot and is about to kill himself." She took a step backward into the galley. "There's no way to get into the cockpit and stop him."

00:12:06

"Captain Krull, this is Thomas Wyatt." Tall and trim in faded jeans and a denim shirt, Wyatt stood on the front porch of his cottage overlooking the dark waters of Alligator Lake in the backwoods of North Florida. "Can you hear me?" he said into the satellite phone.

No response.

"Captain, I'm here to help you."

Static.

Wyatt knew there were at least a hundred people listening to the call that had been routed directly into the aircraft's communications system. He pictured groups of military and civilians at the Department of Homeland Security, the Pentagon, DoD, NORAD, the FAA, and countless other agencies leaning toward the speakers of their electronic devices. And he was acutely aware that he had only a short time before things would turn tragic. Virgin Atlantic Flight 45 was squawking a 7500 hijack code and would not be allowed to land in or even approach New York with a suicidal pilot at the controls.

Pressing the phone to his ear, Wyatt said, "Captain, no matter what brought you to this moment, there's still time to turn back. This is not only about you, Captain, but about two hundred and eighty innocent people onboard your plane. They don't deserve to die. Whatever issue you have, they are not responsible. Let's put it into the hands of experts who can solve it for you."

Wyatt glanced at his watch. He knew that two F-18 Hornets were vectored to intercept the airbus. They were under explicit rules of engagement regarding a 7500 code: force the plane to divert to a secure landing location or, if necessary, fire upon the aircraft and shoot it down. The airbus, big and lumbering, would present no challenge for the fighter pilots.

00:11:04

"Captain, you are a seventeen-year veteran," Wyatt said, glancing at a three-page fax in his hand. "Your record is one other pilots aspire to achieve. You have a family—twin ten-year-old girls. Are you ready to leave them fatherless? Taking the lives of those innocent passengers onboard would affect hundreds, if not thousands, of lives as their friends and relatives grieve. And if you take this aircraft down with you, what about the lives on the ground? Why don't you tell me what you want—I'll do everything in my power to help you get it. It's not too late."

Wyatt knew there were usually three reasons someone takes hostages: martyrdom, murder, or suicide. The information he had been given clearly indicated number three. And number three was Thomas Wyatt's specialty.

00:10:19

"Captain, we're running out of time here." He pressed his palm to his forehead as he looked out over the glassy surface of the lake that reflected the tall pines and palmetto thickets surrounding it. His cottage was the only one for twelve miles. Wyatt managed to retreat to it a few times a year to relax and fish. There would be no fishing today.

"Captain Krull, the world is a tough place. I know. Maybe the others don't understand what stress can do to a man. But I do."

Thomas Wyatt scanned the faxes once more. There was nothing in Krull's profile that he could determine might have made the pilot go over the edge. No marital or financial difficulties. No drug or alcohol abuse. And that made Wyatt's task more problematic. He had nothing to hook onto, nothing to target to convince the pilot that Wyatt was his friend—perhaps the only one he had right now. Wyatt needed Krull's trust, but without finding something he could use to lead the pilot into conversation, Krull would never see him as an ally. That was bad news. There would be little chance of talking him down.

"Captain Krull," Wyatt said, knowing this was his last opportunity to deter the pilot from whatever plan he had. "There are F-18 fighter jets approaching your aircraft from the rear. One is about to pull alongside and signal you to decrease your airspeed, drop to ten thousand feet, and follow him to an alternative landing site. Do you understand?"

The silence was as empty as Wyatt's hopes. He looked at his watch again. "Captain?"

00:09:25

"Oh God!" a woman screamed from a few rows behind where passenger 2K sat. She pointed out the window. "They're going to shoot us down!"

Within the last few moments, the anxiety level in the airbus grew from whispered concerns to panic. Now, as they all glared in disbelief out the port side of the aircraft, passenger 2K saw the threatening, sleek shape of a military jet fighter. Twin tail fins reminded him of knife blades. The long needle nose looked like an insect about to sting. Sitting inside the swept-back cockpit, the pilot motioned to attract Captain Krull's attention.

As passenger 2K glared out the window to get a better look at the fighter, he saw something that caused his pulse to quicken and his breath to be sucked from his lungs. Attached to the wingtip of the jet fighter was a small blue guided missile. Would it be the one used to turn Flight 45 into a raging ball of flames and drop the airliner into the cold waters below?

"Holy shit," a teenage passenger shouted.

"Everyone remain calm," the flight attendant shouted over the screams of the passengers. "This is standard procedure. That plane is just here to escort us safely to the closest landing site."

"Why?" the teen yelped. "What do we need an escort for? What's wrong with landing at JFK?"

"There's another one!" someone cried from the opposite side of the cabin.

The second F-18 was so close that the pilot's face could be seen. Passenger 2K felt his knees give way as he slumped back into his seat. He took his glasses off and closed his eyes. *Standard procedure?* he thought. *Escort us in? If the copilot is dead and the pilot is threatening to shoot himself, who will fly the plane?*

00:04:02

"Captain Krull, I know that by now you can see the F-18s off each side of your aircraft." Wyatt paced his deck as sweat formed on his brow. The weathered two-by-fours creaked under his boots. He heard the screech of blue jays as they argued over the peanuts Wyatt had thrown in the grass for them just before getting this call. If his problem could only be as trivial as theirs right now.

00:03:23

"Captain, those pilots are hearing every word I say. So is the NORAD commander. There will be no hesitation if he feels that you and I are not coming to terms. His sworn duty and that of his pilots is to protect the citizens of the United States. Captain, they are under orders that have no ambiguity, no flexibility. A single word from me and I can call them off. I know you're a good man, a father, a husband. The lives of so many are now in your hands. Please tell me what you want. I'll move mountains to get it for you. I can do that. I've done it for others. Just let me hear your voice."

00:01:02

The muffled pop caused everyone in the business-class section to stop as if someone had pushed the pause button on a DVD player. A bitter taste rose into the throat of passenger 2K as he stood and took a step toward the cockpit door. His glasses fell to the floor. The flight attendant was two paces ahead of him, and another was coming up the aisle.

"Let us in!" the attendant screamed, pounding on the door. "Open up!"

Passenger 2K shoved the attendant aside and kicked the door with all his strength. He felt as if he had kicked a block of stone—his leg flamed with pain. Another passenger came from behind, a fire extinguisher in his hands. Using the bottom as a battering ram, he struck the door repeatedly, leaving behind only smears of red paint.

Suddenly, the nose of the plane pitched down, causing everyone to tumble. At the same moment, a woman a few rows back yelled, "We're going to crash!"

The airbus pitched again.

Luggage, blankets, pillows, drinks, and passengers dropped to the floor and slid toward the bulkhead.

Passenger 2K was slammed to his knees as the man with the fire extinguisher fell onto him, the breath knocked from his lungs. He opened his mouth to call for the other passenger to get off when a sound like the crack of thunder struck his ears. He turned his head to look down the aisle. Without his glasses, what he saw was blurry, but he knew it for what it was. A wall of flame raged toward him like a searing, fiery wave. He cried as he took his last breath, knowing the small blue guided missile had found its target.

00:00:00

GILLEY'S FOSSILS

We are what we think. All that we are arises in our thoughts. And with our thoughts, we make our world.

—BUDDHA

Dinosaur Valley, Texas

"THE WORLD IS ABOUT to change, Ted," Cotten Stone said into the cell phone. She held it in one hand and the steering wheel in the other as she drove the rental car along Highway 67 toward Glen Rose, Texas. "This will stand a lot of people on their heads."

"I'm impressed," Ted Casselman said, his voice starting to cut out.

Cotten looked at the signal-strength indicator on her phone. It flickered between one bar and none. She hoped she wouldn't lose him. Ted had been her boss when she worked at the Satellite News Network. Even though she had landed the chief investigative correspondent job at NBC after leaving SNN, Ted remained her friend and mentor.

"I've seen all the media blitz, Cotten, but of course it's shrouded in mystery. They've done a great job of hyping your exclusive. And that's what I thought it was—just hype. I had no idea. How long have you been working on this?"

"Couple of weeks. I waited for the coverage on the Virgin Atlantic shootdown to cool off. I still can't believe that a pilot of a commercial aircraft would do something so horrific. Don't they get tested for mental stability?"

"It's interesting that the pilot recently went through his yearly evaluation with no problems. We're continuing to do follow-up human-interest pieces on it. Having to shoot down a plane full of innocent passengers was a real wake-up call for a lot of folks. Even after 9/11, I don't think anyone thought it would ever come to this."

"I understand the plane was transmitting a hijack signal."

"Yes," Ted said. "They figure the copilot triggered it to get the attention of the air traffic controllers."

As Cotten Stone listened to Ted Casselman, she pictured the tall, forty-four-year-old black man. He was graying early, and she knew she could be blamed for many of those premature gray hairs. Wanting to move away from the tragic airliner incident and bring the subject back to her story, she said, "I feel really strong about my exclusive, Ted. It's going to be amazing."

"More than amazing. You're going to crumble an entire mountain of scientific data." Ted laughed into the phone before sighing. "I hope it works out," he said. "You've got a lot riding on this."

Cotten felt trepidation trickle through her veins as she caught a glimpse of the Paluxy River, now so shallow it couldn't be paddled. But after a heavy rain, she'd been told, it transforms into raging white water—the only rapids in North Texas. Just as the rain transforms the river, she believed, her news story would bring about a drastic transformation as well.

"What did you say the network paid?" Casselman asked.

"Eight K," she answered, hearing Ted whistle. "Don't give me a hard time. I'm absolutely sure it's the real thing. If the network hadn't bought it, it would have sold on the black market for way more than that. And somebody else would've gotten the story—and the glory. I've checked it out, Ted. The experts say it's the real deal."

"Checking something out and confirming authenticity are two different things, kiddo. Nobody should know that better than you." He paused. "I just don't want you to turn into Geraldo opening Capone's vault—or worse, another Dan Rather debacle. Know what I mean?"

"I had a paleontologist examine the fossil. He gave me a thumbs-up."

"Listen to how it sounds, Cotten—just so you're ready for whatever comes. Good old Gilley—that was the dealer's name, right? God, is everybody in Texas named Gilley?"

"No, there are some George Ws and Lyndons. But honestly, that's how he introduced himself—Gilley."

"Better than Deep Throat, I suppose. Anyway, Gilley the Texan, son of a junk collector with a pile of old dinosaur bones, finds this mind-blowing fossil in his old man's basement in a box with a bunch of other bone fragments. He calls you, all on the q.t., offering you the big story for a reasonable fee—otherwise he's going to sell this thing on the black market for a bundle. But out of the goodness of his heart—"

"No, it wasn't the goodness of his heart. He figures with the notoriety he'll get if we cover the story, his fossil store will reap tons of bucks. He can write a book, do interviews, and have his fifteen minutes. His other choice is to sell underground, and he'll realize the same amount up front, but no flash. Said that either way to him is fine. But he'd prefer the flash."

"And the paleontologist? Where'd he come from?"

"Come on, Ted, give me a break. Why can't you just be happy for me?"

"Because you're like my own daughter. I worry about you. Don't want you to get sloppy amidst all this fame."

Cotten's body relaxed back into the seat, and she glanced at the speedometer. She was doing eighty-nine in a sixty-five zone, so she eased off the accelerator. Ted really did worry about her. "His name is Waterman. That's Waterman with a P-H-D at the end. I met him at a party the Museum of Natural History had for the press a couple of months ago. Worked out perfect. He offered to go down to Texas. Of course, he had to sign a nondisclosure until we air the story. And it took some doing to persuade Gilley to let Waterman see it. Only the brass at NBC, Waterman, Gilley, me—and now you—know about this. And I'd get fired if they knew I was having this conversation with my competition."

"Waterman," Ted repeated. "Got a first name?"

"Henry—no, Harry," Cotten said. "Harry Waterman. Why?"

"Just curious. Maybe I'll see what I can find out about him."

"He wrote the network a letter stating his opinion that it was authentic. If he hadn't, I don't think they'd have sprung for the money."

"So, you're shooting live for the evening news?"

Cotten's muscles tensed with excitement. She was back on top. This evening, her face would be in everyone's living room. God, she loved it.

"Yep," she said. "Today's the big day."

"Guess I'd better start getting *my* crew in place."

Cotten heard anticipation in his voice. "What do you mean?"

"Think about the huge follow-up story. How are the scientific community and the fundamentalists going to respond to seeing proof that the Bible literally got it right? Somebody's going to eat crow—or maybe a brontosaurus steak."

"I like a good roasting," Cotten said.

There were at least three seconds of silence before Ted responded. "Take care, kid."

"Talk to you soon," she said, and flipped the phone closed.

Cotten peered at the bloated, galvanized gray clouds hanging low in the sky. She might get to witness the Paluxy River's transformation.

Up ahead, she saw the faded sign: *Gilley's Fossils and General Store, One Mile.* This was it. The moment she had waited for. The story that would put her on top once again. The Grail conspiracy had been one thing. But this—undisputed proof that man had lived during the time of the dinosaurs. *Her* fifteen minutes just kept getting longer.

During the last visit to Glen Rose, Gilley had taken her a couple of miles down the road to visit the Creation Evidence Museum. She'd found it fascinating, especially the collection of dinosaur and human footprints. She'd talked to several people there who were passionate in their beliefs. Wait until they got a load of what she was about to broadcast.

As Cotten Stone pulled into the gravel-filled parking lot of the rustic tourist attraction, she felt that old familiar rush of excitement. She had created huge headlines over the last two years: when she found the Holy Grail—twice; when she persuaded the Vatican to open its vaults and allow the Jews to reclaim the sacred menorah of the Second Temple brought to Rome by Titus in AD 70; when she covered the amazing find of more ancient scrolls in caves near the Dead Sea; and when she announced the discovery of the thirty pieces of silver that Judas Iscariot was paid to betray Christ. But this would be her crowning achievement. When it came to religious sensationalism, Cotten Stone ruled the airwaves. And now she had the chance to single-handedly debunk the basic scientific theory of evolution right here on a hot afternoon along a dusty stretch of Texas highway. She was riding high, feeling the adrenaline flush her face and throat.

Cotten pulled in beside the NBC 5 Dallas–Fort Worth remote video truck parked in front of Gilley's. It was ready to beam her next world-changing story up to an orbiting satellite and back down to an awaiting audience. She was about to show the world a dinosaur bone with a spear point embedded in it—proof that man had lived alongside the dinosaurs.

As she got out of the car, Cotten looked into the cloudy Texas sky. *Hang on to your shorts*, she thought. *Cotten Stone is about to rock the evening news again.*

* * *

Only a week after what was supposed to be her finest hour, Cotten Stone stood before the cameras again. But there was no burnishing glow of excitement in her cheeks, no perk in her voice. Instead, her eyes wore heavy makeup to disguise the swollen lids. Her whole body seemed to sag, and when she spoke, her voice was riddled with shame.

"I would like to apologize to anyone I have betrayed or offended," Cotten said, avoiding eye contact with the camera. She stared down at her prepared notes, sensing the studio crew glaring at her, their contempt palpable. "It was not my intention to lie or conspire to lie to the viewers of the National Broadcasting Company or its affiliates. Deception was not my goal. I've been accused of ignoring evidence that indicated that what is now being called the creation fossil was an elaborate hoax. I adamantly deny having any prior knowledge that it was a fake, and I never intended to trick or deceive anyone. If I have been an embarrassment to any group or person, I am deeply sorry. I hope that you can forgive me."

Cotten let the notes slip from her fingers onto the studio floor. She walked out of the bright lights and off the news set. No one followed. No one wished her well. She thought she'd never get to the doors to escape the horrible silence.

On the crowded sidewalk outside, news photographers snapped her picture, shouting questions.

"Ms. Stone, is it true you were forced to resign?"

"Are you going to continue trying to prove the Bible was right about creation?"

"What's next, now that you're out of a job?"

She saw Ted Casselman standing beside a yellow taxi. He motioned, and as she approached, he opened the car door.

"Didn't think you'd feel like dealing with flagging one down," he said.

She kissed him on the cheek. "Thanks for coming. You've always been my rock."

"Told you before, you're like my own daughter."

Cotten slipped into the back seat, and Ted leaned in.

"You sure you want to do this? Leave New York?" he asked.

Cotten nodded. "South Florida sounds real good to me right now."

"Remember, you've got friends here."

She gave him a faint smile.

"All right then, kiddo. You've already been to hell and back. You can do it again, I know you can." He kissed her forehead and then closed the door.

As the cab pulled away, Cotten felt her soul sink into the abyss.

PERU

One Year Later

COTTEN STONE LEANED HER head against the airplane's cold window. The earth's surface revealed itself in short clips, most of the time hidden by thick clouds. She checked her watch. Right on time. Her ears had popped as the plane began the final approach into Jorge Chavez International Airport. As if waiting for the other shoe to drop, Cotten listened for the telltale groan of the wheels as they were lowered out of the wells. She closed her eyes. Lima. A new story. A new start. After a painful year of struggling with depression and few jobs since the creation-fossil disaster, this was a chance at redeeming herself, she hoped.

At the sound of the landing gear's thump, Cotten's fingers gripped the armrest. Intellectually, she understood the theories of lift and thrust, but in her gut she still had a difficult time trusting those forces to get something as huge and heavy as an airplane to fly. And then to control the descent without plummeting to the ground and splintering into a million pieces was something else.

That's what made her fingers tighten over the lip of the armrest. Takeoff and landing were praying times for her.

When the word *praying* slipped through her mind, a chill so cold it felt more like a pinch at the base of her neck made her shiver. Memories hacked at the dam inside her. Praying wasn't something she did much. Cotten took a deep breath through her nose and blew it out her mouth. She had gotten a refill for Ativan before she left Fort Lauderdale . . . just in case. Controlling anxiety with visualization and breathing exercises had been working, but right now the combination of the plane landing and the sudden rush of memories blasted straight through her ability to concentrate.

Cotten shifted in her seat, putting her hand between the seat belt and the space just below her shoulder and above her breast. The restraint of the belt added to the restlessness. She wanted it off—not to touch her or bind her. The urge to stand and move bubbled up in her like the carbonation in a shaken soda bottle, and if she didn't get it under control, it would spew out.

Cotten squirmed in her seat, and as she did, she caught a glimpse of lights glittering below. Only fine wisps of organza clouds passed as the plane came closer to the ground. *Almost down. Almost down.* If she'd kept the damn Ativan in her pocket, she could have retrieved it. But the pills were stowed in her carry-on in the overhead compartment. If she stood and dragged out her bag, everyone would look at her—some might even recognize her.

Cotten closed her eyes again, focusing on breathing and relaxing her body, starting with her toes, concentrating on every muscle, moving up, all the way to her scalp. Deep, slow, even breaths. In through the nose, out through the mouth.

The wheels screeched on touchdown. The plane bounced twice before rolling smoothly over the tarmac. The scream of the engines as the jet slowed was more like a beautiful serenade to her. Cotten's breath came easily now, and her fingers loosed the armrest. The nape of her neck cooled from the dampness of sweat. She sank into the seat, glad the "spell"—she preferred that word to "attack"—had passed, but not knowing whether she'd beaten it or if the safe landing had reduced her stress to a manageable level. It didn't matter now. She was on the ground.

This assignment wasn't expected to be much of anything, but she was getting paid for it as a freelancer, and it did help move her up another rung on the respectability ladder. The disaster in Texas a year ago had not only cost her her network job, her image, and her credibility, but it also yanked the rug of self-respect from under her. There wasn't much left that could be squeezed out.

Finally, she heard the soft ding of the Fasten Seat Belt sign being turned off. She waited until the aisle cleared and everyone had deplaned before getting up and taking her carry-on from the overhead compartment. She thought about it, but resisted unzipping the bag and getting out the Ativan.

The airline crew bade the obligatory farewells as she passed through the hatch. Cotten nodded politely and offered what she knew appeared to be an insincere smile. But that was all she could muster.

Making her way through the terminal to the baggage claim, Cotten took her cell from her pocket. She flipped it open to scan her contacts list for Paul Davis. As soon as she turned on the phone, she saw there was one missed call. She pressed the down arrow to bring up the screen of recent calls.

John Tyler. Just seeing his name made her heart trip over itself. She blinked, and in that instant she could see his deep blue eyes in her mind. God, she missed him. If he weren't a priest, she knew their lives would have been different.

Cotten pressed the button to return his call, but before it could ring, she canceled. When she did talk to John, she wanted to be able to gather her thoughts and spend some time. Traipsing through the airport was not the place.

Toggling through the contacts list stored in her phone, she found the number for Paul Davis. He was the cameraman she had worked with on her last assignment, a piss-poor piece on whether the detection of fluoride in what is claimed to be an ancient relic should be considered in the authentication process. The argument was that fluoride is a supplement now added to water supplies, and if it is detected in an artifact, that should prove it to be a hoax. The opposite to that theory is that when someone finds an artifact, what do they usually do? Wash it off in tap water—so voilà, the fluoride. The bottom line was that nobody really cared except a select few in the archaeological community who loved to bicker and banter in efforts to prove one is more brilliant than the other. It just didn't play to the general public. She and Paul had quite a few laughs covering that story. So when she got this gig, she called him to be her cameraman, and in turn he solicited Nick Michaels, a friend and field soundman, to meet up with them in Lima.

Cotten was about to push the send button on her phone when she heard a familiar voice.

"Cotten!"

She looked up to see Paul Davis waving as he approached across the crowded concourse. She greeted him with a hug.

Paul was tall and slender with dark brown hair. He pulled his video equipment behind him in a silver Anvil case that Cotten recognized from their last job.

"This is Nick Michaels," Paul said, introducing his companion, "the best soundman south of Auburn, Alabama. And he makes a mean pot of chili, too." Nick, shorter and stockier than Paul, had brown hair that had been groomed with gel to make it look tousled and spiked—and he had an intriguing, mischievous glint in his eye.

"A Tiger," Cotten said, shaking Nick's extended hand. "I'm a Wildcat myself, born and raised in the Bluegrass State."

"I won't hold it against you, Cotten," Nick said with a smile.

"Fair enough," she said. "How much time do we have to make our Cusco flight?"

"Just long enough to grab a round of Lima's famous *pisco* sours," Paul said, motioning to a concourse restaurant bar.

* * *

After the short flight to Cusco, the trio boarded a train for the start of the forty-three-mile journey to Machu Picchu, the fortress city of the ancient Inca, built in the fifteenth century. The steep, zigzagging ride took them first to Aguas Calientes. Cotten wished they had splurged and taken the luxury train—the *Hiram Bingham*. But the views were breathtaking even when her teeth were clacking together.

From Aguas Calientes, they took a bus that followed the Urubamba River before climbing the mountain by a series of switchbacks to a final destination eight thousand feet into the clouds.

"So, do we get to look around while we're here?" Paul asked when they got off the bus near Machu Picchu.

"I don't think we'll have time," Cotten answered as they worked their way up steep steps to the tourists' reception area. "We've got a guide meeting us at the Sanctuary Lodge around two thirty. And the trek from there to where we are going is a couple of arduous hours."

They did at least manage to find time to get what Nick called the money shot, a photo-op location near the Caretaker's Hut. Cotten pulled out her Canon Elph digital camera and asked a passing tourist to snap a picture of the three of them together with Machu Picchu spread out in the background.

"I wish we had more time," Cotten said before they headed to the Sanctuary Lodge.

"Maybe on the return trip," Paul said. "It would be a shame to come all this way and not get to spend some time here." He looked around quizzically. "How do you think the Inca built all this?"

"Coca leaves," Nick said.

"That was a privilege for Incan royalty and priests," Cotten said.

"I still bet the peasants sneaked a leaf or two," Nick said.

"We actually should get some of the tea they sell that's made with coca leaves," Paul said. "It's supposed to help with altitude sickness." He asked Cotten, "What do you know about the site where we're going?"

Cotten shrugged. "Only that it was recently discovered and is still being explored. They don't know who built it or what happened to the inhabitants."

"Sounds spooky," Nick said.

Great, Cotten thought. *Just what I need.*

RIPPLE

IN THE MEN'S ROOM of the Department of Physics at the University of Illinois at Chicago, Lester Ripple blinked a stream of tears down his cheeks. He couldn't get the damn contact lens in his eye without copious snotting and tearing. He laid his index finger against one nostril to close it off, and he blew his nose into the sink. Then he did the same to the other side. Getting the contact in was always such a pain. Why couldn't it be a simple thing to do?

Lester put the contact on the tip of his finger again. He swept back his dirty blond hair and watched in the mirror as he brought the lens closer and closer. He thought of the contact as a Lilliputian goldfish bowl. Without the goldfish, of course. Having the lens a half inch from its target, both eyes stung and his nose ran. Lester pressed his thick lips together, drawing his fleshy cheeks tighter to the bone, and stretched open his pale blue eyes. At the first touch, finally, the contact sucked onto his eyeball. He blinked again, then dabbed his eyes with his handkerchief, which he had draped over the side of the sink. Lester squinted, scrunching up his nose. At least he could see. His left eye had 20/20 vision, but the right one had 20/200. The defective vision in the one eye had not been caused by an accident or injury; it had always been that way. His entire life, he'd been off-balance, stumbling and bumbling, the perfect target for bullies when he was a kid. At first, eyeglasses had improved his vision, but glasses added another layer of geekiness for kids to pick on. His father had wanted *the kid* to toughen up, fight back, not be such a baby. But his mother understood, so she hid away some money, then forked it over to get him a contact lens for his eleventh birthday.

"Don't tell your father," she had warned.

That had been seventeen years ago, and he still hadn't gotten used to the damn thing. Queerer still, his father had never noticed.

Lester checked his watch. He was early. It was two o'clock and his interview was scheduled for two forty-five. That was all right. He needed the extra time. It gave him a sense of security. After all, the city bus could have been late. There could have been an accident along the roadway. He could have had an attack of diarrhea or hives or hay fever, and then he would have needed time for the Imodium or the Benadryl or the Claritin to work. Lots of things could have gone wrong, and then he would have been late. Can't get a job starting off that way.

Lester folded the handkerchief in quarters. He set it on the edge of the sink and patted it three times, then turned it over and patted again, counting aloud, "One, two, three." Then he tucked it in the left hip pocket of his trousers.

Next he washed his hands, tapping the soap dispenser three times, then lathering. He rinsed, dipping his hands under the faucet.

"One, two, three." He air-dried them, shaking and flapping his hands above his head, with a final swipe down the sides of his pants.

Lester Ripple picked up his tote bag—he was ready.

Down the hall, he found the room where he'd been told to report. The building was old, the wood floors the rich color of Colombian coffee and the plastered walls pitted and flaking in spots. The wood door to the room was nearly as dark as the floor. Light shone through the frosted glass insert and also through the transom above.

Lester paused in front of the door and wondered if he should knock or if he was expected to go inside without formal announcement.

He knocked.

"Come in," a woman's voice responded.

Lester turned the knob and opened the door.

"Good afternoon," he said. "My name is Lester Ripple. I have an appointment with Dr. Osborne."

The secretary never looked up. "Have a seat," she said. "You're early."

"I know," Lester said, sitting in the vinyl chair by the opposite wall. He reached inside his tote and sorted through several magazines and books. He settled on the magazine *Physics Review*, put it in his lap, and flipped it open to the article "Gravitational Waves in Open de Sitter Space," one he'd read at least a dozen times. But he liked it. It was written by Stephen Hawking with Thomas Hertog and Neil Turok. God, he could read Hawking all day. Stephen Hawking was Lester's idol, and whether Hawking knew it or not, he was Lester's mentor. How many times did Lester ask himself

"WWHD"—"What would Hawking do?" They had so much in common, it was uncanny. Both had January 8 birthdays. Both had the middle name William. Both of their fathers had wanted them to go into medicine, but Lester and Stephen preferred mathematics and eventually physics, and more specifically theoretical physics. Both had disabilities—Hawking's ALS more dramatic than Lester's screwed-up eye.

He read the article with as much vigor as he had the first time. When he finished, Lester checked his watch, then glanced at the closed office door behind the secretary and wondered what Osborne was doing in there. His eyes roamed the room for a moment before he decided to read something else. Lester chose *Green Lantern: Rebirth*, a DC comic from his collection. He found reading Catwoman, Superman, and Green Lantern just as entertaining as reading Hawking, Bohr, and Einstein.

"Dr. Ripple?" The voice came from the man who had opened the office door.

"Dr. Osborne?" Lester said, standing, the comic book fluttering to the ground.

Osborne stared down at the front cover. In a creepy, dripping font, the title declared: "UNHOLY TRINITY."

Lester knew he wasn't going to get the job.

DISCOVERY

Chami, a native Inca, was the guide's Quechua name, which translated into "little" or "small." And that he was. About five foot three, Cotten guessed—skinny with deep brownish-red skin that fit snugly against the underlying muscles. He was quick to tell them he spoke three languages and preferred to be called José. Cotten supposed it simplified things. Almost everyone in Peru spoke Spanish; the Inca spoke Quechua and often both Quechua and Spanish.

José brought with him another man of greater stature who helped with the baggage, but he apparently spoke no English.

A footpath that had been hacked out of the jungle led them through the mountain terrain. Sometimes the density of the foliage was suffocating.

Not far from their final destination, they took a side trail that was marked by a red-painted block of wood nailed to a tree. About forty feet down the uneven, partially overgrown trail, they stopped.

"Rimancu," José said. He explained that this site had undergone only preliminary investigation, but Dr. Carl Edelman, the excavation leader, wanted Cotten and her crew to at least see a bit of it as they passed by.

"What does 'Rimancu' mean?" Cotten asked.

"It means 'they speak,'" José answered.

After a short rest and some exploration, the group continued toward the main campsite, finally arriving in the late afternoon. The light was already fading as the sun dropped below the mountains. Cotten, Paul, and Nick were tired and fighting for breath in the high altitude.

"No wonder this place went undetected for so long," Nick said, dropping his backpack and gasping for air. "I think I've climbed all the way to freakin' heaven. It even looks like heaven—the clouds are so low and thick."

José waved them on and led them to Dr. Edelman.

Standing beside a fold-up table outside his tent, Edelman shook hands with the newcomers.

"A pleasure to meet you," he said to each.

He seemed a bit smug or standoffish to Cotten, but perhaps it was just the Brit in him. Or maybe he was simply more comfortable with books and rocks and dirt than with people.

Edelman fit the stereotypical image of an academic archaeologist, not the adventurous type in the movies. He was tall, lank, and pale-skinned, his dark hair needing to be cut, as a swatch of it hung over the left side of his forehead—Errol Flynn but without the good looks, she thought. The British accent topped it off.

After introductions and casual small talk, Edelman had José show Cotten and her team their quarters—small tan tents with flaps for doors. Inside was a canvas cot, a Coleman lantern, a small, firm foam pillow, a roll of toilet paper, and a white plastic bucket with some water in it.

"Latrine is that way," José said, pointing to the other side of the camp. "You want private, use bucket," he said, pointing.

"All righty then," Cotten said, slinging one of her bags into the corner of the tent. *So you'll do anything for a job, Cotten Stone,* she mused. *It's going to be an experience.*

As dusk settled over the mountains, Cotten explored the camp. Edelman had a tent of his own, a tad larger than the rest. The chief, she thought, among his Indians. There was an empty tent next to Edelman's that José explained belonged to Richard and Mariah Hapsburg, the American portion of the expedition, who had recently returned to the States to solicit grant money for more exploration and excavation of this site and Rimancu. Nick and Paul had separate tents close to hers. There was a mess tent in the center of the camp and another in the dig crew's quarters, which was separated from the main camp by a wall of trees. At the opposite end of the encampment was the trail that led to the actual site. She followed the path, a narrow swath chopped and slashed out of the forest. Soon, the first of the ruins came into view. Thick roots, like the tentacles of some ancient sea monster, snaked among the crumbling walls and heavily weathered carvings of the Incan artisans.

Cotten stared in fascination, trying to imagine what it must have been like 550 years ago when the Incan royalty walked along this same path. Sitting on an outcrop of rock, she studied the magnificent sight until it became part of the night.

* * *

Over the next few days, Cotten learned how the American-British archaeological team had uncovered the remains of the royal city, a jewel of the lost Incan civilization, long hidden by the nearly impenetrable vegetation high up in the Peruvian cloud forest. Since the dig had begun, the team had unearthed a remarkable complex of temples, astronomical observatories, residential structures, and preserved textiles.

Fighting altitude sickness and the constant, penetrating dampness and chill of the air, Cotten, Paul, and Nick worked at snapping pictures and recording videotape of the dig team, including interviewing Edelman, José, and some of the other natives. Hours of cover footage was shot of the portions of the city revealed by the expedition.

Once she had completed the shoot list and interviews needed for the story, she told Paul and Nick that they had enough to bring back to Lima and turn over to the Peruvian television network. There was no need to stay any longer. They agreed with her that they were ready for real food, real beds, and real air—at least air with a lot more oxygen content.

On the afternoon of the day before their departure, Cotten took a stroll away from the campsite to think and evaluate. This assignment was small and cheap. Nothing to brag about or enhance her résumé. She would not even get to edit the piece, just shoot the footage and go home.

Cotten found a hammock strung between two trees on the edge of the campsite and stretched out in it. What was she going to do once she got home? All she seemed to get was one shitty job after another. And even those were rare.

Cotten stared at the sky. "Just what do you want from me?" It wasn't praying—she didn't believe in prayer. But in her own way, she needed answers from something—someone—greater than herself. "Just tell me what you want." The clouds seemed to grow darker. "How about a sign? Anything will do." She closed her eyes, thinking she might allow herself to doze off.

"Come quickly!" came a shout from across the campsite. "We have found something. *Haku! Haku!*"

It shook Cotten Stone from her thoughts as she sat up and swung her feet to the ground.

A few yards away, Dr. Carl Edelman rose, placing the artifact he was examining onto the folding table. "What is it, José?" he said.

Cotten watched José burst into the camp clearing. She had learned that the Indian was not only a guide, but also the dig team's foreman, supervising the laborers.

"*Utqhay*. Hurry. You have to see this. Come. *Haku*." José lapsed again into his native Quechua so that everyone within earshot would understand. Waving his hands, he called out, "*Mana ininan kay*. It's incredible. I have ordered no one touch it until you arrive, Dr. Edelman."

As José spun around and sprinted off, Edelman followed. Cotten, along with Paul and Nick, who had just joined her, trailed behind them. Whatever had José so ecstatic might be the break she needed to enhance the footage and impress the Peruvian network into giving her another assignment.

Cotten smelled the pungent aroma of decaying foliage along the now well-defined path. At this altitude, the mountain clouds kept everything perpetually damp.

Soon, the first of the ruins loomed out of the mist. Over the last few days, what Edelman thought was a small ceremonial structure had been uncovered. José entered the site jogging backward, still babbling, and headed for the new location.

When Edelman stepped into view, the group of workers grew quiet.

"There," José said, gesturing toward the circle of coppery-skinned men standing around a trench. "Back up," he shouted. "*Kutiriy*. Give Dr. Edelman room."

Edelman knelt beside the trench. "Brush," he ordered, holding out his hand.

Like a medical assistant, José handed him a four-inch paint-brush.

Delicately, Carl Edelman swept away a thin layer of reddish dirt.

Cotten stood behind him, leaning forward to see what lay at the bottom of the trench. She heard Edelman draw in his breath as he sat back on his haunches.

"What is it?" Cotten asked. Over her shoulder to Paul, she said, "Are you getting this?"

Paul gave a thumbs-up, then flipped on the high-intensity flood atop the Sony digital camcorder. The soft hum of the tape drive blended with the wind sliding across the treetops.

As Cotten turned back toward Edelman, a radiant spectrum of light caught her eyes. Even through the caked-on soil, she saw something out of place—something that didn't seem to belong in this ancient place. It captured the sunlight through a break in the thick clouds and sent it back in splinters of dazzling colors.

Edelman pulled a trowel from his pocket and gingerly dug around the edges of the object.

Glass? Cotten thought.

When Edelman had worked the dirt loose, he probed beneath the object and freed it from the earth. "Get me something to wrap it in."

José translated the command, and one of the workers tossed the archaeologist a towel.

With the dexterity that comes from years of experience, Edelman extracted the object, wrapping it with the cloth. "Amazing," he whispered. "When Richard and Mariah get back, they are going to—"

"What is it?" Cotten asked.

Edelman stood, cradling the artifact like a babe in swaddling clothes. "In my entire career, I have never seen anything like this."

THE CRYSTAL TABLET

The temperature dropped as darkness engulfed the ridge. During the days the sun was brilliant and the air warm, but at night the temperatures fell to fifty degrees or below. Chilled, Cotten pulled her parka tightly around her. On evenings like this, the cloud forest of Peru shrouded itself in mist and mystery. José had said some locals believed that within the clouds was a gateway to another world.

Cotten heard the muffled voices of the native dig team from across the campsite as she, Paul, and Nick gathered with Edelman under the light outside his tent. A generator thrummed in the darkness.

Edelman pointed to two large, soil-encrusted shells with holes in them sitting on the table. "Musical instruments—horns—used by the Chavín," Edelman explained. "The Chavín are known as the earliest Peruvians." From next to the shells, Edelman lifted a small stone that was concave in the center. "A mortar. Probably used to grind *vilca* seeds."

"What's *vilca*?" Cotten asked.

"It is a tree. They roasted the hallucinogenic seeds, then ground them into a powder. They used small bone tubes like straws and either sniffed it up or someone blew it up another's nostrils."

"What did I tell you about them sneaking a coca leaf?" Nick said. "These guys have been into getting high for thousands of years."

Edelman ignored Nick's comment. "We found nothing truly extraordinary at this site until today," the archaeologist said. "I examined the object recovered from the trench before inviting you to come have a look."

Paul turned on the camera flood and started taping while Nick adjusted the audio levels on his portable R-DAT. He held a short boom mic over Edelman's head. Cotten tried to finagle a better look, walking around the table, but Edelman had the object covered with a buffing cloth.

"We have had other insights and evidence that something is different about this place," Edelman said, sipping his Glenfiddich—neat. He had the only real glass in the encampment, having declared that because of his conservative British upbringing, he couldn't abide drinking fine whiskey from a plastic cup. It wasn't fitting.

"What evidence?" Cotten asked.

"The most obvious, and the first striking fact we noticed, was that there was a large gap in time between early Incan habitations of this site. The first Incan habitation appears to have abruptly left the site. Vanished. And the strata remain sterile between that habitation and the most recent."

"Why would they leave like that?" Cotten asked.

"Good question."

"Maybe they were wiped out by another tribe," Paul said.

Edelman shrugged. "Possibly, but there are no graves, no tombs, no human remains—at least none that we have found other than those who recently inhabited the site."

"Isn't that a bit strange for a city this big?" Cotten asked.

"To have no graves, yes. But to disappear is odd, but not unheard of. It has happened a number of times down through history. A great culture or civilization just vanishes overnight. We may never know for sure what caused these people to abandon this city. A good example that you might be familiar with is your American Southwest Indians, the Anasazi."

"Cliff dwellers?" Paul said.

"Yes. Like many other ancient civilizations, they were a resourceful and adaptable people who suddenly disappeared without a trace. It could have been crop failure or drought, disease, conflict." He nodded to Paul. "Truth is, no one really knows why some of these civilizations vanish. There is no evidence of decline, something you would find with crop failure or drought. One day they're there, then poof."

"You'd think with all our modern technology, those mysteries would have been solved," Cotten said.

"Yes, one would think," Edelman said. "Once in a while there is a small scattering of stragglers, but for the most part, they are gone without a trace. Think about Atlantis, for instance. Plato wrote about its existence, but if it did exist, what happened to it?"

Edelman rolled his head and massaged his neck while leaving the chamois draped over the object. "Some of the other artifacts we have found here could indicate this site predates the Inca and Chavín—maybe by thousands of years," Edelman said. "A few of the artifacts point to a totally different culture—one as yet unknown. Now this.

This unbelievable object compounds our indecision about the inhabitants of this site. When Richard and Mariah get back, we will reconstruct our line of thinking."

"Have you spoken to them?" Cotten asked before taking a sip of Cerveza Cristal. The Peruvian beer didn't quite hit the spot. She wished instead for her beloved Absolut and regretted she hadn't grabbed a couple of miniatures on the flight from Fort Lauderdale to Lima. Even though she preferred it straight out of the freezer, she would have been satisfied to sip it chilled only by nightfall's cool mountain air.

"Indeed," Edelman said. "I rang them up on the satellite phone, and as soon as they finish the grant proposal, they will be on the first jet back to Lima. Richard's knickers are in a bit of a twist that he was not here when we found it. You know he goes to work to go on holiday. His work is his pleasure."

Richard Hapsburg was a Yale anthropologist, and his wife, Mariah, was an art dealer and professional grant writer. While examining famous explorer Hiram Bingham's 1911 expedition notes in the Yale archives, Richard discovered references to a second site, one that Bingham considered unimportant and didn't publish enough information on to allow others to follow up. Using the latest in thermal imaging, Hapsburg and his Yale group identified the mystery site's most likely location. After weeks of chopping through the thick wall of vegetation, Hapsburg and Edelman, along with their team of diggers, finally laid eyes on the lost city.

"Here is what causes me to question so much about this place," Edelman said. With a sweep of his arm, he lifted the cloth and scooted back in his chair. "Feast your eyes."

Cotten peered at the object on the table, and her jaw dropped open in awe.

It was a crystal object—transparent, shimmering, almost liquid. It appeared to be about six inches wide, nine inches tall, and an inch or so thick.

"Beautiful," she whispered. "Absolutely beautiful."

The crystal caught the camera flood and threw the light back in streams like iridescent gossamer floss.

"Move over to this angle, Paul," she said without taking her eyes from the artifact. Intricate markings covered the surface. At the top were etchings of sorts—glyphs or symbols—and on the bottom half was a series of dots and lines. "Can I touch it?" she asked.

Edelman nodded, then continued. "Anthropological evidence shows us that in the past, as well as today, quartz crystals play an important role in shamanic ceremonies in Peru. But this . . . this is like nothing I could have imagined. Maybe it explains their fascination with crystals. Do you know much about crystals, Ms. Stone?"

"Not really. Just the high school basics." She slid her finger across the polished surface. "It's exquisite." Cotten pulled her Elph camera from her pocket and snapped several close-ups.

"Yes, it is," Edelman said, edging out of the way so Paul could get a better angle. "It weighs a little over four kilos—about nine pounds. I believe it was carved from a single quartz crystal. Under magnification, I determined it was carved against the natural axis of the crystal. Anyone who works with crystals, particularly crystal sculptors, are intensely aware of this axis—the molecular symmetry of a crystal. If carved in the opposite direction, against the grain, the crystal will shatter. Even the most modern technology for carving crystal—high-tech lasers and the like—still does not always meet the challenge."

"But wasn't this created hundreds of years ago?" Cotten said.

"Looking at the markings, my best speculation is more like thousands," Edelman said.

Edelman drummed his fingers on his chin. He stared at the tablet. "I spoke with Richard Hapsburg earlier and inquired about what kind of tool or technique could have been used to create this tablet. He got back to me perhaps half an hour ago. Said that from the preliminary conversation he had with his colleagues, the initial theory is that the crystal and the glyphs had to be hewn with diamonds, and the finer detail created with a solution of sand and water. Of course, this was all based on my verbal description, since I have no way of uploading images from here." He paused a moment, taking another swig of his single malt. "And the real conundrum would be that if he is right, it would have taken an accomplished craftsman more than a lifetime—even a hundred years or more—to complete this kind of work." He motioned to the crystal tablet with an expression of bewilderment. "Amazingly, I cannot find even a tiny scratch as evidence of what type of tool was used."

"Then what you're saying is this crystal tablet just shouldn't exist," Cotten said.

"Correct. Hapsburg is rounding up some trusted associates to come down here," Edelman said. "We need a bevy of experts to look at this thing."

"Has he spoken to the press yet?" Cotten asked.

"No. We will need better verification before we make any announcement." He glanced at her knowingly. "Do not be concerned, Ms. Stone. You will have your exclusive."

Cotten wondered if maybe this was going to be the story that would salvage her career. She needed any break she could get. "Get some stills, too," she said to Paul.

He placed the camcorder aside and started using a Kodak digital camera. When he had all he needed, he nodded to Cotten, who handed him and Nick each a Cerveza Cristal.

"Now we're getting somewhere," Nick said as they clinked the beer bottles together.

Cotten turned to Edelman only to find him in deep concentration. He had pulled his chair back to the table and stared down at the tablet, shaking his head.

Cotten moved beside him. "What?" she said. "Something else?"

He knocked back another mouthful of his Scotch, followed by a second, draining the glass. "If I am understanding these glyphs—"

"You mean you know what they say?"

"Roughly," he said, using his finger to mark off the perimeter of the top half of the tablet. "And I am basing my interpretation on the fact that the glyphs bear some similarity to early Zapotec and Maya inscriptions. All the early writing of Mesoamerica used complex, square-shaped pictures."

"Mesoamerica? We're in South America," Cotten said.

"Yes, we are, but the newest thinking is that all these ancient peoples moved around much more than what was once believed. Was the crystal created here, or was it brought to this place from somewhere else? That is a question I cannot yet answer."

"So you don't think the Inca or Chavín created it?" Cotten asked.

"They had no written language like this," Edelman said.

"But some group older than the Chavín did?" Cotten said. "I thought you said they had no written language."

"Quite a riddle, is it not?" Edelman said.

Paul tipped his beer to his lips, swallowed, then said, "You mean to tell me the folks who built Machu Picchu and this complex of palaces and observatories had no written language?"

Edelman put on a tolerant smile. "It is naive for us to think that *writing* means putting down words by way of pen and ink, the way we do it. The Egyptians used stone and papyrus, the Sumerians and Babylonians wrote on clay. And the Inca used a different method and medium entirely. They are famous for textiles, so it makes perfectly good sense. They used *khipu*—knots on ropes and strings. It used to be believed that khipu was only a way of accounting, but recent analysis indicates it could be a three-dimensional written language in a seven-bit binary code. Very complicated. Remember, our modern-day computers are also based on binary codes."

"The Inca used the same technology as today's computers?" Paul asked.

Edelman nodded. "When we write e-mail messages, for instance, they exist inside the computer in the form of eight-digit sequences—a binary code made up of only ones and zeros. The coded message gets sent to another computer, which translates or decodes it back into the script typed by the sender. The Inca invented such a system at least five hundred years before Bill Gates launched Microsoft."

"Maybe we aren't as smart as we think," Nick said.

"No, we certainly are not," Edelman said. "Arrogant is more the case. The Spanish recorded capturing one Inca trying to conceal a khipu, which he told them was a record of everything about his homeland, both good and evil. And so, in their pious wisdom, instead of keeping it to study and learn from, the conquistadors burned it as an idolatrous object and punished the poor native for having it. What was done to these cultures in the New World in the name of God is an atrocity we tend to ignore. They were obliterated."

Edelman again leaned in close and studied the markings on the crystal while writing in a notebook, all the while shaking his head as if he couldn't believe what he was transcribing.

Paul elbowed Cotten. "What's up?"

Cotten shrugged. "So what do you think it says?" she asked.

Edelman didn't answer right away, but kept writing. Paul raised his eyebrows at Cotten as they stood by patiently.

Finally, Edelman looked up. "If someone thousands of years ago took on such an incredibly difficult task creating this remarkable object, he must have had something profound to say. You agree?"

Cotten cocked her head as she noticed the mountain mist growing thicker around them. "I suppose so."

Edelman continued. "As I said, I have only a rough translation based on similar glyphs I have studied, but the most remarkable thing that helps me understand these markings is that I am familiar with the message. I have heard it before, and so have you. The crystal itself is an incredible enigma on its own. But you see, it is not simply the message inscribed on the crystal that is so amazing. It is the fact that the writer had prior knowledge of *this* particular event at all."

"What event?" Paul asked.

"Noah's Ark and the Great Flood."

VENATORI

"Mr. Wyatt, I want to thank you for coming on such short notice," said Archbishop Felipe Montiagro, the Vatican apostolic nuncio to the United States.

"I was intrigued by your call, Your Excellency," Thomas Wyatt said. He shook hands with the archbishop, a tall man dressed in a black suit with a simple Roman collar—no visible indication of his diplomatic or Roman curia position.

Wyatt had thought a lot about why he would get a request from such a high-ranking diplomat to come to the Vatican embassy for a job offer with what he assumed was the Swiss Guard. Since the loss of the Virgin Atlantic plane a year ago, he'd found himself considering a thousand times if he should leave his job. For weeks after the shootdown, he would lie awake at night debating what else he could have done to convince the pilot to reconsider suicide. He had experienced a few other failures in the past, but mostly dealing with a single suspect or terrorist. Nothing approached the loss of the 280 innocents on Flight 45.

Montiagro motioned for Wyatt to sit as he went around to the other side of his desk. "It's not often we have such special needs and can find a man of your stature and experience."

The two men sat in a modern but modestly decorated office on the second floor of the Vatican State embassy on Massachusetts Avenue in Washington. The spacious room was wood paneled and windowless, and on the wall behind Montiagro was a large portrait of the pope.

"Just what *are* your special needs?" Wyatt asked. "I thought that to be a member of the Swiss Guard, you had to be Roman Catholic and hold Swiss citizenship."

"That's correct, Mr. Wyatt. And if I were really recruiting you for the Guard, you would of course not qualify. There are other levels of Vatican security," he said.

Wyatt gave him a curious look, wondering where Montiagro was going. With degrees in criminal psychology and international law, Wyatt had spent the last seven years as a senior analyst expert on human behavior for the National Security Agency in Fort Meade, Maryland. He had received the call from Montiagro just before leaving his office for the day. Maybe this was the opportunity to finally move on with his life and get out of the shadow of the Virgin Atlantic disaster. He wondered if perhaps a position with Vatican security might be just the change he needed.

"So if you're not offering me a job with the Guard, then what?" Wyatt said.

"Are you familiar with the Venatori?" Montiagro said.

"Of course, Your Excellency. Along with the FBI and the CIA, the NSA exchanges data with the intelligence arm of the Vatican on a regular basis."

"Very good," Montiagro said. "The Venatori is the information-gathering agency of the Holy See and is responsible for briefing the pope on international affairs. The agency processes the data you send each day. As you know, we also have a daily report that is forwarded to the NSA and other Western agencies as well."

Wyatt nodded, realizing that little was known about the Venatori other than that it was one of the oldest spy organizations in the world.

"We feel we need to bring on a special field analyst to work out of this office. Unlike the Swiss Guard, a Venatori agent does not have to be a Catholic. In some instances, we have agents in other countries who are not even Christian. You see, Mr. Wyatt, the Holy See is governed by the laws of man *and* God. We sometimes get caught up in our own agendas and forget that there are things that can and must be explained by logic and facts. We value a person like you to keep our feet firmly on the ground as we analyze data and information."

The proposition was certainly curious, Wyatt thought. What made them seek him out? "As much as I respect your position and the place the Holy See occupies in the international community, I'm not sure what needs you have that would require someone like me."

Montiagro laced his fingers and rested his hands on the desktop. "We have watched your involvement with hostage negotiations and suicidal fanatics over the past several years. We have monitored your work in a dozen or so national and international situations in which you took part in negotiating with terrorists. Saving lives is important to the Vatican."

"Well, I appreciate your confidence, but I'm not always successful. I've had my share of losses."

"We understand," Montiagro said. "And we know you took the loss of the Virgin Atlantic flight personally."

Wyatt's chest tightened. He hoped Montiagro didn't keep on with the same point.

"What we are impressed with is that the United States government has enough faith in Thomas Wyatt to call upon him in the most critical situations."

If he was going to leave his job for another, Wyatt needed a better understanding of what that job was. "I am still unclear what assets I bring to your table. You're not at war. You have no standing army, no physical threats other than the usual religious fanatics we all deal with daily."

"Maybe," said Montiagro. "Maybe not." The archbishop placed his palms flat on his desk. "Unfortunately, you're incorrect on all the issues you raise concerning war, armies, and physical threats to the Holy See. For instance, from the standpoint of war, we—"

Wyatt's cell phone chirped. He held up his hand to the archbishop as he pulled it from the belt clip and read the caller ID. "I deeply apologize, Your Excellency, but I must take this call. It's from the agency."

"I understand," Montiagro said.

Wyatt stood and walked away from the desk before pressing the talk button. He listened intently for a moment before turning back to the archbishop. "Excellency, do you have a TV available? There is breaking news that I think we both should watch."

"Of course," Montiagro said. He rose and opened a large cabinet, revealing a wide-screen TV. After pushing the power button on the remote, the image and sound of the Satellite News Network sprang to life.

The first image was of a massive fireball streaking across the night sky. Although there was no point of reference, Wyatt assumed something large had caught fire and burned in flight.

The announcer said, "This is video shot from off the east coast of Africa as the International Space Station tumbles out of control and burns up in the atmosphere. The spectacular sight in the night sky could be seen for thousands of miles. The terrible tragedy started with the report from the Russian Space Agency that the three-man crew—a United States Navy captain, a colonel in the Russian Air Force, and a Russian cosmonaut—all committed suicide just after causing the station to leave orbit. A short time later, it crashed into the Indian Ocean."

Archbishop Montiagro seemed frozen, his gaze transfixed on the images as Wyatt came to stand by his side.

"This is unbelievable," Wyatt said.

Montiagro turned to Wyatt. "Actually, no." He placed his hand on Wyatt's arm. "This, Mr. Wyatt, is why we called you."

BATTLEGROUND

MONTIAGRO MUTED THE SOUND on the television.

"I don't understand, Your Excellency," Wyatt said.

"You will soon enough. Thomas, we are at war. Every moment, every second, every breath we take, we are fighting for our lives—our souls. As real a war as those being fought in a dozen other terrible, painful, bloody places on this planet. The war we are engaged in started a long time ago. And it will not end until one side—those who believe in the goodness of man or those who see only the blackness in human hearts—wins."

The nuncio gazed at the live coverage on the TV screen. "You would never know it, but we are in the midst of a battleground. The Church is the center of the war for human souls." He looked at Wyatt. "We need someone like you to help fight this battle. You understand human behavior. One way that our enemy wins a battle is to cause a soul to commit the ultimate sin against God—the sin of suicide. The army we fight is led by Satan. The Nephilim have meticulously planned for the day they will strike back at God and take away the one thing he treasures most, his prized creation—man."

"Nephilim?"

"Offspring of the Fallen Angels, the rebel angels cast out from Paradise after the Battle of Heaven."

"You think that all suicides are some kind of demonic possession?" Wyatt asked. Actually, he'd like to think that was the explanation, though devils and demons were more on the periphery of what he believed. But it would lessen the weight of failure he felt about the Virgin Atlantic incident. Talking down a man from committing suicide would seem a whole lot different from talking down a demon.

"Not all," Montiagro continued. "But we believe the war is escalating."

"Why?" Wyatt asked.

Archbishop Montiagro pointed to the TV. "Because, Mr. Wyatt, the signs are escalating as well."

THE PREDICTION

"Noah's Ark? In Peru? You've got to be kidding," Cotten said, beer sloshing from the bottle she waved in reaction to Edelman.

"That doesn't compute," Paul said as Nick nodded in agreement.

Edelman pasted that same tolerant smile on his lips and looked at Paul before turning to Cotten. "No, Ms. Stone, I am not kidding. But maybe I did mislead you. Let me qualify. The Great Flood story is common amongst many cultures, usually passed on from generation to generation through oral tradition and then later turning up in written language. Even the Inca had a flood myth. The Incan legends profess that the early Andes people were survivors of the Great Flood and that they then populated the region. There are literally hundreds and hundreds of flood myths around the world—Scandinavian, Asian, African, Australian, Near East, Pacific Island. Not a corner of the planet is without a flood story.

"Theologians are always happy to point out that fact because those cultural legends and early texts corroborate the event recorded in biblical scripture." Edelman paused, staring at the artifact. "But the inscriptions on this crystal do not chronicle the account of a Great Flood."

"Didn't you just say it did?" Paul asked.

"Not exactly," Edelman said. "You see, the inscriptions on this tablet *predict* a massive flood. It reveals that a flood is *going* to occur, and it spells out specific directions for how to prepare."

"You mean as in build the boat and gather up the animals two by two?" Cotten asked.

Edelman traced his finger beneath some of the glyphs as he spoke. "It gives specific instructions for building a vessel, yes—an ark, if you will."

"Look, I was brought up in the Bible Belt," Paul said, "and we tend to lean toward the fundamentalist side. I remember being taught that the whole point of the Flood was God cleansing the earth of sinners—everyone but Noah and his family."

Cotten set her bottle down. "But this would mean there was more than one Noah."

Paul smacked his lips after taking a slug of his beer. "You said these people moved all around the world. How do you know this wasn't a crystal given to Noah? Or maybe he created it or had it made. Like an instruction manual or something. Then someone brought it here."

"The glyphs," Edelman said. "They were not part of Noah's writing or reading repertoire."

Paul shrugged, a pinch of embarrassment in his expression.

"If the inscription proves to be a *prediction* of the Great Flood here in Peru," Cotten said, "the multiple-Noahs thing is going to fly in the face of the Bible story of Noah."

"Fundamentalists aren't going to be happy if this screws up Genesis," Paul said. He turned to Cotten. "Just the opposite of your creation-fossil story." With a caring smile, he said, "Sure you want to go down that road?"

"It's the only road I've got right now." Cotten looked at Edelman. "Paul has a point about the multiple-Noahs thing, doesn't he?"

"Yes," Edelman said. "But even more than that. It is not just *what* is written here. We have an object thousands of years old inscribed in a language encompassing a variety of symbols, none of which are native to any one culture. By the best estimates, it would have taken an ancient scribe at least a lifetime to complete, and that is if he had precise diamond-cutting tools and the like. And its message predicts an event that tradition says occurred over five thousand years ago." He gestured toward the crystal tablet. "So the big question is not what it says, but who wrote it?"

Cotten felt her heart stutter. "Maybe we're looking at the handwriting of God."

THE MIST

IT WAS PITCH-BLACK AND cold as Edelman, Cotten, Paul, and Nick sat around the large folding table and ate a special farewell dinner in the mess tent.

"We should have hired an American cook instead of a native," Paul said. "I don't know if I can ever get into eating guinea pigs."

"Don't think of it as guinea pig," Cotten said. "Call it by the Peruvian name, *cuy*—it might help. I find it pretty tasty, actually."

"It is all in what you are used to," Edelman said before taking a fork of potatoes. "You know, women are more likely than men to perceive something as disgusting. Disgust is nature's way of protecting us from disease. It follows that women would have a higher sensitivity—they are the child bearers and the caretakers. Interesting fact from research done in the UK: as reproduction ability declines with age, so does the sensitivity to disgust."

Paul thumped his fork on the butterflied *cuy*, hesitating to take the first bite.

"If we were in Korea, you could have a marvelous soup called *bosintang*," Edelman said.

"I'm afraid to ask," Paul said.

"Rover," Cotten said, and gave a little barking sound.

Paul groaned.

"I can give you the URLs of sites that post recipes for exotic foods," Edelman told him.

"Pass," Paul said, poking the *cuy* with his fork.

Nick leaned over to Cotten and whispered in her ear. "You getting as tired of that know-it-all-prick as I am?"

She acknowledged the question with a slight nod. Cotten had grown weary of Edelman's constant encyclopedic mind as well, but she knew they should respect their host. She turned to Paul. "Go on. Don't be such a wuss. Take a bite."

"Yeah, man, do it," Nick said. "As for me, I'm starving. Shit, I'd eat the south end of a northbound llama about now." He jammed a chunk of meat in his mouth. "Mmm, mmm, mmm."

Paul lifted his fork. "You're gonna tell me it tastes like chicken, right?"

"Doesn't everything?" Edelman said.

"Maybe I was a—what'd you say, child bearer or caretaker—in my other life," Paul said. "I can't even get past frickin' tofu, and now I'm expected to eat . . . *cuy*." He cut off a piece and slowly lifted it to his mouth.

Nick grinned as much as he could while chewing some more, then gulped and washed it down with bottled water. "Pretend you're on a reality show and there's a million bucks at stake."

Paul slipped the meat past his lips. He held the fork in the cave of his mouth for a tentative moment before scraping the guinea-pig meat off with his teeth. His nose flared and wrinkled, his jaw muscles working slowly. "Not too bad, I guess," he said, still chewing. Finally, he swallowed.

Edelman raised his bottled water. "Here is to living on the edge, young man."

Cotten heard a yelp from the direction of the dig team's campfire, though its faint glow was no longer visible in the ever-thickening mountain mist. She knew they too were celebrating, as they did every night, but with something stronger than water—a concoction they home-brewed daily.

"I'd like to propose a toast," Nick said. "Here's to the discovery of Doc's crystal artifact, along with Paul's new sense of culinary adventure." He held his water bottle high, reciting, "Some Guinness was spilt on the barroom floor when the pub was shut for the night, when out of his hole crept a wee brown mouse and stood in the pale moonlight. He lapped up the frothy foam from the floor, then back on his haunches he sat. And all night long, you could hear the mouse roar—bring on the goddamn cat!"

Paul and Edelman laughed while Cotten shook her head. "Cheers," she said, raising her water.

"What we need," Nick said, "is some of that stuff our friends drink every night." He motioned in the direction of the dig team's laughter and hollering.

"Then go ask José to share," Paul said. "He told me earlier they just whipped up a new batch."

"Think I might," Nick said, standing. He brushed off his pants and trotted into the mist.

Cotten pulled her Elph camera out and snapped a few pictures of Paul finishing his guinea-pig dinner. "Now you've really got something to write home about," she said to him, putting the Elph in the pocket of her cargo pants. "And I've got the evidence."

A few moments later, Nick returned with a whiskey-type bottle encased in a dark leather sheath. As he held it up for all to see, Cotten admired the multicolored markings. On one side were the words *Lineas de Nazca* and several drawings of the famous Nazca lines—a monkey, spider, and bird. There were also depictions of a distant snow-capped mountain and a colorfully dressed native woman.

"Just what the doctor ordered," Nick said, smiling broadly. He passed out paper cups, pulled the cork from the bottle, and poured a small amount into each. "Doc, José said this shit will make those markings on the tablet crystal clear in no time. Get it? *Crystal* clear."

When everyone had a cupful, Paul raised his. "Here's to the Great Flood. Oh, and to Noah—one hell of a shipbuilder."

"Cheers," said Edelman. "To all the Noahs."

Cotten took a small sip and immediately fought back a gagging reaction. Rather than the smooth velvet taste of her favorite Swedish vodka, this was more like drinking razor blades. The first swallow was a struggle, but she discovered a distinctive pepper aftertaste that was somewhat pleasant. And it was strong, heating her insides all the way down.

"I must say, this isn't bad—after the first shock, anyway," Edelman said. He finished his cup.

"There's plenty left, Doc," Nick said, holding out the bottle.

"Well," Edelman said, "one more couldn't hurt."

"Yes, to all the Noahs," Cotten said, raising her cup. She turned to Edelman. "What about what's on the rest of the tablet, after the Flood prediction—those lines and dots? What does it say?"

"I can only muddle through the top half of the tablet," Edelman answered. "I was lucky with the semi-recognizable glyphs, and of course being familiar with the story of the Flood helped. But the glyphs stop midway down the tablet with the remark that God will cleanse the earth a second time, but not by flood. Then the whole language of the tablet changes—no more glyphs. Those dots and lines look like a graphic rendering of a form of khipu, and that is not my field if it is being used as a language. But I imagine, since the first half describes the Great Flood and how to survive, the other half might do the same—maybe something dramatic like how to stop Armageddon. The last that I can make out of the glyphs says something like the second cleansing is still to come and will be led by the daughter of an angel."

* * *

Cotten Stone staggered into her tent, finding it hard to remain on her feet, hard to breathe. After only one cup of the native brew, her head had spun. But what she had just heard Edelman say overshadowed the effects of the potent local drink.

Led by the daughter of an angel.

A burning sensation started in her abdomen and moved in throbbing waves through her body. Her vision blurred, and her fingertips tingled as if she'd touched a light socket. Cotten cupped her hands over her nose and mouth and breathed in and out to ward off hyperventilation. She focused on easy breathing and relaxing, slowing her heart rate.

Even over her panic, she still heard Edelman, Paul, and Nick in the distance—their laughter and blather sounding more like gibberish than speech.

Cotten dug through her bag, finally latching onto the plastic pill bottle. She struggled with the childproof cap, cursing it. At last the cap popped off, and Cotten dumped the Ativan into her palm. She took one and threw it onto the back of her tongue. She swallowed hard, getting the pill down her throat. Then she put the rest back in the bottle and dropped onto her cot, pressing her palms to her temples. They throbbed like kettle drums. She wondered if the tightness growing in her chest meant she was having a heart attack.

Cotten lay motionless for what seemed like an hour, until the throbbing in her head subsided. Even in the chill of the mountain air, she was bathed in sweat—unable to stop Edelman's words.

Led by the daughter of an angel.

She heard Edelman in the distance, his proper English accent distorted and slurred. Were the guys still awake? Still partying?

Edelman called out her name—asking if it was Cotten who approached from the mist.

Then he screamed.

FIREFLIES

Be sober, be vigilant;
because your adversary
the devil, as a roaring lion,
walks about, seeking whom
he may devour.

—1 PETER 5:8

COTTEN SAT UP AND swung her feet onto the dirt floor, blind in the blackness. Was she sure she'd heard Edelman scream? It had to be a mistake, she thought.

She stood and brought her hand to her face—her skin cold and clammy, her hair sodden, her balance shaky.

She felt under the cot for her flashlight. Flipping the switch revealed the thick mist filling her tent. The beam barely penetrated the distance to the entrance flap a few feet away. She was enveloped in a cloud—droplets of moisture moving slowly in the shaft of light like plankton in the depths.

Cotten reached for the tent flap. She stepped outside and felt a chill beyond what could be attributed to the altitude.

"Dr. Edelman?" she called. "Paul? Nick?"

No answer.

The fools had gotten sloppy drunk and decided to spook her. She didn't find it funny. Of course, they couldn't have known how Edelman's translation had traumatized her. If they had, they wouldn't be pulling this stupid prank. She'd done her best to hide her reaction, excusing herself from the party, claiming she'd had too much to drink and wasn't feeling well. They were probably too loaded to conclude anything else was wrong with her.

She saw a faint glow approaching in the distance. The idiots were creeping up on her, but their flashlights gave them away. She didn't want them to realize how much their practical joke scared her.

"All right, guys. I know what you're up to," she called out.

The glow brightened, turning from light orange to vibrant rose to brilliant red. And with it came the disturbing sound of flapping—like sails in a gale.

Suddenly, José bounded out of the thick mountain mist—at least she thought it was José, but the flames engulfing him made it difficult to tell.

"José!" she screamed as he ran past before disappearing back into the night. This was no prank. "Oh Jesus, what's happening? Paul? Nick?" Where were they?

Then other screams ripped through the encampment. One sounded like Nick, but she could not be sure.

Again, from out of the mist, Cotten realized something was approaching—a radiance emerging from the dark wall of clouds.

Fireflies.

Here in the high mountains, Cotten saw thousands of fireflies. In a flickering mass, they moved toward her until they orbited her in swirling light. Spiraling, they coiled tighter, so near she could feel the air stir against her skin. Their motion seemed to radiate heat. She sensed the distinct odor of sulfur as she clamped her hand over her mouth and nose. Frantically, she batted at the tiny points of light. They swarmed as if they wanted to penetrate, to find a way inside her. Though she willed her feet to move, they didn't, and her hands suddenly came to rest at her sides, her flashlight dropping to the ground. Not even her eyelids had the power to close. Paralyzed. Had the fireflies done it, or had she scared herself into this state? For a moment, she wondered if she was breathing.

Then, in an instant, they were gone—a streak of light in the darkness.

Cotten blinked as if coming out of a trance, her faculties returning.

More screams of terror—someone shouting in Quechua. One of the dig team?

Picking up her flashlight, Cotten tramped through the camp, afraid to run, afraid she would stumble and fall. As if fulfilling her own prophecy, her foot snagged, and she fell prone on the ground, mouth in the dirt, arms flailing, knees thudding. Immediately, she scrabbled up on her left elbow and shone the light toward her feet to see what had tripped her. Paul's body lay in the dirt, his throat slashed and gaping. In his hand was a large, bloody knife.

"Oh God. Oh shit." She kicked herself away from Paul's body, scooting backward. Had he slit his own throat?

Cotten scrambled to her feet, the flashlight's beam jumping wildly in the fog. Ahead, just inside the mess tent, was the table where she and her friends had eaten their last dinner together. There was still *cuy* left in an aluminum tray in the center of the table. The bottle of native brew rested on its side.

"Nick?" she called lowly. "Where are you?"

She switched off the flashlight, immersing herself in the night. The beam would make her an easy target. The only light came from inside Edelman's tent. Cautiously, she moved toward it.

"Edelman?" she whispered, peeling back the tent flap. She heard a soft hum and felt a subtle movement of the air. She turned as a bright light came from behind her. A thick swarm of fireflies flooded into the tent, bringing with them a suffocating heat and that choking sulfur odor. This time they ignored her, instead gathering and hovering over the table. They descended and shrouded the crystal tablet. Beside it, Edelman's papers ignited and turned to ash, blowing away and floating in the air.

Cotten shrank toward the rear of the tent. Bumping into a crate, she looked down and gulped back a cry when she saw what lay at her feet.

THE RUINS

Cotten looked down at Edelman's body sprawled on the ground. He had apparently crashed onto a crate and then rolled off onto the dirt floor. A pistol lay next to him. The dark smudge of gunpowder on his right temple surrounded a small, almost bloodless entrance hole. Cotten knelt and lifted his head. His eyes were open, the pupils fixed and dilated. His head lolled to the side, revealing the exit wound. "Oh God," she whispered, covering her mouth. The left side of his head was gone.

A small plopping sound made her look up. A glob of Edelman's brain had slid from the canvas and dropped onto the ground. Cotten's stomach contents gurgled up into her throat. She shuddered and fought back the urge to vomit. José—burned alive. Paul—throat slashed. And Edelman had blown his brains out. What the hell was going on?

Suddenly, the glow from the fireflies intensified. Cotten stared transfixed as the crystal tablet levitated a few inches above the table beneath the mantle of glowing insects. She was captivated by the surreal sight, unable to turn away. A feeling of rapture swept through her—that she was in the presence of the supernatural, that it was a part of her. Then, just as quickly, she felt nauseated, realizing that whatever was in the tent with her was pure evil.

With all her strength, Cotten forced herself to her feet and carefully maneuvered around Edelman's body, sidestepping the artifact table and slipping past the fireflies to the tent entrance before bolting out.

Quickly, she made the decision to avoid the dig crew's encampment, terrified she would find more of the same horror. Aiming her beam at the ground, Cotten ran in the opposite direction, toward the path to the dig site. She stumbled along the uneven trail, exposed roots making it hard to maintain her balance. The mountain mist rolled past her in waves—thick in places, thinning in others. The flashlight barely penetrated the clouds.

She tried to push the images of death to the back of her mind, but it was impossible to think of anything else. Her friends appeared to have killed themselves or each other. "Oh God, oh God, oh God." Her words kept the rhythm of her feet pounding the ground.

Cotten looked back once and thought she saw tiny pinpoints of light—the fireflies.

And what were they? Some form of aggressive insects, like killer bees? Had they levitated Paul's knife like they had the tablet? Had they set José on fire just as they had burned Edelman's notes? Forced him to shoot himself? Maybe they were only a product of her imagination, brought on by the native drink—hallucinogens from some local drug mixing with her medication—or due to her earlier panic attack.

No, she'd fallen over Paul's body, she'd felt the heat of the flames that had engulfed José, and she'd held Edelman's head, still warm. Although she hadn't seen Nick, one of the screams had sounded like his voice. Those were no hallucinations.

Winded from the high altitude, Cotten struggled to stay on the path. She'd become familiar with the intricacies of the trail leading to the ruins over the past few days.

Suddenly, the first of the massive structures loomed out of the darkness, the wall of white granite stones. She dodged the trenches and tools that littered the site and moved up the steep ascent to the domed structure she'd asked Edelman about. An Incan observatory, he had told her. Although she couldn't see it through the darkness and heavy mist, she remembered it clearly. Glancing backward, she saw nothing following her as she climbed to the observatory.

The round outer wall appeared, and the path became steps. Cotten heaved for air, her lungs laboring and her legs burning. She remembered the narrow pathway that hooked around to the trail, which they had followed when they'd arrived the first day.

Rimancu wasn't that far from here, Cotten thought. If she could find it, she could hide there until daylight—until she could figure out what was going on. Then she would go to Machu Picchu and get in touch with the authorities.

The mist flowing around her seemed to have a life of its own, moving in undulating waves like a giant invertebrate swimming slowly past. Deep in the jungle, far from camp, she finally stopped, pressing her back against the trunk of a tree. Rimancu had to be near. She waited until she caught her breath and then continued on. Shining the flashlight ahead, Cotten finally spotted the red block of wood.

Shortly, she found the entrance to one of the Rimancu structures. Bent over with her hands on her knees, she cried with relief. Cotten wiped her nose with the back of her hand, feeling dirt smear across her face. Inside the ruin, she found a room congested with debris from a collapsed wall overgrown with heavy vegetation. A black tree trunk, twisting like a strand of licorice, grew up from the stone floor and disappeared into the darkness overhead—its base as thick as a large man.

Cotten shuffled over a carpet of live and composting plants. She crouched in a far corner behind the tree trunk. Swinging her flashlight in an arc to take in her surroundings, she leaned against a stone fallen from the crumbling wall. She flipped off the switch to conserve the battery.

Her thumping pulse was the only sound she heard. The pungent odors of jungle, perpetual dampness, ancient stone, and soil filled her nostrils.

Cotten closed her eyes, straining to make sense of what had happened.

Paul and Nick had joked on the flight from Lima about scoring some local drugs—stuff that they heard could make you crazy. Was that what happened? Was the native drink to blame? Had the side effects of the brew made them suicidal? Then why not her? But the fireflies . . .

The fireflies.

Cotten opened her eyes and jerked back against the wall.

Thousands of them filled the ancient room. The luminescent mass took on a pattern, first like a swirling desert dust devil, then more complicated—a double helix glowing bright enough to cast the shadow of the twisted tree on the stone wall.

She got to her feet and edged along the wall, coming to an opening just big enough for her to squeeze through. Cotten stooped and pushed away the clinging growth that blocked her, finally emerging into the jungle again. She ran, searching for the footpath. Suddenly, a coil of vine caught her ankle, and down she went, slamming her head on a stone, a stone hewn by Incan hands over five hundred years ago.

ELI

RICHARD AND MARIAH HAPSBURG sat in their Cadillac Escalade on the shoulder of North Racebrook Road near the gates to Eli Luddington's estate in Woodbridge, Connecticut. Mariah stared out the window as a silver Mercedes passed. The occupants were probably headed to Luddington's dinner party, she guessed. Her husband, Richard, sat behind the SUV's steering wheel, sulking, and it was pissing her off. She knew she could wheedle anything out of Richard, get him to do whatever she needed if she handled him right. And that was her responsibility . . . keeping him in line.

Tonight she had blown it, losing her temper because of his whining. He didn't want to go to the party, preferring to stay home and work on some research project. He'd complained the entire drive over, and finally she had cracked, letting loose with a savage outburst. Now she had to backtrack and smooth the little prick's feathers.

Mariah sidled over to him and put her hand on his knee. "I'm sorry. I should be more sensitive to your feelings. I know you don't enjoy these kinds of things, but it's good for the business. These people head the foundations that feed the gallery's coffers. And they fund the private grants. We have to schmooze with them."

Richard removed her hand from his knee and held it down on the leather seat.

"Richard," she whispered, leaning so close her lips touched his ear. "Come on, baby. I said I'm sorry, didn't I?" She nipped the top of his ear as she curled her long legs up on the seat.

Richard retreated toward the driver's door. "Mariah, I'm well aware of why we have to suck up to these people."

"Then why make it so difficult?"

Richard shook his head. "It's Luddington."

"But you know you have to deal with Eli. There's no way around that." Whether he liked it or not, Richard and his sort ultimately answered to Luddington. But in her case, she had made the choice herself. And every day she was thankful for it. Eli was her savior.

A little more work on Richard and he'd be fine. She knew his weakness. Mariah slid her hand along his leg and stroked his inner thigh. "Let me apologize," she whispered, breathing on his neck before taking a soft nibble just below his jaw. "You know how much I want to please you," she said, caressing his crotch with one hand while unbuckling his belt with the other.

Richard leaned his round, shiny head against the headrest and sighed.

"That's a good boy," she said. "Just let me do all the work. You like it when I apologize, don't you? I think you like me to be naughty just so we can make up."

The belt fell away, and her fingers went to work on the button at the top of his fly.

"Mariah," he said, his voice husky, "we—"

"Shh," she whispered, slipping the zipper down and sliding her hand inside. When Richard moaned, she smiled.

So easy.

"Move the seat back," she whispered.

Richard pressed the button and the power seat glided silently away from the steering wheel.

"Someone might see," he said. But his eyes were already glazed with desire, and he made no attempt to stop her.

Mariah freed him from his trousers as she kicked off her spiked sandals. No sense in bruising the leather.

Richard's eyes closed as she took him into her mouth. His abdominal muscles fluttered against her cheek. When he was ready, Mariah lifted her dress, climbed on top, and pulled her panties aside. Gazing intently on his face, she lowered herself.

She watched the lustful haze come over him, the lost-in-ecstasy squint, the blank stare, and the clenched jaw. Working him slowly, she let the heat build as she teased him. Mariah took Richard's hands and placed them over her breasts.

"Take it off," Richard said. "Take the dress off."

She moaned, moving his hands from her breasts to under her hem, placing them just below her small waist onto the crest of her hips. There was no need to take the dress off. This wouldn't take long.

"Oh God," he uttered. "You feel so good. What are you doing to me?"

It was a rhetorical question, and there was no need to answer. She held his sweaty head in her hands, rising and falling to a vigorous rhythm.

"Yes, baby. Oh yes, Rumjal," she whimpered, knowing his real name would electrify him. She was a pro at sex talk, knowing just what he liked to hear. She let her long blond hair fall across his face as she rocked. She knew he could smell her hair, her sex. "Rumjal, Rumjal! Oh God, I'm so close . . ." Mariah knew her words would put him over the edge. When she led him to believe that he was exciting her, bringing her to orgasm, it quickly took him to his climax. After all, it was getting late. They had to get on to the party.

She groaned and made her body shudder.

He tensed beneath her with a choked-off breath and bucked for an instant. She felt him shoot into her.

Then it was over.

Richard went limp as she leaned onto him.

"My sweet baby," she said. "Give me your handkerchief. I need to clean up."

He wrapped his arms around her, holding her tightly. "That was so goddamn good," he said. "Let me catch my breath."

Mariah sat up. "Can't. We'll be late." She eased off him and took the handkerchief from his inside jacket pocket. On her knees, she wiped his mess from between her legs.

"There," she said, tossing the handkerchief onto the floor mat before readjusting her panties. She climbed back to her side of the seat. "You tidy up, too. Can't look like you just got fucked in the front seat of your SUV."

Mariah put her heels on and smoothed her dress. She opened her small handbag and took out her miniature brush before switching on the visor light and looking in the mirror. "Not too much damage," she said, brushing her hair and then finger-combing and fluffing it up. Good thing she hadn't worn it up, or she would have had trouble becoming presentable.

Mariah leaned forward, inspecting her makeup in the mirror. Suddenly, she flinched and recoiled.

"What's the matter?" Richard asked.

She knew that what she saw reflected was the work of her imagination—a nightmare from her past. The hideous face with the horrible keloid scars tracking across it like mole tunnels, the missing eye, the disfigurement—the monster—it wasn't really there.

"You okay?" Richard asked, reaching to touch the bare skin of her arm.

She inched back to the mirror and touched her face with her fingertips. She was beautiful—flawless skin, full lips, seductive mouth, captivating blue topaz eyes with coal black lashes.

"Yes, I'm fine."

Eli Luddington was indeed her savior.

* * *

Richard and Mariah Hapsburg sat on the dark Concorso Italian sofa in Eli Luddington's study. Richard's finger tapped on one of the copper nail heads on the armrest. Across from them, Luddington sat in a matching wingback holding a glass of François Voyer Extra Grande Champagne cognac, its rich caramel color radiant in the light of the huge fireplace. The other guests had departed, and the three were alone. As always, Eli was impeccably dressed. Tonight he wore a three-piece cashmere navy blue suit and a heavily starched white dress shirt with French cuffs—every crease crisp, every nail manicured, every hair in place.

Richard felt rumpled and ragged in Eli's presence.

"Excellent work," Luddington said. "You've done well."

Though the voice was composed and articulate, it rasped in Richard Hapsburg's ear. He didn't like Luddington, but had no choice. Unlike Mariah, Richard was born to this servitude—it was in his blood.

Richard brushed his hand over the top of his bald head, feeling the stubble of his red hair with his palm. He wished he had shaved it this morning.

"Aren't you going to say thank you?" Mariah said to her husband. "Eli just gave you a compliment."

"Of course," Richard answered, with an effort to disguise his irritation. He knew that he shouldn't allow any display of displeasure, because in the grand scheme, Eli Luddington regarded him as expendable.

"Did Edelman translate the tablet?" Luddington asked.

Richard composed himself. "We can't be sure. We don't think Edelman or anyone else present was capable of deciphering anything other than the glyphs."

"Did you not speak with Edelman? What did he tell you?" Luddington asked.

"He seemed more concerned about *how* the tablet was made," Richard answered. "Said he had a vague notion about the upper portion but hadn't settled entirely on all the inscriptions. He wanted us to bring some other experts down, in particular someone who could translate khipu into a language, which tells me he did not decipher the complete message. He had no idea what he was looking at. The cameras, audiotapes, and notes—everything was destroyed. No one is left to tell what they saw. The authorities will assume they died from drinking a bad batch of the local Indian brew. It's an acceptable theory. There has been so much research recently on the influence of drug-induced suicide. And of course, with the added element of native hallucinogens, the drink did its job. They ingested a concoction riddled with such an array of drugs that they were not only hallucinating and experiencing paranoia, but they were also driven to suicide. At least that is the evidence they will find."

Luddington stood and walked toward Richard and Mariah. "Then it appears you have taken care of everything." He stopped in front of Mariah, reached out, and stroked her cheek. "To Richard," he said, raising his glass.

Richard had declined the cognac, but Mariah was on her second. She touched her glass to Luddington's and toasted. "Yes, to Richard."

Richard looked at his wife as she sipped the cognac. How could he be so lucky? When he entered a room with her on his arm, he knew every person there asked that very same question. She wasn't just beautiful. Mariah had an exquisite elegance that was so striking it took their breath away. Not glamorous or flashy. Those words fell far short. The simplicity of her beauty was what set her apart. She was perfection. And she was his.

Richard smiled at his wife.

The toast complete, Luddington moved to the fireplace and set his cognac on the mantel. He picked up a small box tied with a ribbon. "And for you, Mariah. Something special. A little Arabian opulence."

"Oh, Eli," Mariah said. "What have you done?"

Eli strode across the room and presented Mariah with the gift.

She smiled at him as she untied the ribbon and opened the box. "Oh my goodness," she gushed, seeing the contents. "Amouage!"

"They say it is the most expensive perfume in the world," Eli said.

Mariah held the lead crystal and gold bottle to her throat. "You spoil me so," she said. "Thank you, Eli." She held the perfume out toward Richard. "Can you believe what Eli has done?"

Richard said nothing.

When Mariah opened the bottle, the aroma of its ingredients filled the air. Rose, jasmine, lily of the valley, sandalwood, silver frankincense . . .

"You deserve to be spoiled," Eli said before returning his attention to Mariah's husband. "So now, Richard, what are we doing about the Stone woman?"

Richard Hapsburg felt sweat bead up on the top of his head. "We can't seem to rid ourselves of her. You've said that repeatedly." His voice came in jittery spurts, and he instantly regretted his nervousness. He twisted his Rolex to the inside of his wrist and glimpsed at it. He had no interest in the time, and it didn't register in his brain. He needed to appear nonchalant, unshaken, and noting the time might give that impression.

As calmly and with as much control as he could, Richard said, "She is out of the picture, at least for now. We've already discredited her, and now we've got her traumatized. She witnessed an unspeakable horror and saw something that was not of this world. She won't tell anyone—who would believe her? It would sound like another sensational attempt to make headlines and recover from her last debacle. Right now, she can't be sure of anything, even if deep in her mind she senses it was all done by our hand." Richard tugged at his cuffs, satisfied with his response.

"You know where she is now?" Luddington asked.

"She fled into the jungle, as predicted." He chose the word "predicted" purposefully. "As far as we can tell, she hasn't emerged."

Luddington paced across the late-nineteenth-century Ushak Turkish carpet, finally stopping and stroking the head of a stuffed Bengal tiger that stood forever poised to attack. "She will always be a concern, Richard. That is why she was created."

Richard was perfectly aware not only of who the woman was but also of the fact that she wasn't going away anytime soon. Because of his well-executed plan, though, there might at least be a reprieve. Couldn't Luddington show some gratitude for that?

Richard buried the anger threatening to surface. "I only meant that we may have frightened her enough that a part of her is so terrorized she will choose to stay hidden. She won't want to pursue the tablet or us."

Luddington returned to the mantle for his cognac. He took a sip. "For a while, maybe," he said, seeming to savor the velvet liquid. "Richard, you must stay focused. Be the jeweler with your loupe to your eye, and she the stone beneath. You will document every facet of every move, every step, and every breath she takes. She is our Achilles' heel, Richard. Cotten Stone is our nemesis."

THE SHAMAN

FIRST, COTTEN FELT THE bumping along, the dangling of her arms, the pressure in her head. Then she fought to open her eyes.

She struggled to focus.

Heels. She looked down on old and weathered bare heels traipsing along a jungle path. Someone carried her, a bony shoulder digging into her abdomen. She hung head-down, her chin knocking against sweaty skin.

Jumbled, disconnected thoughts formed in her brain, but nothing coherent. She moaned.

A buzzing sounded in her ears, then turned to ringing, and she felt herself fading out.

* * *

Smoke.

It stung in her nose. Cotten turned away.

Then chanting.

Low, rhythmic. What language?

Same words, over and over, and the harsh smoke coming back to her nostrils.

Cotten turned her head and groaned.

Something moist, a cloth maybe, dampened her lips. She wanted more. A drink. Her tongue was stuck to the roof of her mouth, and her throat was so dry it burned.

A little more from the cloth drizzled through her lips.

Water. Sweet, sweet water.

The chanting stopped, and the smell of smoke diminished.

Her mind seemed to be coming together. Finally, she forced her eyes open.

A man, black eyes surrounded by a dark olive face netted with lines, stared down at her. He arched a brow.

"Good medicine," he said.

Cotten blinked.

Another face came into focus, peering over the man's shoulder. A woman's face, leathery, with glittering black eyes and long black hair pulled tight at the nape of her neck.

Who were they? Where had they brought her? Cotten tried to think of the answers. Had these people raided the campsite? She flinched as the man leaned toward her.

"Good medicine," he repeated. Then he said something to the woman.

The woman nodded and smiled as she spoke in a language Cotten thought was Quechua. The tone was not threatening. Maybe they did not intend to hurt her.

The man also smiled. Perfectly shaped white teeth.

"Ah," the woman said, her face backing away and out of sight.

Cotten's head hurt, especially the right side of her forehead just above her eye. She touched it lightly with her fingertips. There was some kind of bandage, thick and sticky.

"Good medicine," the man said again.

The woman reappeared and held a small pot to Cotten's lips.

"Drink," the old Indian said.

She sipped, and the woman grinned, muttering words that were obviously meant to encourage and approve Cotten's effort.

The taste told Cotten the liquid wasn't just water. There was a tart, fruity aftertaste, but not unpleasant. Cotten swallowed, and the elixir soothed her throat. Some of it spilled out the corners of her mouth and rolled down the sides of her neck.

The woman chattered on as she repositioned herself to tilt Cotten's head up and give her another chance at drinking her concoction.

Cotten took a good gulp, and the woman lowered her head back to the mat.

"Thank you," Cotten said, her mouth finally moist. She looked around and realized that she was in a hut made from stone, thatch, and timber. Suspended from the beams above her hung hundreds of—what could she call them—ornaments? Collections of brilliantly colored feathers, red, yellow, green, teal; plants, dried and fresh; and cordage.

The man noticed her curiosity, stood, and plucked one down to show her. It seemed to be made of a fresh plant material, somewhat like corn tassels, and bound at the base with rough twine. Dragging his thumb across it, he fanned it open so she could see in the center.

It took a moment to register what she was looking at. Threaded in the middle of the tassels was a long, thin white bone, hollow in the center.

"Condor," he said, moving away.

She tracked him with her eyes as he moved to a small pit dug in the dirt floor. A thin trail of smoke coiled from it, rising up and seeping out through the thatch.

The man crouched and held the tassels in the pit until they caught fire. He blew on them, killing the flames, leaving them smoldering and smoking.

He waved it beneath his nose and breathed in and out. He moved back to her and waved it for her to breathe in. Reluctantly, she did so. This was the same smell, the same smoke that was in the air when she'd awakened.

"The smoke calls out the bad spirits. The condor carries them away." Then he took her hand and pressed it to the bandage on her head. "They go with the condor."

Fetishes and talismans, she thought. That's what all those things were hanging above her. It was a medicine man, a shaman, who treated her wounds.

Suddenly, she recalled her flight from the camp to Rimancu, and her fall. She had struck her head and must have lost consciousness.

"How long have I been here?" she asked.

He fumbled for a stick propped against a basket, then brought it close for her to see. Three notches had been etched in the bark-stripped stick.

"Three days?" she asked.

The shaman touched each notch with a long, gnarled, and brown index finger. He flashed his white-toothed smile at her, seemingly proud of his record keeping.

"Rimancu," he said. "It is not a good place for you. They do not let anyone stay."

"Who?"

The man drew back, his face solemn. "*Mahorela*—descendants of the dark heaven."

From the expression on his face, she surmised that she had touched on native myth or theology. Not a subject to be discussed with an outsider.

"I tripped and fell. You found me there—in Rimancu?"

He nodded.

"I guess I'm lucky you were around."

"I was told to go there and find you." He stood, ending the conversation.

"Wait," she said. "Who told you? How would—" Cotten rose up on her elbows and tried to sit erect, but dizziness swamped her.

The man turned and left the hut.

She wanted to ask him more—especially about her friends. Cotten fell back on the woven mat. Like shrapnel, questions embedded themselves in her brain.

Uneasiness swept over her. She had to leave. Get back to civilization. As soon as she was able, she would start the trek out of the jungle, contact the authorities, get help up to the camp.

As she closed her eyes, her mind filled with the vision of the warm, sticky blood flowing from Edelman's head wound, the singeing heat from the flames engulfing José, and Paul's lifeless body on the ground.

But the one vision that dominated them all was of the blinding light from the column of fireflies.

And the levitating tablet.

THE HEALER

THE FOLLOWING MORNING, COTTEN awoke feeling her strength growing and her alertness sharpening. With the brilliant morning sunlight streaming into the hut, she had a fresh clear-headedness that provoked her inquisitiveness.

She looked under the blanket at what she wore. Her clothes had been replaced with a wide drape of soft cloth wound around her. It was bound at the waist with a cloth belt and was fastened at the shoulder with a pin, about five inches long, that had a square head decorated with geometric designs. It appeared to be made from hammered copper. Cotten readjusted the dress and watched the doorway.

As expected, her daily visitors soon arrived, and she sat up.

"Ah, you feel well this morning," the shaman said, entering the hut. His clothing was different from Cotten's—he wore a poncho with bands of fringe hanging below his knees and on his ankles.

The woman followed him, grinning as she always seemed to do. She was dressed like Cotten.

"I feel like I have finally awakened from a bad dream," Cotten said. She touched her head wound—there was no bandage, only a rough patch of skin.

"The medicine is good," the man said, "and the condor is good."

Cotten didn't think they had told her their names, and she was certain she hadn't asked, nor had she told them hers. "I don't know where to start, what to ask first." She decided to begin with her name and in return learn theirs. The man's name was Yachaq, meaning "wise man and healer." The woman was called Pilpintu, which meant "hummingbird."

"She was named that when she became a woman," Yachaq explained, "because she flutters from place to place."

Yachaq liked Cotten's name. "Your name comes from *Pachamama*—Mother Earth," he said.

Though she explained that her name was not spelled the same as the cotton plant, he still seemed to approve and connect it to nature.

Yachaq instructed Pilpintu to help him get Cotten to her feet.

She felt as if she had just climbed out of a pool, her body extraordinarily heavy and her legs weak. She experienced a fleeting moment of lightheadedness that made her grip the forearms of Yachaq and Pilpintu for balance. "Wow, being off your feet for a few days . . ." Her head spun, and her legs started to give way.

They took several steps, guiding her outside. In the bright morning light, Cotten had her first real glimpse of the village—stone huts with thatched roofs, cobbled lanes, llamas and alpacas grazing, bronze-skinned men and women moving about doing daily chores, children playing. There were agricultural terraces carved out of the mountain above her, and the river flowed below the village. She was closer to the valley than she had been at Edelman's campsite. Cotten felt like a time traveler, knocked on her head and transported to a time before Pizarro and his conquistadors. There were no T-shirts, no Nike Airs, no cars or bikes, no sign of modern civilization at all.

Yachaq and Pilpintu guided her to a nearby stone bench. Once Cotten was seated and comfortable, she asked, "Where is Rimancu?"

As she spoke the word, Pilpintu gasped and covered her mouth, her brows pinching.

"There," the man said, pointing up the mountain. "A half day's walk."

She remembered him saying that he had been told to go look for her. How could that be? "Who told you to find me?"

Yachaq stared with his black eyes into hers. "You are not ready yet," he said. "Perhaps tomorrow or the next day."

"I don't understand. And how is it that you speak English? Does anyone else here speak English?"

"You rush . . . like your life, I suspect. Let it unfold, Cotten Stone. If you rush, you will pass thresholds and byways without ever seeing them. All things—all answers—are given to us when we are ready to receive them."

"You've never lived in New York," she said, laughing.

He stared at her with a head slightly cocked to the side. Then he closed his eyes and breathed deeply three times before looking at her again.

She thought he stared because he didn't understand her comment about New York. But when he spoke next, she knew that wasn't what he had been thinking.

"Cotten Stone, I have received your name. To me, to us, to Viracocha, the creator god, you are Mayta. Mayta—the only one."

Cotten choked, craving air as if she were being held under the water.

LIQUID LIGHT

DURING HER DAYS OF recovery, Cotten got to know much of the daily routine of the people in the village. She watched them plant and work the fields. The women chewed corn kernels, along with seeds or fruit, and spit the pulp into jars with warm water to ferment, yielding *chicha*—the Incan version of beer. They domesticated ducks and guinea pigs for food, sheared alpacas and an occasional wild vicuna for wool, and spun the wool into thread with simple spindles and whorls. There were rituals and traditions Cotten discovered dated back centuries.

No day started without prayer.

Yachaq spent considerable time with her, but he had not revealed much about himself. Instead, he prodded, led her, guided her, until finally she confessed what had happened in Edelman's camp that terrible night. Yachaq listened intently, but to her surprise, showed no shock at what she described. He questioned nothing she told him, not even showing a subtle arch of the brow.

One afternoon she watched two young boys participate in a coming-of-age ritual. As she looked upon their blood-smeared faces, Cotten thought of Passover. Her sparse religious upbringing, those early days of summer Bible school, brought back the story of the night when God unleashed the tenth plague upon Egypt—the night all firstborn children were slain, except for those of the Israelites. God instructed them to mark their doors with the blood of a lamb, and they would be *passed over*. How would she ever understand or explain how she was *passed over* that terrible night in Edelman's camp?

Cotten looked around the village. She could learn to live here—to blend in, become invisible. Staying here, hidden in this remote village, would keep her safe. She was a lost cause, and she wanted to remain so.

Sitting at the base of a red-trunked coloradito tree, Cotten watched the ceremony as she fought the onset of tears. She covered her face with her hands, seeming incapable of making a decision on what to do next. Suddenly, she felt a gentle touch on her shoulder.

"Come," said Yachaq. "Let us go for a walk. I think there are things you are now prepared to see."

As they wandered to the perimeter of the village, Cotten asked, "Why don't you ever talk about yourself? I don't know anything about you, yet I've told you almost everything about me." *Almost.*

"There is not much to tell."

"Will you answer if I ask questions?"

"Perhaps," Yachaq said. He smiled at her. "What is it you want to know?"

"Who are you? And how did you come to speak such excellent English?"

Yachaq looked straight ahead as they walked. "When I was a boy, my mother took me into the city to the Monasterio del Cusco, an old Jesuit monastery. Our lives had been hard, and she did not want me to grow up in poverty. So she left me with the monks, making me promise to stay and not follow her home."

"How sad," Cotten said.

"Eventually, I was put up for adoption, and an American family took me in as their son. They moved me to Oregon, where I grew up. I loved them, but still in my heart I ached for my homeland and the way of my people. I never grew accustomed to the American way of life—the lack of spirituality, the lack of respect for *Pachamama*, I could not understand. And so, after my adoptive parents' deaths, I came home to Peru."

"They call you a wise man and a healer," Cotten said.

"Mostly because I am of the two worlds—the ancient and the modern," he said.

Yachaq led her to a trail that angled down toward the Urubamba River. "This path is old," he said. "Generations of my people have left their footprints here."

"I have another question."

Yachaq nodded his willingness to hear it.

"You said you were told to go find me at Rimancu. Who told you?"

The shaman spread his arms to their surroundings. "Your cries were brought to me upon the wind, your fear was swept along with the dark river below us, your pain I felt seep up from the earth itself."

"That's impossible," Cotten said. "How can it be?"

"Patience, Mayta, you are about to learn." With a motion of his arm, they started along the trail.

After what Cotten thought was close to half an hour of walking, Yachaq stopped at a large rock formation with steps carved into its side.

"What is this place?" she asked, touching the wall of carved stone.

"To the *Runa*, the people—that is what we call ourselves—this place is a *huaca*, a holy, mystical place. Go up the steps," he said. "On top, sit and become calm."

At the top, Cotten found a smooth, level plane. As she sat cross-legged on the cool stone, Yachaq joined her.

"Close your eyes." His voice blended with the breeze through the trees.

Cotten obeyed.

"First, you will cast out the thoughts that obstruct your vision. I want you to imagine yourself floating in a pool of sacred light, pure light. Liquid light. Light so brilliant it blocks out every other object. Put yourself there, in the clear, brilliant, liquid light. It bathes you in its warmth—shining, glittering, brilliant light washing over you."

Yachaq waited for her to follow his instructions before speaking again. "Allow the light to pour inside you. Let it come in from every surface of your body. Welcome the light into the center of your being, where it collects and spins—spinning pure light."

Cotten felt the intensity of the light she imagined and experienced tiny vibrations as she envisioned the light spinning inside her core. It was a sensation like none she had ever felt before.

"Do not let go of the light," Yachaq said in a soothing voice. "Set your mind free so it moves effortlessly, not stopping on any thought, traveling through space and time in absolute stillness. The light spins inside you, brilliant, clear. Pure energy, pristine, virginal energy. It moves inside you, the spinning growing larger, an oval now from your base to the crown of your head. Exist only in this perfect moment."

Cotten didn't speak. She was overcome by the sensation. She blocked out all thoughts, concentrating only on the pureness of the light.

"Let it spin down now," Yachaq said. "It grows smaller. Smaller still. Smaller still. The light is fading." He paused.

Cotten felt the diminishing of the light, its glow not as intense, the spin slowing.

"Release it," Yachaq whispered. "Feel the warmth left behind." He paused, then said, "You are ready, Mayta?"

Cotten felt totally at peace, completely cleansed, and reveled in it.

"Say nothing. Listen. Your mind has the clarity of pure energy. There is no clutter. Listen."

She sat in silence, wondering what she should hear.

"Tell me," Yachaq said, "what sounds come to you?"

"I don't hear anything," Cotten said. "Only the rush of the river . . . the wind in the grass and brush . . . the distant, shrill cry of a bird."

"What else?"

Gradually, more sounds came to her, sounds that startled her—many sounds. "The whisper of my clothes against my skin . . . a small animal moving through the grass—I hear its breathing . . . water tumbling a pebble along the river bottom . . . an insect moving among the flowers."

"You learn fast," Yachaq said. "Faster than any of my other students. The spirit of nature dwells in you, does it not?"

He knew, she thought. He knew when he named her Mayta—*the only one*. What's more, he knew what she was.

The daughter of a Fallen Angel.

She could still hear his voice the first time he called her by the Incan name. It was as clear as the water pushing the pebble along the river below.

Cotten Stone opened her eyes and gazed at the surrounding jungle, the valley carved by the mighty river, the mountains beyond. She felt as though she sat atop the world.

"Your first lesson," Yachaq said. "As I told you before, let it unfold. With practice, all answers will come from within. You will create the world in which you live. But in time. This is just the beginning."

Cotten turned to him. "How do you know who I am?"

"We are all of the same energy," he said. "In everything we do, we must respect the entire universe. We *are* our thoughts. Using the energy of the liquid light is the beginning—the first lesson to help you open yourself, recognize yourself as part of the source, the single energy that is everything. It will be important for you when you return to your world." He held out his hand. "Take this. Keep it close. It will remind you that just as the condor has wings to soar, so does your spirit." Yachaq handed her a hollow condor bone and feather fetish.

Cotten looked up at him.

"Take it," he said, spilling it into her hand. "The *cuntur*, the condor, as you call it, does not feed on the living. It depends on carcasses. And so you can send away the dead inside you on the wings of the *cuntur*."

Cotten held it close, then swept her hair from her face. "But I think I have decided to stay here. I could continue to learn your ways. You could be my mentor," she said, hoping to please him.

"Why do you think the liquid light came to you so easily? You are special. Yet you still do not accept that you are chosen?"

"I don't know. I've tried to put that out of my mind. And what if I don't want to be special, to be chosen? I had nothing to do with this life I'm now leading. What if I don't believe it?"

Yachaq looked at her curiously. "We all make deliberate decisions about our lives. You can live your life however you want. But unconsciously you may make doors open that you think you have closed."

Cotten looked away. "It was decided for me, or so I've been told . . . a contract without my signature."

"You have a destiny, Mayta. We all do. What you make of it is within your power."

"I didn't choose my destiny. My father did . . . and God."

"You are not really that different from any of us. We all have our place. Just as there are many paths in the forest leading to different destinations, all the paths of life lie before us each day, each minute. All the paths exist at the same time—we simply choose which to follow. Once you understand the power of the liquid light, you will see the paths before you and choose the one resulting in the most good."

"It just seems that so much of my life has already been chosen for me—especially in the last three years."

Yachaq sat quietly, watching her wring her hands as she tried to find the words.

"You doubt yourself? Your greatness?"

"There's nothing great about me. And yes, I do doubt myself, my decisions. Sometimes I wonder if I really have control over my actions at all. Is it really up to me to decide if I should go home? That's the eventuality of it, isn't it? If I choose not to go back, something outside of my control will come along and force me."

"There can be no forcing. You will open the door that will lead you home, whether you are aware of it or not. Mayta, staying here will not relieve you of your burden."

Yachaq was right. She knew it—had known it for some time now. That was why she was born, why she existed. She knew God's enemies—Viracocha's enemies—were responsible for the creation-fossil hoax, for setting her up and discrediting her. But it was easier to blame herself for not doing her homework. And maybe she hadn't. How easily she'd been led to a place so high just so she could fall. Discrediting her meant she could not expose them. Terrorizing her would cause chaos, fear, and insecurity—and, in the case of Paul, Nick, and Edelman, death.

Cotten choked back the fear. The life she imagined ahead was more than she could bear. "I can't," she said, her voice clear and resolute. "I want to be courageous and brave and . . ." The conviction faltered. "But in truth I'm only a reporter who got too big for her britches. I'm not ready for any valiant task. I'll fail. Don't you see? The world can't trust me. God can't trust me."

PETER PAN

LESTER RIPPLE CUT THE banana into small disks, three in rapid succession and then a pause before the next three. "One, two, three." The pale yellow circles fell onto the bread, which was already spread with chunky Peter Pan peanut butter. Lester left the small pointed butt end of the banana in the peel and threw it in the trash.

He gathered his supper—the sandwich, a Kosher dill pickle, and a glass of buttermilk, which was hard to find these days, and headed for the sofa and TV tray. He already had NPR on the radio, and it was Science Friday—the best.

Lester adjusted his eyeglasses. The Scotch tape he had wrapped around the hinge had a tiny exposed piece of adhesive that tugged at a hair from his eyebrow. He grimaced as the hair pulled out of its follicle, and the glasses sat squarely on the bridge of his nose.

Next to him on the sofa was a test he'd found on the Internet that determined a person's "nerd factor." So far he was batting a thousand—well, almost.

Are you socially inept?

Is your vision worse than 20/40?

Do you know pi past five decimal places?

Were you ever on a chess team?

Do you know more than three programming languages?

He'd answered ninety-nine questions like this, and then came the last one, which made him discount the entire survey. Actually, it had done more than make him disregard it, the last question had made Lester angry because of how it demonstrated society's total disrespect for intelligence.

Have you ever reached sexual climax while programming a computer past 4 a.m.?

Didn't that just prove his observations of today's society? It was athletes and entertainers who got all the millions and the respect. And they didn't need any sort of brain in their heads. And who was to blame for this? The common man. That's who determined what and who is valued. Mankind had lost its integrity.

So be it, Lester thought.

He took a bite of his sandwich and focused his attention to Science Friday. He listened intently. The dialogue was about the future of computers. The person being interviewed was Dr. Benjamin Faigel.

Lester took a big swallow of the buttermilk to wash down the sandwich while registering the radio dialogue in his head. Faigel was leaving something out. Something important. Lester was going to have to call in to the show.

He chewed another bite of sandwich three times—one, two, three—slid his hands down the front of his shirt to wipe off any peanut butter or banana remains, then stood and went to the kitchen wall phone.

He dialed the number for Science Friday, which he had written on a tablet on the counter. He couldn't let this program go on without mentioning how he had already demonstrated qubit operation of a silicon circuit using standard fabrication techniques. He had proved that it could be done. The key was having a high number of operations within the characteristic coherence time of the qubits to control the coupling between qubits . . .

"Yes, this is Lester Ripple," he said when the NPR operator answered. "I need to speak to your guest."

SUNRISE

Prayer is the key of the morning and the bolt of the evening.

—MOHANDAS GANDHI

COTTEN COULDN'T SLEEP. THE liquid light experience had intrigued her, making her want to try it again. If she practiced, maybe it would bring her peace, as Yachaq promised. It certainly worked for Yachaq—and for those few brief moments that it had provided some tranquility for her. She wasn't sure what he meant by saying she could create her world. This had to be the kind of meditation so much of the New Age culture was about, but it seemed to go beyond what she had seen and heard, she thought. Maybe it was the Andes, the mysticism of the Incan culture, the distance from civilization, and of course Yachaq's guidance that had captivated her. She wanted to try it again—this time alone—and see if she could conjure up that same harmony she felt with *Pachamama*. She wanted to recreate the serenity, make it last longer and go deeper.

Cotten sat up on the cot. Sunrise would be the perfect time.

The village was quiet. A faint scent of smoke from a nearby cooking fire, long turned to embers, was all she smelled. In the distance, a dog barked once. She could slip away to the *huaca* and be there at dawn.

To protect herself from the cold, Cotten slipped on the Incan poncho given to her by the women of the village. Stepping from her hut, she looked up at the full moon. Plenty of light. All she had to do was follow the trail. She hesitated for a moment, wondering if she should wait until sunrise and have Yachaq accompany her. No. She wanted to see if she could bring about the same experience on her own. She felt drawn to it—almost compelled.

Heading quietly across the center of the village, Cotten searched for the path Yachaq had shown her. The eastern sky was already changing from coal to charcoal—dawn less than an hour away. She saw the faint outlines of the mountains against the sky.

Cotten was determined to be sitting upon the rock, ready for her passage into the wondrous liquid light, when the sun moved up the sky and silhouetted the great Andes peaks. She wanted to be there as the world first felt the warmth of the new day.

Navigating the path was easier than she thought. Still, she moved slowly and cautiously, fearing that a fall could result in not being found for hours. She had already spent long enough recuperating from her last fall—she wasn't ready to go through that again.

Finally arriving at the *huaca*, she stood at the outcropping and quickly climbed the carved steps to the top.

The glow from the east grew brighter as she took in a deep breath. The cool morning air invigorated her, bringing energy and excitement to her spirit.

Cotten thought back to the way that Yachaq had taught her. Once again, she imagined herself floating in a pool of the liquid light. It became so brilliant that it blocked out the ever-brightening dawn. Cotten felt it flooding her center, spinning down into her core, cleansing her of all but the pure essence of the light.

She allowed her body to be fully immersed. Soon, she heard the sounds of the river and the forest, a few animals moving in the underbrush, the whisper of the wind, the distant call of birds, the—

Suddenly, a voice interrupted. "*Es ella?*"

Cotten jerked back. Her eyes flashed open, immediately becoming blinded by a bright light. She brought her hand up, shielding her eyes from the pain of the light. As her vision slowly adjusted, she saw three figures standing before her. One held a paper in his hand, holding it up and appearing to compare what was on it to her. The other man's flashlight beam was trained on her face.

"*Sí,*" another one said, looking at the paper and back at her. "*Se parece a ella.*" He peered up at Cotten. "*Sí.*"

"*Parate,*" one of the men said. Then, with a heavy accent, he said, "Up."

Getting to her feet, she saw that the three men held weapons—submachine guns—aimed at her.

One motioned for her to proceed down the steps, punctuating his command with the barrel of his weapon.

Cotten did as she was told.

As soon as her foot touched the ground, strong hands twisted her arms behind her, spinning her around. Her wrists were bound and her eyes blindfolded with a bandana. With a shove, she was forced down the path.

She sensed the river to her left and realized they were leading her away from the village. Somehow she knew she would never return.

SHINING PATH

After hours of stumbling blindfolded along the uneven mountain trail, Cotten felt the first drops of rain hit her face. In another minute, the freezing mountain rain fell hard, soaking her and causing the muddy path to become treacherous.

The men who had taken her prisoner had said little since surprising her atop the *huaca*. She knew so little Spanish that she wouldn't have understood anyway. But she did catch one word—*recompense*, reward. Whoever these men were, they had come looking for her to claim a reward. The paper they held when she first saw them must have shown her picture and description. This definitely meant the authorities were searching for her. She hoped it also meant she would be kept alive so they could collect the reward.

In one of their conversations, Yachaq had mentioned pockets of rebels—remnants of the old Shining Path insurgent organization that still could be found in the region. They would jump at the chance to collect a few *nuevo soles* to pay for food, clothing, and ammunition, Cotten thought.

She shivered from the freezing rain that pelted the group as they slowly moved through the forest. More than once she slipped, only to be jerked to her feet by the man gripping her arm.

Suddenly, Cotten was shoved to the ground. She could still hear the rain, but she no longer felt it. They must have found refuge beneath some type of rock formation or in the mouth of a cave.

She lay on her side, her knees drawn up to her chest, trying to keep warm. Although she couldn't see them, she heard the men around her in whispered conversation. They had moved away from her. She wished she could understand what they were saying.

Cotten hoped she had guessed right about their intentions. Then again, maybe they would kill her. Maybe all they needed to collect the reward was her body.

She listened, trying to catch a word or phrase that would give her a clue. There was a quick burst of static and chatter, probably from a walkie-talkie. One of her captors spoke into the radio, bringing a short response.

She heard a man laugh as if he felt festive. It gave her the creeps. But then the voices grew louder, sounding agitated. She smelled something that she thought might be rum, and she also detected the scent of marijuana. Soon, a few of the men began arguing. Maybe they were preoccupied and not watching her. Cotten twisted her wrists, seeing if she could loosen the rope. It was already looser than when they had first bound her, probably from so much movement and the effects of the cold. Finally, she snagged one coil of the rope under her thumb and began driving it up her palm. The closer she got the rope to the tips of her fingers, the deeper the opposite part of the coil cut into the tender flesh of her wrist. She bit down on her bottom lip. The rope moved steadily. At last, she forced it over her fingertips, and the single coil fell loosely to the back side of her hand. Cotten wriggled her hands back and forth, feeling the restriction give way. If she could only see exactly where the men were and what they were doing.

Suddenly, their voices grew silent.

Shit, Cotten thought. They knew what she had done. She lay perfectly still, afraid to breathe.

Footsteps. Someone approached.

One of the men called out, and the footsteps stopped. Then another spoke. There was a moment of silence, followed by shouting. The footsteps reversed. More yelling. Why had the one been coming in her direction? Obviously, he hadn't noticed her wrists or he would have done something about it. Was he planning to rape her, and the others objected—or maybe they wanted their turn with her first?

She had to get away. Cotten slid one hand free from the rope and slowly brought it under her cheek, edging the blindfold down.

Three men stood about fifteen feet from her and to her right at one end of a rock overhang. If she could get to her feet fast enough, she could bolt in the opposite direction and get a quick enough start to lose them in the jungle. She had to believe that they needed her . . . needed her alive to collect the reward, so they wouldn't shoot. At least they wouldn't shoot to kill. She couldn't allow herself to think of the alternative, that all they needed was a corpse.

She lay frozen, working up the courage to make the sudden move. *Just do it*, she thought. *Just get up and run.*

The men's voices sounded more civil, and the pitch had fallen. She should have made her move while they were so engrossed in their argument. The rain seemed to be letting up. Everything was working against her, minute by minute. If she was going to make a break, she had to do it now. As soon as the rain stopped, they would come for her and notice her wrists immediately.

Now.

Cotten sprang up and bolted. She heard shouts as she ran from the shelter of the overhang and fled into the trees.

Instantly, the voices were drowned by the blast of gunfire.

THE LAIR

THE COLD WET LEAVES stung Cotten's face and hands, slapping against her skin as she ran. Bullets zinged past, ripping plants and spraying her with tiny fragments of vegetation. Once she cleared the overhang and left the path, running became impossible. Thick vines and undergrowth covered the forest floor, and she had to fight her way through the wall of brush and trees. She wasn't getting far enough fast enough, but she didn't dare take a chance on moving back onto the trail, where she would be an easy target.

Cotten made so much noise that she knew tracking her would take little effort. Every step was a grueling effort, and with no machete to chop her way through, she was exhausting herself. She had to keep ahead of the bandits and stay out of sight.

Glancing back, she saw that the forest was so thick it filled in behind her, barely leaving any signs that she had trampled through. Cotten plowed forward, feeling briars and dead twigs in the undergrowth pierce her poncho and long Indian dress and prick her skin. The rebels knew the jungle, and in her brief glimpse before being blindfolded, she remembered sheaths dangling from their belts that must have held machetes. They could easily slash their way through this, coming right behind her. She couldn't control her sobs and grunts as the jungle and fear tore at her.

Keep going. Keep going. The words in her head formed a mantra, forcing one foot ahead of the other.

She found it hard to breathe—the exertion and stress at this altitude were suffocating. She was going to die at the hands of some two-bit rebel outfit in the jungles of Peru. And no one would know. She had been missing for almost two weeks already.

If they caught her, would they rape her first before hacking her to pieces—the brutal trademark the Shining Path used against their enemies? If she was lucky, they would just shoot her and get it over quickly.

Reeling from fatigue, Cotten knew she had little chance of going on much farther. She didn't have the physical stamina—the altitude alone was killing her. To the rebels, these mountains, this jungle, was home. She couldn't outrun them, but she was not ready to give up yet.

"Gotta have a plan," she spoke aloud on a winded breath. "Think, Cotten, think!"

Suddenly, she had an idea and stopped briefly to look about. Then she forged on, purposely stomping the foliage, grabbing the vines and peeling them down, crushing the brush under her feet. Methodically, she left behind a less and less obvious trail, attempting to gradually deaden her track until it seemed to just disappear into the forest. But she had to hurry.

Finally, she backtracked to where she had seen a particularly dense clump of underbrush. As delicately as she could, taking her time not to crush sheaves of grass or snap twigs, she made her way to the place she had spotted moments earlier and dropped to her knees. She crawled beneath the lush leaves and the fallen deadwood. Terrified of finding a snake or spider in her lair, she cringed.

But she had to do this. Hiding was her only chance. The rebels would expect her to keep moving, however slowly, away from them. They would think she would stay on the run, keep trying to distance herself.

Cotten drew up into a ball and adjusted the wild brush surrounding her so that she was completely covered. If she remained silent and still, they might not detect her unless they stepped directly on her. What were the chances of their feet landing on just this spot? If they tracked her, they would notice her trail grow smaller and smaller and finally disappear. They might give up.

She prayed they would give up.

The moist soil and composting foliage were dank and cloying. It made her need to cough, but she fought the sensation, clamping her hand over her mouth. After several more minutes, the urge to simply clear her throat became nearly intolerable. She wanted to cry but knew that would exacerbate the problem.

When darkness finally poured over the Andes like molasses with its thick, impenetrable blackness, Cotten felt completely powerless. And with the darkness came the mist. Just like the terrible night of death, it crept through the jungle, cloaking every leaf, twig, and branch in its heavy grip.

Cotten's clothes were as soaked as the earth she lay upon. Every fiber and bone in her body steeped in the chill that came with the night. She felt safer from the men but more defenseless against nature—the cold air and the nocturnal creatures that inhabited the jungle.

Cotten wondered at what point she would decide that she'd rather be dead.

If she could just see the stars, she might feel less anxious. She huddled, shivering through each hour, physically and emotionally weary. She wanted to sleep but was too afraid, needed to empty her bladder but didn't.

Where were the rebels? How close or far were they? Not knowing was worse than if she knew they stood beside her. She thought about the liquid-light experience. Maybe she could replicate it even though she was not in a sacred place, nor in a state of peace or calm. But if she could, perhaps her senses would be elevated to where she could hear her pursuers, know where they were and what they were saying.

Cotten concentrated on moving all her thoughts aside, driving away anything that could interfere with her internal vision. She mentally moved her concentration to each portion of her body, starting at her feet and working upward—relaxing, calming, comforting. The chill and dampness of the mountain air diminished—slowly at first, like portions of a sandcastle being eaten away by each lapping wave.

She tried to visualize herself in a pool of light, floating on its surface. But the light came only in splinters moving in and out of her thoughts.

Without warning, she lost her concentration. It felt like she had been drifting under water and then suddenly burst to the surface. The light and its warmth vanished. She wasn't going to be able to do this. The idea was foolish anyway. Incan magic.

As the hours passed and the cold deepened, she gave in to trying it again. There was nothing to be lost.

Cotten followed the sequence of finding serenity and harmony. She pictured the brilliance and purity of the light, inviting it inside her. This time the light flowed into her as if her body was a perfect conduit. Its oneness with her filled Cotten with tranquility and warmth. She imagined it beginning to spin, willed it to spin by imagining it spinning, small circles at first and then growing in wider and wider bands of purity, from the crown of her head to the pit of her belly. With it came increasing calmness, less fear, more warmth.

She listened intently to her surroundings just as Yachaq had taught her.

Sounds previously lost in the noise of the forest became sharp. The breathing of an animal—deep and haunting. The delicate crunch of insects feeding. A slithering. Even the sound of decay.

Then something else.

A heartbeat. A yawn. The sourness of human sweat.

Someone was near.

Fear blazed through her, evaporating the liquid light. Cotten's ears filled with the drumming of her blood.

The bandits were near. Awake, like her. Waiting for daylight.

* * *

It seemed forever before she caught a glint of gray light in the sky above the blanket of green. The dawn came slowly and overcast.

Cotten looked around her with only the movement of her eyes. She dared not move her body, even though her muscles begged to be stretched. Her neck was stiff, and the shoulder that she rested on ached for relief from the constant weight. Her bladder was so full now that it was acutely painful. But she dared not get up. Grimacing at what she had to do, Cotten felt the heat of her urine drain down the inside of her thigh and seep into the earth below.

Suddenly, she heard a sound—something, someone slipping slowly and carefully through the forest nearby. Ever so faintly, the leaves and soggy earth squished, and the foliage swished and crackled.

And just as suddenly, the rain came, falling in torrents as it had the previous day. She strained to hear over it, but the sound of the downpour pounding the leaves and earth was too strong.

A surprising nudge of something cold and hard probed the brush and poked into her side. She knew without even looking—it was the barrel of a gun.

THE EXCHANGE

"*Está aquí*," THE REBEL shouted. "*La encontre!*"

Cotten didn't need a translation—he was shouting that he had found her. She tried scrambling to her feet, but a kick to her side with a pointed boot laid her out flat in pain. Then the rebel fired a shot into the air.

"*Puta*," he said, yanking Cotten up. He fired a second shot, and within moments the other two men who had kidnapped her materialized out of the jungle.

They blindfolded her and secured her wrists once more before guiding her out of the thick underbrush back onto the trail. Soon they were continuing on their delayed march through the mountains.

By midday, the trail became less uneven, eventually leveling off. Occasionally she heard the squawk and hiss of the walkie-talkie and the spurts of conversation as her captors communicated with someone.

In late afternoon, the walking became easy. Cotten's feet splashed through puddles along what she guessed was a muddy mountain road. She tilted her head at the sound of an approaching vehicle. The rebel who had kept a tight grip on Cotten's arm jerked her to a halt. She could tell the vehicle stopped, but the engine kept running. There were brief words exchanged between her captors and the newcomers. Then one of the rebels pulled the bandana from her eyes.

Cotten focused on a Jeep-like truck in the road ahead. Two men in army-green uniforms jumped from the vehicle and then pulled a bony man with several weeks' growth of beard from the back seat. His wrists were bound like hers, and he flinched at the gun barrel jabbed in his back.

One of the men approached with a paper in his hand. Standing in front of Cotten, he glanced at it before scrutinizing her. The brim of his hat was trimmed with gold braid, and a bright metal badge glistened on his chest. *Policía Nacional.*

"Cotten Stone?" he said with a heavy accent.

"Yes," she answered, trying to sound unintimidated.

The uniformed man hiked a dark brow and nodded to the rebels.

There was a quick burst of conversation, and then one of the officers put an envelope in his prisoner's fist and shoved him toward the rebels and Cotten.

At the same moment, she felt a hand nudge her from the back.

"*Vaya*," the rebel said, heaving her forward and pitching his head in the direction of the vehicle.

This wasn't just the claiming of a reward, she realized, but it looked like it also involved some type of swap—the bony, bearded prisoner for her.

She kept walking toward the truck, aware that just as the uniformed men kept their gun sights trained on her counterpart, the rebels must be aiming at her.

Cotten passed the prisoner, glancing at him out of the corner of her eye. The authorities had not only paid for her, but the rebels had also negotiated an exchange.

A few feet from the vehicle, Cotten looked back. With a round of handshakes, backslapping, and laughs, the rebels departed.

One of the officers helped her into the back of the truck before crawling in to sit beside her. The other, the one who had compared her to what she assumed was the equivalent of a wanted poster, took the driver's position. He checked the paper once more before he turned and smugly gazed at her.

Maneuvering in her seat, Cotten managed to turn around for one last look at the men who had captured her, but they had already disappeared into the jungle. Along with them vanished any thoughts she had of remaining forever lost in the Incan mountain mist.

* * *

"I am Chief Inspector Merida." The man spoke in stiff but clear English. He sat across the table from Cotten in a concrete-block-walled interrogation room somewhere within the Policía Nacional del Peru headquarters in downtown Cusco. He was slender, had black hair gelled and combed straight back and a partial beard, and also wore the green uniform, but with epaulets and yellow bars over the shirt pockets. His hat reminded her of those worn by Nazi officers.

He tapped the ash from his cigarette into an ashtray. "So, you are Cotten Stone?"

"Yes," she said. "I hope you're going to explain to me why I have been put through so much over the last few days."

Cotten was irritable and uncomfortable and realized she would have to watch her temper. She had been given the opportunity to wash her face and hands before being brought into the small room for questioning, but she still felt filthy and knew she reeked of stale urine.

"Why are you in Peru?" Merida asked.

"I'm a freelance reporter hired by TNP in Lima. I'm here to shoot footage for a documentary on the discovery of a new archaeological site near Machu Picchu."

"Correct," Merida said.

This man is really pissing me off. "Is this a test? Why are you asking me if you already know?"

Merida leaned back in his chair and rapped his knuckles on the table. The cigarette hung from the side of his mouth, the smoke wafting up, making his eye blink. "A little over a week ago, the bodies of twelve men were discovered at the archaeological dig site you referred to. They included your American camera and sound men, and Dr. Carl Edelman, a British citizen, and nine others. All dead. And in such a horrendous manner, it disturbs me to describe it. Murdered. Burned. Shot. The only one who escaped was you." He took a long drag from his cigarette. "And here you are, safe and sound. Do you not think that curious? Ms. Stone, why are you here safe and sound?"

Cotten wanted to say that it was because while the fireflies were levitating the five-thousand-year-old crystal tablet, they didn't bother to cause her to go insane and commit suicide like everyone else. Instead, she said, "I don't know."

"Why don't you tell me what you do know?" He crushed out the half-smoked cigarette.

Cotten threaded her hair behind her ears. "That night we ate dinner and drank some of the local moonshine brewed by the natives on our dig team."

"Moonshine?"

"Liquor—homemade liquor."

"Ah, *guafarina*," Merida said before writing a few notes on the pad before him. "And then?"

"It was strong stuff and made me ill, so I left the others and went to my tent. I tried to sleep but couldn't right away."

Merida opened a paper bag that sat beside the notepad on the table.

Cotten stopped talking as she watched him remove a brown plastic pill bottle. He turned it in his hand to read the label.

"Ativan. CVS Pharmacy, Fort Lauderdale. Prescribed for Cotten Stone."

"Yes," Cotten said. "They're mine. So?"

"You have been suffering from anxiety? Feeling too much pressure?" He gave the container a shake, the hollow sound of the pills clattering against the plastic and echoing off the bare walls of the room like a rattlesnake. "It must be difficult to rise to the heights of fame like you have, only to fall so far. Is that why you suffer from anxiety?" Merida paused, as if pondering his next question. "What would you be willing to do to regain your celebrity status?"

"My life is complicated right now. But that has nothing to do with what happened in the mountains. Yes, Ativan is for anxiety, but not for treating patients who have psychotic episodes. I'm not being treated for violent behavior, if that's what you're alluding to. I didn't have anything to do with the death of Edelman or anyone else. Something happened that night. Something made them homicidal or suicidal."

"Well, you may profess not to have violent tendencies, but I do not believe any clinical trials have been done on the effects of your prescription when mixed with *guafarina*. Perhaps the two together could change your personality significantly."

Merida abruptly stopped talking and had a strange expression on his face, as if he had just experienced an epiphany. He leaned forward. "Or let us suppose a large dose of your medication *mistakenly* ended up in the drink. We don't know what kind of effect that might have had on those who drank it. Suppose such a mixture induces hallucinations, homicidal and suicidal thoughts? Such side effects are not unheard of. And maybe you chose not to partake in the native drink. How lucky for you—the only one in the entire encampment not to drink the concoction. That would explain why you are alive and well. Hmm, how could your medication have found its way into the drink?"

His arrogant and condescending tone grated on her. "I don't like what you are proposing. Look, Chief Inspector Merida, I had nothing to do with what happened to my friends and Dr. Edelman. I'm as devastated as anyone over their deaths. That night, I didn't feel well, so I returned to my quarters and fell asleep. The next thing I knew, there was chaos in the camp."

She left out the part where she'd been freaked out by Edelman's translation of the tablet markings referring to the daughter of an angel. Merida hadn't mentioned the crystal tablet. Had the fireflies really taken it? But then, there was no one left alive who knew about the tablet. Edelman's notes had been incinerated, so there was no documentation of the find anywhere. Only the conversation Edelman had with Richard and Mariah. What was their last name?

"Ms. Stone?"

"Sorry. I was trying to recall what happened. Perhaps an hour later, I was still trying to sleep when I heard Dr. Edelman yelling—screaming, actually. I ran from my tent and called to him. I heard other screams. Then José . . . I saw José . . ."

The image rushed back, clear and frightening, putting a tremor in her rising voice. "He ran through the camp, past me, on fire, engulfed in flames. I didn't know what was happening. I searched for my friends. That's when I tripped over Paul Davis's body. He'd been stabbed . . . his throat slashed. He had a knife in his hand. I found Edelman in his tent, shot in the head, and a gun on the ground right next to him. I thought I heard Nick Michaels scream, but I never saw him." She felt sick, the images coming so fast, so vividly. She could smell José's burning flesh and could still hear the plop of Edelman's gray matter sliding off the canvas tent wall and falling to the floor. "I was terrified, and I didn't know what to do. I ran—ran from the site and—"

The door to the interrogation room opened, and a man in a navy blue business suit stood in the doorway.

"I have a report here that you need to see, Chief Merida," the man said in English.

Merida abruptly pushed his chair back and stood, his face reddening. "You do not come in here unannounced. Whatever you have can wait."

"No, sir," the man said, tossing a folder onto the table. "It can't."

FORT LAUDERDALE

Thank God for the American embassy, Cotten thought as she trudged up the flight of steps to her second-floor Fort Lauderdale efficiency. If not for their interceding, she'd still be in a cell in Merida's jail, or worse.

The night was balmy—a draft of ocean breeze still brisk even though the beach was three blocks away. A strand of her pecan-colored hair spun free, and she pinned it behind her ear. In the pink tarnish of the mercury-vapor streetlights, the coconut palms waved and rustled, casting ghostly shadows on the stark stucco walls.

The building, constructed in the 1950s, was originally a motel catering to the seasonal tourists referred to as snowbirds. In the early eighties, it was converted to rental apartments. Twenty-five years later, it was two clicks past quaint, as Cotten liked to describe it. Cheap in the off-season—just inside her budget. The building maintained the front desk since apartments could be rented by the week or the month, even by the weekend.

Her neighbors stayed to themselves, most of them transients or laborers. First and last months' rent in advance and no lease. A far cry from her Midtown apartment in New York. The creation fossil had changed all that. It was hard for her to complain about her fellow tenants—the old pot calling the kettle black.

Cotten had stopped at the front desk for a duplicate key since hers was still somewhere in the Andes. The only thing the Peruvian police had returned to her was her wallet. No cash, of course, but at least it did have her credit cards and driver's license. Everything else they had collected from the site was to remain in their possession until the investigation was complete.

She rang the bell a half dozen times before the night clerk dragged herself from the couch in the rear of the office. Cotten paid the five-dollar fee for the lost key to the yawning clerk, who didn't even offer a greeting.

"Welcome home," Cotten said, unlocking the door and nudging it open. The apartment spewed out mildew-soured air. Mildew was a byproduct of living near the ocean, the air being perpetually humid. There was a saying about South Florida especially heard around hurricane season: "The good thing is that we live in the tropics. The bad thing is that we live in the tropics."

Before Cotten left for Peru, she'd turned the thermostat up to eighty-five degrees. A mistake, she decided, sneezing from the pungent stench of mildew. But then, she hadn't anticipated the extended stay.

Cotten flipped on the light switch. Luckily, she paid her rent in advance for three months at a time, which kept her from spending it anywhere else. Not knowing when she'd get another paycheck, this assured her a place to live. She considered it practical and disciplined. And even though she was certain her electric payment was late, they hadn't cut her off—yet.

She dropped the small bag given to her by the wife of the American consulate in Peru onto the terrazzo floor and climbed on the sofa. Then she reached through the Venetian blinds and cranked open the glass jalousies. Sweet ocean air flurried in.

Cotten had promised Ted Casselman that she would call as soon as she got home, but it was 2:15 a.m.

She glanced at her watch—8:15 a.m. in Rome.

Cotten picked up the cordless and dialed. She didn't need to look up the number, as it was permanently embedded in her memory—the private Vatican City phone number to the most important person in her life, John Tyler.

Archbishop John Tyler.

"John," she said, picturing his smile, his eyes—the bluest she had ever seen.

"Cotten. Are you home?"

"Yes," she said. "I just needed to hear your voice." Cotten felt herself wanting to tear up, but she fought it. "You're the only one who knows me. The good—the bad."

"I read of the terrible tragedy in South America. You've been in my prayers every day."

"I need as many as you've got." She took a heavy breath. "In Peru—," she started, but choked.

"Take your time," John said.

Cotten started again. "At the dig site in Peru, an artifact was found—a crystal tablet. It was covered with inscriptions predicting the Great Flood." Cotten shook her head as if John could see.

"The Great Flood? You mean as in Noah?"

"Yes, but that was just the beginning." Again she hesitated because of the pinching of her throat.

"Are you all right?"

"There was something in the inscription about a second cleansing. John, it said that a second cleansing would occur, and it would be led by the daughter of an angel." She gulped a sob, unable to dam it any longer. "And now, everyone that was there is dead. Everyone except me. And, oh Jesus, John, there were insects—fireflies, millions of fireflies. They swarmed around the artifact and took it away." The words came in spurts and fragments, spoken faster than she could connect the thoughts. "I know what they were, John. You know what they were. But how can I ever explain what really happened? No one will believe me. Only you . . ."

"Cotten," John said. "It doesn't matter. The truth is, you know what happened, and you realize what you are up against. I have something important to ask you. Was there a second part of the inscription?"

"How did you know that?"

"Could you describe it or perhaps draw it?"

"No. Edelman couldn't read it, but he thought it looked like khipu. It's just lines and dots. John, how did you know about the second section?"

"I can't explain now. Just try to get some rest."

"I have no idea what to do next. I—"

"Follow your instinct. It proved true the last time you were tested. You understand that, don't you?"

"But you were there for me—with me. Now I'm alone."

"You're never alone."

Cotten wiped the tears away. "Promise?"

"Yes," he said.

Cotten pushed the off button. John Tyler may have been the only man she had ever truly loved. But he was a priest. And like so many things in her life, she forever seemed to want what she couldn't have.

Cotten glanced at the single bed on the other side of the room. The sheets and pillows probably smelled as dank as the stale air. She would wash the linens tomorrow and give the pillows a good dose of sunshine.

She pulled the chain on the ceiling fan before stretching out on the couch. A moment later, she was deep asleep.

* * *

The golden sunrise sliced through the slits in the blinds and projected rungs of light on the opposite wall. Cotten squinted to see across the room and read the LED clock on the nightstand by her bed. Eight thirty. Stiff from the night on the sofa, she sat up. Twisting around, she spread open two of the blind slats to look outside. Scrubbed-clean blue sky. From her second-story window, between two of the tall buildings that stood along the beach blocks away, she could catch a small glimpse of the ocean—aquamarine water with sunlight glittering off its surface. It wasn't what she could call a view, but it was her little secret peek at the Atlantic every morning. Her eyes wandered over the small pink, white, and blue buildings of her street and their marquees standing like sentinels, survivors of a bygone era that rested in the shadows of the new high-rise hotels and condos on A1A. Her eyes stopped on a man propped against the cement flower box in front of the motel across the street, reading a paper. He seemed out of place. Too young to be a retiree. Too clean-cut to be a rent-by-the-month tenant. He wore a light green golf shirt tucked into belted jeans and stood out against the gold and garnet crotons that grew in the flower box. The man folded the paper and glanced up. Cotten let the blinds spring back into place, feeling like a voyeur.

* * *

After a hot shower and a cup of instant coffee, Cotten went to the bedside phone. Her conversation with Ted Casselman would be considerably different from the one she'd had with John Tyler.

"I'm back," she said when Ted answered. "I would have called last night, but it was so late."

"Flight okay? Any trouble?"

"No, it was fine. Boy, am I indebted to the American embassy down there. I have to tell you, Americans look after their own. As soon as the toxicology report came back, they had it in Inspector Merida's face."

"You started to tell me about that when you called from the airport. What did the report say?"

"Whatever the dig team brewed up that night was loaded with all kinds of hallucinogens and other drugs—all derived from the local plants. I don't know all the specs, but essentially they told me that the side effects were similar to those of Prozac and other anti-depressants. At lease that's how they explained it to me. Remember Andrea Yates?"

"The mother who killed all her children?"

"Right. There is speculation that she did it because of the antidepressants she took. There are plenty of other cases where patients have killed themselves or others while taking those types of drugs. This native concoction was sort of like that, but with the addition of strong hallucinogens. Nobody at Edelman's camp was murdered. They were the victims of some bad homemade potion and killed themselves."

Silence.

"Ted?"

"My God, you're lucky. You could have easily been a victim, too."

"I guess I didn't drink enough. It made me feel sick right away. The others must have kept at it, drinking the stuff until . . ." She felt her stomach turn. "All they wanted was to have a good time and celebrate finding the artifact. They shouldn't have died because of that. Ted, it was so awful." Her throat clutched up.

"I know, kiddo. But you're home now, and it's over. Put it out of your mind."

Cotten paced with the cordless phone. She didn't want to think about it anymore. "The embassy took care of everything. They were amazing, arranging for a replacement passport and getting money wired from my account. Got my plane ticket and even took me to the airport." Cotten looked through the blinds. The man who had been across the street was gone.

"You all right?" Ted asked.

"I'll be fine. Just need to find some answers."

"Like what?"

"Like the complete translation of the crystal tablet. Edelman had most of it, but there was more. I have to find out what it said."

"What are you talking about?"

"The tablet, Edelman's discovery at the site. I thought I told you."

"I'm sorry, Cotten, you've lost me. There's no report of any crystal tablet."

TABLOID

No mention of the crystal tablet? How can that be? Cotten thought after hanging up from her conversation with Ted Casselman. She remembered things being haphazard with the Peruvian police—and then realized that there was no mention of the tablet during the interrogation. She recalled telling Inspector Merida that they had been celebrating Edelman's discovery, but he never asked what the discovery was. But she was sure that the crystal tablet was not a hallucination. Everyone at the dig site had seen it. She and her friends had heard Edelman take a stab at the translation. And she had clearly heard the archaeologist say—

Cotten stopped herself, trying not to repeat Edelman's voice in her head.

Led by the daughter of an angel.

"All right, then," she said aloud. If she was going to get some answers, she would need money. That meant selling a story.

* * *

Leaving the Sprint store after buying a new cell phone—which put her back more than she'd wanted to spend or could afford—Cotten slipped the small unit in her handbag. At least she was able to keep her old phone number, but unfortunately she had lost her list of contacts.

Her next stop was the grocery store. She had cleaned out the fridge that morning, an old cucumber exploding in her hand in the process. She would restock, fix herself a sandwich for lunch, and then start making calls to look for work. There was a story she had been putting together before leaving for South America that she thought had possibilities.

Cotten made a trip down each aisle of the grocery store, filling her basket with all the necessities. In the checkout line, she caught sight of a tabloid headline.

Mass Suicide or Murder in Mysterious Dig Site in Peru?

Mysterious Peruvian dig site? Murder? What the hell were they talking about? Edelman's camp?

She snatched a copy of the *National Courier* off the rack and scanned the article. There it was in paragraph two—her name. Turning the pages to the continuation of the article, she found her NBC staff picture with the caption "Cotten Stone, embattled reporter pictured here in better times." Words seemed to jump from the page at her: "investigation," "murder," "suspicion," "disgraced," "mass suicide." Cotten felt the panic starting to uncoil, first with her palms icing, then the tremor in her hands, her mouth drying, her throat closing. She recognized the start of a panic attack and needed to get out of the store.

Air. She needed air. She couldn't get enough air.

Lightheaded and in a full sweat, Cotten paid with her credit card and burst out into the parking lot. She chucked the plastic bags of groceries in the trunk of her Tercel before sliding into the driver's seat.

Cotten pushed back the seat and leaned her head on the headrest. Eyes closed, she focused on the breathing and relaxation techniques the therapist had taught her. But her heart kept racing, and she couldn't stop the panic rushing through her. Suddenly, a voice whispered in her head, and she pictured Yachaq:

Cast out your thoughts that will obstruct your vision. You are floating in a pool of sacred pure light. Liquid light . . . light so brilliant it blocks out every other thing . . .

Slowly, as she continued with her vision of the light warming her from her core, the panic subsided, and Cotten opened her eyes. She'd been doing so well. But at least she had controlled this attack without medication. That was good news.

Cotten looked at the tabloid on the seat, knowing she had to read it. Unhurriedly, she spread the *National Courier* open against the steering wheel.

As she read, anger swelled, but no panic. Just straightforward anger. When she finished the article, Cotten skipped back up to the byline: Tempest Star, senior staff writer. "Jerk," she said. "Who has a name like that, except a stripper or a hooker? She's probably a flunky who couldn't get a decent job and had to settle for a stinking tabloid. No ethics. Only out for the headline. And that name, for God's sake."

Tempest Star's article reported the official announcement made by the Peruvian police that the team at the dig site had ingested a homemade brew laden with a combination of hallucinogens that could have caused suicidal tendencies. Slut Star went on with her own rant, not directly making any accusatory statements that would leave her and the scum paper libelous. But rather, in a despicable, almost subliminal way, she intimated that Cotten Stone, once a dynamic, renowned journalist, could have possibly entertained the idea of constructing a catastrophe that would make global headlines, just to be in the middle of it:

> Was it possible that a former world-class journalist could conceive of and carry out a diabolical plan to regain her stature? Could the psychological damage from a devastating fall from grace on the world stage result in something so unspeakable? Inquisitive minds want to know.

Cotten slammed her palms on the steering wheel. *What is wrong with people?* she thought. *Could anyone possibly believe this shit?*

Cotten drummed the steering wheel repeatedly, shaking her head before grabbing the tabloid, crumpling it into a loose wad, and tossing it in the passenger seat. "Inquisitive minds can kiss my ass."

Back at her apartment, she put her groceries away and then threw herself onto her bed. Maybe she should sue. Someone had to be accountable. Slut Star was totally irresponsible. That wasn't even news reporting, it was slander, vile, hurtful. It was mindless trash.

And millions across the country were reading it.

* * *

An hour later, after consuming a turkey sandwich and a Diet Coke, Cotten went to her laptop. First, she checked her bank statement online. It confirmed what she already knew—she needed money, and the way she could get it fast was by selling the story she'd been working on for several months before she left for Peru. If she could hook up with one of the networks, it could put her back on track. She opened the folder "Toxic Dump" on her desktop and scrolled through her notes.

A few minutes later, Cotten lifted the cordless phone and dialed her contact at NBC. "Fran, it's Cotten," she said when the familiar voice answered. "Sorry I haven't checked in lately. I got a little delayed on my last assignment, but I'm back." When there was no response, she said, "Listen, I've been putting together this incredible story that I know you'll be interested in." Without a pause, she started the pitch. "There is this upscale, gated golf-course community down here. Real affluent neighborhood. Several months back, I had a landscaper call me. I won't go into all the particulars, but when the place was being built, all the landscaping died—twice. The landscaper pulled out of the deal at that point and had already lost a bundle. He'd never seen *acres* of land fail like that before, so he started digging, forgive the pun, and discovered from old aerials that the land in question appeared to have at one time been an illegal dump, probably for stuff that was toxic—paints, solvents, and the like—and was supposed to be hauled to special dumps, but wasn't. This neighborhood is sitting on toxic waste." Cotten paused. "So what do you think?"

Cotten's shoulders slumped at Fran's reply. "I don't understand," Cotten said. "What do you mean, it's not for you? But this could be a huge story. Honestly, Fran, we can blow this wide open."

She listened for a moment longer. "Okay. You, too."

Unbelievable, she thought. This was an A-1 story. Scandal, probable health issues, cover-ups. It had all the elements of a ratings booster. Why would Fran turn it down?

Okay. No problem. She would try the other networks. There were lots of fish in the television ocean. But Fran was her most solid connection. There was something wrong. She'd always liked Cotten's stuff. Why the cold shoulder?

She could beg Ted Casselman, her forever friend, mentor, and guardian angel, at SNN, but with the blotches on her record, she didn't want to blemish his. He would send her work if she asked, but she couldn't bring herself to do that. It wasn't right. He'd done enough. Too much.

The next few calls went the same as the first, until Cotten reached an old buddy with a network affiliate in Tennessee.

"Cotten?" The voice sounded sincerely happy to hear from her.

"Billie, yeah, it's me. How are you?" Billie was really Billie May, spoken as all one word, typical of the South, but being the ball-busting woman she was, she preferred stand-alone Billie.

"I'm great, Miss Hotshot," Billie said. "Fantastic, actually. Hubby and kids are terrific. So, how the fuck are you?"

"I've been living a Margaritaville life down here in paradise. Now I figure it's time to come out and get back to work." Cotten feigned a laugh into the receiver, catching a glance of the Atlantic through her blinds.

The not-renting-by-the-month man was back, sitting on the corner bus bench. This time he didn't have a paper.

Billie said, "Honey, if you think anyone believes you've been hiding in Jimmy Buffet land, you're living in a fantasy world. Listen, baby doll, everybody knows where you've been, and ain't a soul in the industry gonna touch you since that Peru shit. I'm only telling you this because you're my friend. I don't want you going around embarrassing yourself."

Cotten reeled but then stood stock-still.

"Face it, baby doll, you've been blackballed," Billie said. "It's a bitch, I know, but that's the reality of it. Nobody's going to touch you. My station would have me in thumbscrews if I picked you up. I know the rumors aren't true. Hell, everybody in the business knows it's not true, but the damage done by the gossip can't be ignored. Doesn't matter what your peers really believe. It's all about the image."

Cotten drew up the blinds, desperately needing the white heat of the Florida sun to bounce off the glass in sharp shards to shear off what she was hearing.

"You mean it's more than tabloid trash? The rumor is circulating, and people believe I could have masterminded the whole thing just to get a shot at the headlines again?"

"That's it, baby doll. That's the word on the street. You've got a mountain of rumor control and image repair on your plate. I'm just telling it like I hear it."

Cotten couldn't speak.

"Hang in there, sweetie," Billie consoled her. "It'll run its course."

Nausea turned Cotten's stomach. "I really appreciate your honesty, Billie. You're a good friend."

"Gotta go, baby doll."

Cotten glanced through the window again. The bus bench was empty.

"Yeah," Cotten said. "Me, too."

QUAKE

A CRISP MOON ROSE over the New Mexico desert as the third-year astronomy student sat on a boulder and slipped off his backpack. A flat area along the sandy wash would be a good place to camp. The heat of the day was gone, and the night chill swept across the landscape; a soft breeze whispered through the sage and rabbit-brush. Runoff from a hard summer rain two days previous filled a rocky depression nearby. Bone-tired, having walked seven miles on one of the ancient roadways radiating out of Chaco Canyon, he strayed off the road for another five miles, finally stopping atop a hill to survey the scene. Nothing left but rubble here. Unlike the other outliers, communities built near the hub of Chaco Canyon, this place was all but destroyed. The student drank from his canteen and decided on the direction he would take. From a distance, he heard what sounded like a fingernail scraping along a comb—the call of a spadefoot toad.

Freedom, that's what he felt, total freedom. In the near silence of the desert and the shadows of the great Anasazi Indian ruins, he was at peace. This trip was devoted to the Anasazi, the mysterious culture that had disappeared seemingly overnight after inhabiting the area for thousands of years. He felt a strong spiritual kinship to the Indians of the Southwest, especially those who had constructed such magnificent buildings.

He also shared the Anasazi's love and knowledge of astronomy; they were systematic sky watchers who understood much about the heavens. His trip up the remote canyon was to search for something he'd only seen in pictures. At the Peñasco Blanco ruins overlooking the Chaco Wash and the Escavada Wash, on an overhanging rock along the dark walls of the canyon, there was an Indian painting. Found in the early 1970s by archaeologists from the University of New Mexico, it depicted the images of a crescent moon, a rayed disk, and a hand. From years of study and recreation of the night sky from when the painting was made, it was theorized that the Anasazi saw and chronicled a spectacular celestial event: an exploding star.

At the same time those images were painted, on the other side of the world, Chinese astronomers documented the appearance of a "guest star," probably the bright explosion of a supernova, marking the death of an exceptionally massive star. According to their accounts, the guest star appeared on July 5, 1054. On that day, the predawn sky blazed with the brightest star ever seen by humans. Its remnants became the Crab Nebula.

The young student hoped to find another, as yet undiscovered painting of the exploding supernova. Tired as he was, his excitement made him want to begin his search for the painting right away. He was eager to stand in the footsteps of the original artist and gaze upon the horizon. Electrified at the thought, he decided to begin his search immediately.

The young man slipped on his headlamp, turned it on, and adjusted the bezel to direct the light. He trudged up the wash. The temperature dropped rapidly as the dark walls of the canyon rose like silent sentries on either side of his path. He stopped for a moment and gazed skyward as he snapped the front of his jacket closed. The stars spread a spatter of silver across the heavens.

Finally, he found a low ledge and started climbing, slipping on the loose gravel. Regaining his footing, he moved more cautiously. The incline was gradual, but he could tell in the delicate moonlight that the wash was falling farther and farther below.

After ten minutes of steady progress, he suddenly came upon the remains of a pueblo sunk back in a narrow alcove. Then beyond it, he stared up at the ruins of a tower *kiva* that he guessed could have stood over thirty feet high. It could be reached only by a set of precarious hand- and footholds if he kept on in the same direction. Instead, he hooked right onto a ridge that narrowed as he rounded a bend in the canyon wall. He came upon a flat stone ledge jutting out slightly about one hundred feet above the floor of the canyon before it ended abruptly.

He must have chosen the wrong route, he thought. Just as he turned to retrace his steps, the headlamp illuminated the wall ahead, catching something in its beam that made him stop short. There, just below an outcrop of rock, was the object of his search. He gasped at the painting's vibrant colors, glowing back in the light. The Indian who had painted this had been so moved by what he saw in the night sky that he was compelled to preserve it forever.

With his fingertips, the student traced the images of the crescent moon, a multipointed star, a sun sign, and a handprint.

He glanced back in the direction of the horizon to the place where the magnificent event had occurred. The moon was high, bathing the desert in a dusty pastel blue.

As he took in the sight, he heard an unfamiliar sound. At first, it was faint, nothing more than what he thought was the rush of the desert wind up the side of the canyon.

Suddenly, he lost his balance, staggering against the wall. Then came the rumble—low but building rapidly as the earth seemed to moan. The canyon wall leaned out as if taking in a breath, and the ground rippled, forming waves that passed by like great swells on an ocean.

The rumble grew to a roar of cracking and ripping—chunks of the wall rained down. The young man turned and sprinted down the path. At times the ground dropped from under him, and he fell hard. But it almost immediately swelled up, throwing him forward. Struggling against the liquid motion of the earth, he fought his way along the path until he was at the bottom and racing along the wash. Finally clear of the falling debris, he knelt, out of breath, watching the ground move back and forth, shaking and trembling.

Then, along the sloping cliff face, he heard rumbling as tons of earth roared downward. To his astonishment, as the land slid away, it exposed an expansive, dark cavity. Like the curtain opening on a Broadway play, the pale moonlight revealed a theater-like setting of massive stone walls, narrow doorways, steep staircases, and dozens of windows framed in stone masonry. All that was missing were the ghost actors moving across the desert stage.

Standing alone under the silver brush stroke of the heavens, the student gazed wide-eyed as he breathed in the ancient air rushing from the ruins. He knew the spirit of the great Anasazi was now a part of him forever.

* * *

Eli Luddington watched the evening news with interest. He had received a call the previous night telling him about the earthquake before reports hit the airwaves. Camera crews, reporters, and scientists had waited for daylight to converge on the location and check the damage. The quake had caused a major landslide, the result of which took them all by surprise. As Eli listened to the TV reporter recap, exhilaration surged inside of him.

"A magnitude five-point-five earthquake rattled the desert floor late last night in a remote area of New Mexico," the announcer said. "Seismologists reported the epicenter was located about thirty-three miles south of Farmington. Though not considered a major earthquake, it did cause a landslide in a canyon wall, exposing a phenomenal discovery. Authorities first on the scene who observed and inspected the area were in awe. What they found were newly uncovered ruins of an ancient Indian civilization. Initial reports were that archaeologists and anthropologists are completely puzzled. A young astronomy student hiking in the area was the sole witness to the event and was not hurt. No casualties have been reported."

"At last," Eli whispered, "we have found your secret hiding place." He strode to his private bar and made a hefty Tanqueray and tonic—four fingers gin, two fingers tonic, screw the ice.

“Mother Nature always provides,” he said. Eli lifted his glass and his eyes, as if he could see through the ceiling. He didn’t nurse his drink but swallowed it in three gulps, taking the smile off his face only long enough to get the alcohol down. This was extraordinary news.

He immediately mixed himself another Tanqueray and tonic, but he babied this one as he continued watching the news of the quake. Just as the segment was over, the chimes from the front entrance rang.

Eli had dismissed the house staff early that evening, so he answered the door himself, drink in hand. He already knew who would be there—he had summoned them.

Mariah and Richard Hapsburg stood on the expansive marble portico flowing out from the entrance to the Luddington estate house.

“Eli, this is such wonderful news,” Mariah said, then kissed him on the cheek.

Eli ushered the couple inside.

“We need to celebrate,” she said.

“Good evening,” Richard said, passing Eli in the doorway.

“You should be more cheerful, Richard,” Eli commented, closing the heavy oak door. “This is a great day.” Moving past them, he said, “Let me get you both a drink.”

Setting his cocktail on the bar, he studied the labels of several bottles of champagne. Finally choosing a 1983 Salon Le Mesnil, he popped the cork and caught the overflow in a starched white cloth napkin he held at the neck of the bottle.

"Mariah," Eli said, pouring champagne into a Waterford flute and handing it to her. "Richard?" he asked, raising the bottle and his brows.

"Sure," Richard said, "why not."

"That's the spirit." Eli filled a flute with champagne for Richard and retrieved his gin and tonic. "So we finally come to this moment. We knew three tablets remained of the original twelve. After finding the one in Peru, there are only two left. Again, let me commend you for your work there." Eli set the bottle in a silver champagne bucket. "My dear friends, one of the two tablets still lost most certainly is in this new location so conveniently provided for us by the earthquake. We have extensively searched the ruins of the Four Corners region for years with no success, never knowing of this most secret place. We must find the tablet before anyone else has a chance. I have arranged with the State of New Mexico and all the local authorities for you, Richard, to be the dig master on the site."

Mariah smiled endearingly at Eli, and Eli reciprocated.

"Mariah, you will assist," Eli said. "When you find the artifact, contact me, and I will see that it is destroyed immediately. As always, we will take no chances on anyone else seeing and deciphering the message."

Mariah downed her champagne and held out her glass.

"What about the last tablet?" Richard asked.

Eli understood the simple pleasure Richard derived from reminding him of the only tablet held by the enemy. It was like sandpaper on Eli's ego. So he momentarily ignored Richard, stroking Mariah's cheek with his fingertips. He turned her head, brushing her eyelid with his thumb before palming her other cheek. "Exquisite," he said.

Mariah held his hand against her face, then pressed the back to her lips and kissed it. "Thank you, Eli. I will never forget."

Eli finally turned to Richard. "Beware of Cotten Stone," he said, regarding Richard's question of the last tablet. "She will soon be given the key."

* * *

In the Escalade, on the way back to their townhouse, Mariah patted Richard's thigh. "Why so grumpy?"

"You know why," he answered, steering the SUV along the tree-lined road. "He irritates the shit out of me. Always touching you . . . and you . . . when he does, you turn into someone I don't know. As if you like it. You encourage him." He paused, staring at her. "No, let me rephrase that. You tease Eli, make him think that if I wasn't around, you'd fuck him until his heart gave out. And to tell you the truth, sometimes I wish it could."

Mariah said, "Look at me."

Richard shook his head.

"Richard, look at me. Look at my face."

He finally took his eyes from the road for an instant and glanced at her.

"I will always be thankful to Eli. I owe him everything. You may never understand, because you didn't see me after the accident."

"It wouldn't have mattered to me, Mariah. You know—"

She cut him off. "You can never ask me to deny Eli anything." Her voice was strong, to match her words. "I love him, but not in the same way as I love you, my husband. You serve him because that is your legacy, your bloodline. You have no choice in the matter. I made a very conscious choice to serve him. Never forget, Eli raised me from the dead."

* * *

What the hell are their names? Cotten thought, trying to recall the American part of Edelman's team. Edelman said he had called them on the satellite phone about the tablet. They would be able to vouch for the existence of the artifact, and it may be the answer to what had happened in Peru. Everyone who had seen it was dead. Just like the pilot on that Virgin Atlantic flight, they had gone crazy and killed themselves.

Maybe what's-their-names could verify the tablet. And maybe Edelman even described the second part of the message well enough that they took notes or made sketches from his description.

What were their names? "M," Cotten said aloud. The woman's name started with an M. She ran through a string of names. "Mary, Maureen, Marilyn, Mindy, Margaret. M, M, M. Maria." Suddenly, it came to her. "Mariah. Mariah and Richard Hapsburg. But she couldn't recall if they were associated with Yale or Harvard. It was the same place the great explorer Hiram Bingham's records were stored.

Cotten launched her Internet browser and Googled Hiram Bingham. It was in Bingham's old files that Richard had come across the mention of the site and then gone on with Edelman to investigate.

"Bingo," Cotten said, finding Bingham's bio at the Yale website.

After combining the Internet searching and 411 information, she located Richard Hapsburg in Woodbridge, a suburb near New Haven.

Cotten bunched the throw pillow in her lap, sat the phone on it, and dialed the number.

The voice that answered surprised Cotten. It was sultry and young, not consistent with the down-in-the-dirt person she had imagined.

"Hello," Cotten responded, "my name is Cotten Stone, and I am trying to locate Dr. Richard Hapsburg or Mariah Hapsburg." She hesitated, hoping the woman on the other end would identify herself as Mariah Hapsburg. But the line was silent, so Cotten continued. "I was on a dig site in Peru with Dr. Carl Edelman. I was there to do a news story, but the Hapsburgs had already left and I didn't get to meet them." Cotten paused again.

Nothing.

"Can you help me? Do you know how I can get in touch with them?"

"I'm Mariah Hapsburg," the woman said.

"Oh, thank heaven," Cotten said. "I am so glad to be able to speak with you."

Cotten explained how she felt the entire massacre-suicide might have been about an artifact Edelman had found—a crystal tablet. She wanted to know if Edelman had described it in detail to her or her husband. "Edelman deciphered a portion of the message on the tablet. But he thought the second part was a possible depiction of khipu. He wanted experts like yourselves to—"

"I have no idea what you're talking about," the woman said before hanging up.

THE GARDENS

"AGENT WYATT?" ASKED THE young seminarian wearing a black cassock.

"Yes," Wyatt answered. He sat in a high-back upholstered chair in the waiting area on the fifth floor of the Vatican State Government Palace.

The seminarian handed him a red folder. "Please review this. Someone will be with you in a moment," he said.

Wyatt glanced at the cover of the folder. In bold white lettering was the word *MONDAY*, followed by *FOR THE EYES OF THOMAS WYATT*. He realized how tired he was, having just flown all night from D.C. and only lightly dozing. Whatever the reason he'd been called to Rome, it had to be important.

As he waited, Wyatt unsnapped the three metal clamps on the red folder and opened it. Across the top of the first page was the logo and letterhead of the Central Intelligence Agency. The topic summaries followed:

Suicide bombings and attacks in Israel.
Car bomb explodes in Spain after ETA warning.
Taliban commander surrounded and killed.
Reputed abuse in Iraq prison by military.
U.S. nuclear envoy leaves North Korea in frustration.
Missile strike kills Hamas leader.
Somali al-Qaeda leader convicted.
Suicide rates on rise.

Wyatt immediately went to the briefing on suicide rates.

The overall rate of suicide among youth has increased 248% in the last 12 months worldwide. Suicide is the second leading cause of death for all U.S. men, up from eighth just 12 months ago. In 2004, over 30,500 deaths were attributed to suicide. Worldwide rates are increasing rapidly. According to the latest official figures released by WHO and the individual national bureaus of statistics, the suicide rates among reporting countries are escalating at alarming rates. Since the beginning of the official registration, Hungary has been the country with the highest suicide rates in Europe (if not in the world). However, Hungary is now surpassed by some of the Russian and Baltic states. The highest male rates are found for Lithuania, the Russian Federation, Latvia, Estonia, Belarus, and Hungary, all showing an increase of over 500% in just 12 months.

Wyatt looked up as the sound of footsteps approached across the marble floor.

Archbishop John Tyler, the prelate of the Pontifical Commission for Sacred Archeology, introduced himself and apologized for being late. "I hope you've had a chance to look at the documents, Thomas," he said, nodding at the folder in Wyatt's hands.

"Briefly."

"There's an urgent matter needing your attention."

Wyatt said, "How can I be of assistance?"

"Let's take a walk," Tyler said, motioning to the doorway.

The two men left and headed for the elevator near the middle of the building. On the ground floor, Tyler led the way through the back entrance and into the ancient Vatican Gardens.

"In medieval times, the gardens were vineyards and orchards that extended to the north of the Apostolic Palace," John said. "In 1279, Pope Nicholas II enclosed the area with high stone walls."

"Beautiful," Wyatt said.

Soon the two men approached the replica of the grotto of Lourdes. Along the way, they passed dozens of men in black suits moving among the hedges and fountains. Wyatt assumed they were security—but for who?

A hundred yards farther along the path, Wyatt saw a man sitting alone on a bench, a thick red folder in his lap. He seemed to be reading intently as they approached, as if he were a corporate CEO taking a break from a business conference. His hair was white, like the Polo pullover that he wore tucked into dark trousers. As Tyler and Wyatt approached, the man glanced up.

"John, good morning. Are we not blessed by such a glorious day?"

"Your Holiness," John Tyler said, dropping to one knee and bringing the outstretched hand of the pope and the papal ring to his lips. Tyler then rose and stepped aside.

"I'd like you to meet Thomas Wyatt, a senior intelligence analyst and newest member of the Venatori."

Thomas Wyatt tried to disguise his surprise and awe. He was totally unprepared for this. The last thing he'd expected was meeting the spiritual leader of one billion Roman Catholics and the political head of state of Vatican City—especially so casually dressed.

"Thomas, thank you for coming," the pope said, closing the folder. Like the one Wyatt had received earlier, it too was labeled *MONDAY*, but this one read *FOR THE EYES OF THE PONTIFF.*

"Your Holiness," Thomas Wyatt said.

The pope stood and, with the folder under his arm, led the two men along the path past the largest of the ninety fountains found throughout the Vatican Gardens, finally stopping in the shade of a large palm. There, he turned to them.

"Thomas, we have a problem."

SHADOWS OF GHOSTS

The pope motioned toward two stone benches in the shade, a few paces off the garden path. Once the three men were seated, he said, "Thomas, I know you have already seen a copy of this." He held up the red folder. He placed the briefing folder on the bench. "As you know, we have been dealing with a rapid rise in suicides throughout the world for some time. But this spike in the numbers is unprecedented." He glanced at Archbishop Tyler. "We believe it is tied into something John is working on—something a bit out of the ordinary." Looking at Wyatt, the pontiff said, "First, tell me the status of Eli Luddington and his associates, Richard and Mariah Hapsburg."

"Over the last few days," Wyatt said, "there's been a flurry of activity. My contacts at the FBI reported that right after the news of the quake in New Mexico, Luddington was scrambling to arrange for the Hapsburgs to go there and start excavating. He has a great deal of influence and somehow managed to shut out all the universities and state archaeological organizations. The Hapsburgs and their team are en route to the site as we speak. I doubt they barely took time to pack, they left so fast." He glanced at Tyler. "What's so important about this new site?"

"Do you remember the network reporter Cotten Stone?" Tyler said to Wyatt.

"Of course, Your Excellency. She, along with you, delivered the Holy Grail to the Vatican about three years ago. She has gone on to maintain a rather high profile in sensational, religious-based news. I was particularly impressed with her discovery in the Holy Land of the thirty pieces of silver Judas received for betraying Christ. However, she's had a streak of bad luck that has taken its toll. I understand it was the so-called creation fossil that finally did her in."

"That was a setup," Tyler said, "meant to destroy her credibility."

"Set up by whom?" Wyatt asked.

"The same organization that attempted the cloning of Christ using His DNA preserved in the Cup of Christ," the pope said.

"So what does this have to do with the spike in suicide rates?" Wyatt asked.

"We're getting there, Thomas," the pontiff said. "Have you followed the recent incident involving Ms. Stone in Peru?"

"Yes," Wyatt said. "It dealt with a number of people believed to have committed mass—" He glanced up at the medieval St. John's Tower in the distance as his thoughts came together. "This is all connected, isn't it?"

The pope nodded.

"Cotten Stone is the only survivor of the incident," Tyler said. "Everyone was killed by their own hands."

"Strange that only she survived," Wyatt said.

"You will understand momentarily," the pontiff said. "What I'm about to tell you is not based in science or fact but in myth and faith. At this point at least, you are going to have to trust me. Can you do that?" He gave Thomas Wyatt a look of apprehension.

"Of course, Your Holiness." Wyatt felt a tinge of uncertainty in his gut. Ever since he took the job at the Venatori, he had a feeling this day would come—a day when his duties would take him to a place he had never gone before, into a world that few knew or had the courage to know. He was about to cross the threshold.

"Cotten Stone is not like the rest of us," Tyler said. "She is . . ."

"She is the offspring of an angel," the pontiff said.

"Excuse me?" Wyatt said, exhaling.

The pope held up his hand. "Patience, Thomas."

Tyler explained. "Cotten Stone's father was Furmiel, the Angel of the Eleventh Hour. Furmiel decided to go along with the rebellious angels led by Lucifer in the great Battle of Heaven. In the end, they were defeated and cast out. In the Bible, they are called the Fallen Ones—the Nephilim. Over the ages, Furmiel repented and asked God's forgiveness. The Almighty accepted his repentance but would not take Furmiel back to Paradise. Instead, he made Furmiel mortal and gave him twin daughters—one to return at birth to take her father's place in Heaven, and the other to remain on Earth and do the will of God. Furmiel's daughter is Cotten Stone."

Wyatt stared at Archbishop Tyler before shifting his gaze to the pope. "I suppose it wouldn't do me any good to assume this was some sort of a joke or test?"

When neither man responded, Wyatt said, "Okay. Let's say I go along with what you're telling me. Where is all this headed?"

The pope responded, "I told you that it had something to do with what John is working on. It involves an artifact we believe can be found in the newly uncovered site in New Mexico. This artifact will reveal a secret that will give us all hope in winning this war."

"Artifact?" Wyatt asked.

"A crystal tablet," Tyler said. "Inscribed on it is a message written by the hand of God. If we find the artifact first, we can use the words of God to stop Armageddon."

"First?" Wyatt said, shaking his head in confusion.

"The outcome of the war, Thomas," the pontiff said, "could be determined by who possesses the tablet. If our enemies get it first, they will destroy it, thereby forever keeping the secret from us all."

"So there is only this single tablet that we have to find?" Wyatt asked John.

"The myths and legends, even one of the scrolls found in the Dead Sea, say there were twelve. One was given to Noah. The rest were delivered to the spiritual leaders of different civilizations around the world before the Great Flood. The most recently discovered tablet was found in Peru."

"The site where Cotten Stone was?" Wyatt asked.

"Precisely," the pope answered.

Tyler continued. "Each tablet has two parts. The first tells how to prepare for the Flood, and the second holds the secret of winning the last battle. We don't know exactly what the second part of the message is, but we must assume that it tells us how to stop the End of Days."

"But if Stone was at the site, then she must have seen the tablet," Wyatt said.

John Tyler nodded. "Yes, but she isn't able to describe it accurately enough. The best she could do was say it looked like khipu—a drawing of knots on a rope."

"But there wasn't any khipu in Noah's time," Wyatt said.

The pope smiled. "No, there was not. And that implies that God did not mean for Noah's generation to be able to decipher the second part of the message. He wrote it for a future generation."

"We believe there are only two tablets left," John continued. "One we think is in the ancient ruins exposed by the earthquake. Your account of the recent activity of Eli Luddington confirms our conjecture. The other tablets have been methodically found and destroyed by our eternal enemies."

"But you said there are two?"

"Yes," John said, looking at the pope, then at Wyatt. He paused before going on. "There is another."

"Where?" Wyatt asked.

"We don't know," the pontiff said.

Again, Wyatt shook his head.

"Let me give you a bit of history," said John. "Just after Titus took the city of Jerusalem in AD 70, a group of righteous men formed an organization. Their task was to recover and protect the religious documents, relics, treasures, and secrets that had been plundered from the great city. Not until just prior to the first Crusade do we find record of the organization's name. So deeply underground was the group, they referred to themselves only as the *Ombres des Fantômes*—'Shadows of Ghosts.'"

"*Ombres des Fantômes?*" Wyatt said. "Isn't the seal of the Venatori inscribed with the same statement, only in Latin—*Umbrae Manium?*"

"Correct," the pope said. "You are a member of an organization that has its basis, however distant, in the Shadows. There is little documentation on them, and what does exist was locked in the archives here in the Vatican.

"We know that one of the crystal tablets was in the possession of the Shadows during the first Crusade, around the year 1095. For generations, the organization continued its task of protecting the treasure and the tablet. By the fourteenth century, when Philip the Fair of France came into power, the ferocity of the Crusades was at its peak, and the Shadows realized the objects they guarded with their lives were in danger. Not only was there the army of the Fallen—the Nephilim trying to get their hands on the tablet—but now there was also Philip the Fair's army of men. Recognizing the gravity of the threat at their door, the Shadows devised a plan. Their leader was to take their treasure trove and hide it. Only he would know where. In this way, none of the members could be tortured into telling the location. The leader took an oath that he would never divulge where the treasures were hidden. As he lay on his deathbed in Languedoc, France, many years later, he grew anxious that all would be forever lost at his passing. So he revealed the location of the treasure to his trusted successor, who proceeded to take the same oath of secrecy. Each successive leader of the Shadows bore the burden of the treasure's location and the oath. This went on until 1398, when a Shadow leader by the name of Sir James Gunn retrieved the treasure and took it on a voyage to Nova Scotia, accompanied by the famous Scottish aristocrat Henry Sinclair."

"Weren't the Sinclairs connected to the Knights Templar?" Wyatt asked.

"Very much so," John said.

The pope said, "This was kept secret until a bundle of three documents was found buried beneath a small church in Orkney, Scotland, in 1722. Two of the documents were written in a cipher, and Pope Innocent brought in experts to decode them. One told the location of the treasure, and the other document gave explicit directions how to recover it. The third document was a map made by the famous cartographer and fellow Templar Nicolos Zeno, another companion who sailed with Sinclair and Gunn. Pope Innocent immediately launched vessels to a place called Oak Island, Nova Scotia."

"The famous Oak Island Money Pit?" Wyatt said. "I thought it was believed to have been dug by pirates to hide their treasure. From what I've read, the whole thing is booby-trapped. Every time someone attempts to dig it up, the shaft floods."

"It's a distracter," John said. "Gunn and the lot dug the money pit in case anyone suspected what they were up to. They put all kinds of diabolical barriers and obstacles inside the shaft to keep the interest of whoever investigated the pit. The tablet was hidden elsewhere on the island."

"I assume the tablet was recovered," Wyatt said.

"Yes," the pope answered. "It was brought to the Vatican. We're told that the inscription on this tablet was written in an ancient language called Enochian—what some consider to be the tongue of the angels, the language that everyone spoke before Babel—and, because of her heritage, a language Cotten Stone knows. Like the other tablets, it gave instructions on preparing for the Great Flood. But there was a second portion. Although the Vatican linguists were able to translate, what it said made no sense to them. At best, they guessed it might be a scientific formula. What it actually said remains a mystery. That's because, in 1878, the tablet and all records, sketches, documents, and translations relating to it were stolen." The pope opened the red folder and withdrew a single sheet of paper, yellowed and fragile. "Thomas, like Cotten Stone, you too have a special legacy. It is the crux of why we selected you to become a Venatori."

"Legacy? Well, I assure you *my* father was no angel."

"No, he was not," the pope said, "nor was your father's great-great-grandfather. But he *was* a thief." The pope extended the sheet of paper to Wyatt. "This is what he left behind after stealing the crystal tablet."

THE SIZZLE

Cotten couldn't believe what she had heard, couldn't make sense of it. Her thoughts shattered into a million shards ricocheting inside her head. Mariah Hapsburg said she'd never heard of the crystal tablet.

What tablet? The fucking crystal tablet, that's what tablet, Cotten thought. What was going on? Edelman said he called the Hapsburgs on the SAT phone. He'd been specific enough to request experts in the new scientific domain researching khipu as a language, not just an accounting mechanism, to take a look at the tablet. He'd talked to Richard about the impossibility of the technology to make the inscription.

Cotten sat like a rock, unmoving and unblinking, and searched through her memories of Peru, her conversations with Edelman, and her thoughts.

A few moments later, though she fought to push the notion out of reach, she couldn't. This was *their* work. It had to be. She wasn't crazy. The creation fossil and everything from that point on had been crafted by the Fallen, the Nephilim. John had agreed with her. They'd capitalized on her ego with the creation fossil, setting her up in order to humiliate and discredit her. Then on to the mountains of Peru. They hadn't gotten her charged with a crime, but they had planted seeds in the minds of her peers and the world—enough damage that no respectable news organization would ever listen to or believe what she said—and they did this with a purpose in mind. From this bottomless place, she couldn't combat them.

Who would heed anything she said or claimed? And as far as the tablet was concerned, they had destroyed everyone who could corroborate the existence of the tablet. And look at the toxic-dump story. That should be headlines, but it was dismissed. Why? Because she was attached to it.

"Oh, man," she said, leaning back on the couch.

Deep inside, Cotten reckoned with why this was happening. *Led by the daughter of an angel.* Something on the tablet was about her, the daughter of Furmiel, *the only one.* They didn't want her or anyone else to know what it said.

She had to come face to face with the Hapsburgs.

Cotten raked her hair back, drawing it into a thick cord at the nape of her neck. She would ask them about the tablet and what it said. She'd look hard into their eyes. What would it be like to peer into the windows of Hell?

* * *

The following day, Cotten tried to reach the Hapsburgs again to set up a date and time to meet, but to no avail. They ignored her calls, identifying her on caller ID, she supposed. She slung the throw pillow over the coffee table and onto the floor. "Somebody give me a break."

She rested her chin on the back of the couch and looked out her window through the narrow slit between the blind slats. The neighborhood pulsed with traffic and pedestrians in swimsuits. Where was the no-name, not-renting-by-the-month guy? He must have found a job or a better neighborhood, she thought. Good for him.

Well, if the Hapsburgs were not going to answer the phone, then she was going to take the plunge and show up on their doorstep. She could probably get one of those no-frills flights to New York and take the train to Connecticut. It would put a dent in her overextended credit card, but she had to confront them.

The folks at Yale should know how to get in touch with them, she decided.

It wasn't as easy as she first thought. It took a number of calls to find someone at the university willing to help her, so she resorted to a bit of deception.

"Dr. Hapsburg is in the field," the woman said.

"He and his wife are going to be so pleased that I have talked to you," Cotten said. "I've been trying to reach them with recent information about the grant they applied for. It's wonderful news. Do you have contact information?"

At the news of a grant acceptance, the woman was more than happy to tell her the Hapsburgs were in New Mexico at a newly discovered archaeological site.

"Shit," Cotten said after hanging up the phone. Booking a cheap flight to New York was one thing, but New Mexico was a different story. It wasn't even worth checking the fares; she already knew she couldn't afford it.

So it was back to selling a story first. Cotten couldn't even get a bite on the toxic-dump piece, but Tempest Star could get headlines.

Suddenly, she had an idea. Cotten remembered the other tabloid that was always sitting right beside Tempest Star's *National Courier*—the *Galaxy Gazette*. "If you can't beat 'em," she said. She was going to go head-to-head with Tempy baby.

* * *

Cotten pulled her carry-on bag through the Four Corners Regional Airport. Her laptop and purse were slung over opposite shoulders. Tempest Star and the *National Courier* didn't know what they were in for. With Cotten's name and story idea, it hadn't taken an instant for the *Galaxy Gazette*, the *National Courier*'s main competition, to bite. In the world of tabloids, the *Galaxy Gazette* was like Avis in the rental car business: they weren't number one, but they tried harder. Cotten Stone was pretty much a household name—good or bad didn't matter, she could attract a huge audience. And the editor-in-chief of the *Galaxy Gazette* couldn't wait to sign her up. He told her that she would add a new level of class and sophistication to the *Gazette* that he had never been able to achieve with his current no-name staff. Building on her reputation in religious and spiritual themes, he wanted her to focus on stories that took the reader deep into the mysteries of life—the myths, legends, and unsolved disappearances. Cotten knew exactly what to propose. Since returning from Peru, she had spent considerable time pondering all that Dr. Edelman had said about ancient cultures and how many had vanished into thin air. Cotten suggested that her trip to New Mexico be the first in a series covering the seemingly overnight disappearance of ancient civilizations. The editor was thrilled. By the end of the conversation, Cotten had her ticket to New Mexico and a small but welcome advance.

In addition to the airfare, she had motel and rental-car charges and meals. It wasn't just the headlines they were selling. The editor knew it, and Cotten knew it. They were selling the sizzle *and* the steak.

Cotten stopped at the rental-car desk and filled out the forms. The clerk handed her keys to a Dodge Neon. The *Gazette* had sprung for the compact instead of the economy. Be thankful for small perks, she thought.

Cotten took the keys and picked up her baggage. As she hoisted the laptop strap over her shoulder, she caught sight of a man off to her right, standing just beyond the exit doors of the airport. He slowly turned and walked away.

She froze, and the strap slipped down her arm.

The clerk stared at her. "You all right, lady?"

Cotten ran toward the doors. "Hey, you!" she shouted. "Stop!"

The man paused and faced her.

Only inches away from the no-name, not-renting-by-the-month guy, she said, "Who the hell are you, and why are you following me?"

A voice behind her said, "Cotten Stone?"

She spun around to see a tall man in faded jeans and a navy Nautica long-sleeved shirt a few feet away. Dark hair and a tiny sprinkling of silver at the temples. In his hand, he held a ringing cell phone. Handing it to her, he said, "It's for you."

DEMONS

Cotten hesitated before taking the cell phone. She looked away from the stranger just long enough to push the talk button before bringing the phone to her ear.

"Hello," she said.

"Cotten."

Even through the digitized, long-distance static, the voice had an instant calming effect on her.

"What's going on here, John?" she asked. "Who are these men?"

"Friends, Cotten," John Tyler said. "Special friends who are there at my request. The man who gave you the phone is a member of Vatican security. The other is with our diplomatic corps. He's been on special assignment—looking out for you. I don't want to explain over an open phone line, but believe me when I say that you can trust them just as you trust me. You do trust me, don't you?"

Cotten felt a smile form. "With my life and my soul. But you already know that."

"Yes," John said, followed by a pause, as if he was thinking of saying something else.

Cotten wanted to say more, too. That no one else knew her as he did. That she missed him.

Finally, John spoke again. "They will explain everything to you. I'll be here if you need me."

She needed him with her now, she realized as she pushed the button to end the call and handed the phone back to the stranger.

He slipped it into his pocket before extending his hand. "Cotten, I'm Thomas Wyatt. This is Monsignor Philip Duchamp, assistant to Archbishop Felipe Montiagro, the Vatican apostolic nuncio. Do you need help with your bags?"

* * *

Mariah Hapsburg stood at the base of the cliff, staring up at the Indian ruins. The setting sun bathed the towering rock walls, plateaus, and mesas in hauntingly beautiful purple and gold light. A wind whipped up the canyon and tossed her hair into her face—she smelled the sharp, arid desert air. Her pulse quickened as she realized she would be the first person to walk among the ancient buildings in perhaps thousands of years. She wondered what it was like the moment the inhabitants of this remote place had followed the instructions on their crystal tablet.

"What are you thinking, my love?" Richard Hapsburg said as he came from behind and stood next to his wife.

The reality of the situation and why they were there shook Mariah from her musing. It also reminded her of their ultimate goal: preventing anyone from ever learning the secret of the tablet.

"I was only trying to picture what it must have been like to live here so long ago." She touched Richard's arm. "Let's go," she said, leading the way up over the landslide debris to the entrance of the ruins.

She and Richard seemed alone in this desolate place as sunset gave way to dusk. During their long Land Rover ride through the canyons and washes to the remote location, she saw no one—another example of Eli Luddington's power. He had the ability to keep the press, academics, and curiosity seekers away. Power excited her, both mentally and physically. And she was surrounded by power. Mariah considered herself the luckiest woman on earth. For so many reasons.

They moved past the first of the structures that Richard speculated were constructed by Chacoans or descendants of one of the other Pueblo cultures, such as the Mogollon or the Hohokam. The area had been inhabited on and off for thousands of years until literally overnight everyone seemed to have disappeared. It was an ongoing mystery to the archaeologists and anthropologists who studied the Four Corners area. A mystery to everyone. But not to Richard. Not to Eli. And not to Mariah.

The walls, doorways, and windows were well preserved, sheltered from the elements for centuries. In an outcrop of rock near the base of a wall, Mariah noticed a strange, rust-colored tube shape about the thickness of her thumb that appeared embedded in the sandstone. "What is that?"

"Fossilized shrimp burrows," Richard said.

"Shrimp in New Mexico?"

"This was once part of the coastline of a shallow inland sea. It's not unusual to find sharks' teeth and clamshells in the local sandstone, too."

Mariah shook her head in amazement, trying to imagine an ocean covering this barren, dry place.

What seemed to be left of a narrow road led past small apartments—the walls built thick with precise masonry. All that was needed, Mariah thought as she shone her light into each doorway, was furniture. She could almost hear the shuffle of sandaled feet along the dusty paths.

"Probably the elite lived in these," Richard said, aiming his lantern into a large room. "Some areas were for living, others for working. These people were highly sophisticated and well organized."

"So what are we looking for?" Mariah asked.

"A special place," Richard said. "What they considered a holy place."

"How will you know it?"

"I will know."

* * *

Cotten Stone sat across from Thomas Wyatt and Monsignor Duchamp in a booth at the rear of the Farmington IHOP on East Main. She sipped hot green tea and glanced from time to time out the window. In the dim twilight of sunset, she could see her Dodge Neon parked beside Wyatt's SUV, a Chevy Tahoe.

"Venatori?" she said, looking back at Wyatt. "Interesting name. What does it mean?"

"Hunter," he said.

"When I was with SNN, I heard the name once. A story about a member of the Swiss Guard who murdered a Venatori agent at the Vatican and then committed suicide. Very little info came out. You guys play it close to the vest, don't you?"

"It's the nature of their business," Duchamp said.

"And what business is that?" Cotten asked.

"Intelligence analysis," Wyatt said.

"Sort of like the sacred CIA?" she said.

Wyatt smiled. "Sort of."

"I still don't see why I need your help. I'm here to do a story for the *Galaxy Gazette*."

"And you want to know about the crystal tablet," Wyatt said.

Cotten placed her cup on the table. "John told you?"

"He said you had seen the one found in Peru," Wyatt said.

Sitting up straight, she said, "You make it sound like there are others."

"In all, we believe there were twelve," Wyatt said.

Maybe these two men could help her after all, she thought. If they assisted in proving the existence of the Peruvian tablet, she might be one step closer to getting her credibility and life back. And most importantly, they might help her find out more about what the inscriptions meant for her. "Why twelve?" she asked.

"We're not sure," Duchamp said. "Twelve plays an important role in history—twelve months in a year, twelve tribes of Israel, twelve Apostles, twelve signs of the zodiac. And in Revelation, chapter twelve, verse one, tells of a woman who appears during the End Days clothed with the sun, the moon under her feet, and a crown of twelve stars."

"And the twelve days of Christmas," Cotten added with a nervous laugh.

Duchamp ran his palm down his chest. "For that matter, there are twelve pairs of human ribs, twelve major joints in the body."

"And twelve orders of angels," Wyatt said.

A wave of anxiety crashed inside her.

"We have found references to twelve tablets in several ancient documents," Duchamp said. "The point is, we believe God gave a tablet to Noah and eleven other spiritual leaders of different civilizations throughout the world to help them save their faithful from the first cleansing—the Great Flood. We also believe that there are references on each tablet predicting a future cleansing and how to prepare. And we think one of those tablets is in this new archeological site."

"But if the prediction of a future cleansing was on the tablet given to Noah way back when," Cotten said, "what's the rush? How do you know it's not referring to something that will happen a hundred or even a thousand years from now?"

"Because of you, Cotten," Wyatt said.

Duchamp nodded. "Because of you."

* * *

Richard Hapsburg paused and flooded the narrow path ahead with light from his lantern. A few yards ahead was a structure unlike the others. This one was circular—a *kiva*.

"Is this it?" Mariah asked. She set her lantern on the ground and took the flashlight from her backpack. Sweeping her beam across the surface of the high brick wall, she heard Richard's response.

"Yes," he said.

Richard led the way through a tall doorway into a room about fifteen feet in diameter. A fire pit made from smooth stones formed a circle in the middle of the floor. A large black smudge still marked the spot where a thousand fires had once burned brightly. Along the far wall, opposite the door, sat a rectangular stone box appearing to be about three feet high and four feet wide, open at the top. It was made from bricks similar to those in the walls of the buildings. Mariah and Richard looked inside the box.

"There's nothing there," Mariah said. "Just dirt."

Richard handed her his lantern and removed a small triangular trowel from his backpack. He leaned over the edge of the box and scraped away a thin layer of dirt at the bottom. Twisting and poking the point of the trowel, Richard was able to penetrate the base of the box a few more inches. "Nothing here," he said.

"How do we know this place wasn't looted a thousand years ago, Richard? And if not, wouldn't they put something as valuable as the tablet in a more secure place than this box? Seems to me this would be too obvious. Wouldn't they choose a place no one would ever think to look? Maybe not even in this building."

"I believe they would have kept it here. This was their holy of holies. The shaman came here to pray, to make offerings to his god. Sacred ground only he could step upon. I'm sure he kept the fire pit burning constantly to show that the spirit of the people—"

Richard straightened and took his lantern from Mariah. He held the light over the charred stone circle in the middle of the floor. "A place where no one would think to look."

* * *

The ride was bone-jarring as the four-wheel-drive Chevy Tahoe slowly crunched along the washboard road. In the distance, Cotten watched the headlight beams bounce across a desolate landscape. The high-intensity lights attracted flying insects that appeared to relish giving their lives as they flew into the front of the vehicle.

Cotten sat in the passenger seat while Thomas Wyatt drove. Duchamp had remained behind at their motel. Now that Wyatt was here, the monsignor would fly back to Washington tomorrow.

"How do you know the location of this place?" Cotten asked, holding onto the strap over the door.

"The earthquake and landslide made national news. They gave specifics. I plotted it on my GPS." He tapped the dash, where a handheld Magellan rested. "We'll need it when we leave the road."

"And how can you be certain the Hapsburgs will be there at this hour?"

"Trust me, Cotten. They'll be there."

She looked out over the expanse of desert and moonlight-silvered mesas. Thinking of Yachaq, she wondered if there was a sacred place in this remote spot that was like the one in the Peruvian mountains.

"What did John tell you about me?" she said.

"That you are special."

"We went through a lot together."

"So I've heard." Thomas Wyatt switched off the Tahoe's headlights. "We're going to depend on the full moon," he said as he turned off the dirt road onto the beginning of a wide wash. The ride immediately became more uncomfortable.

"What's the deal? Why can't we just drive up to the site?"

"It's been closed off. They don't want anyone going in there except their own."

"Who is 'they'?" Cotten asked.

"Eli Luddington and his legion."

"Luddington?"

"One of the same group you faced with the Grail conspiracy. The Hapsburgs are two of Luddington's own. He sent the Hapsburgs here to retrieve the tablet."

Now it all made sense to her. The Hapsburgs had been in Peru, and when the tablet was found, Edelman called them. They were the link to what had happened that night. When the word of finding the tablet spread, fireflies—or whatever they were—were sent to destroy it. No one who had seen the tablet was left alive. No one but her . . . because of who she was.

Furmiel's daughter.

The daughter of a Fallen Angel.

Half Nephilim.

"Cotten, I've been told things that I don't understand—probably will never understand. But my job is to help you stay focused. I know a great deal about human behavior. John chose me because he trusts me. He knows you're going through a tough time, and maybe I can help smooth out the rough spots a little."

"So you're a shrink?"

"More like a guardian angel."

* * *

On his knees, Richard Hapsburg dug the point of the trowel into the black smudge in the center of the fire pit. Mariah watched over his shoulder as the layers of soot and charcoal were scraped away. A few inches down, Richard hit a hard object. With a four-inch paintbrush from his backpack, he cleaned the surface of the stone slab. It was a little over a foot square, and on it was painted a series of markings.

"What do they mean?" Mariah asked.

"This one is the symbol for the sun, this for the earth, this for water, and this for fire—the elements of life. I'd guess pre-Chacoan."

"Looks like another dead end. Just a stone with common petroglyphs."

Richard glanced over his shoulder at his wife. "You simply have no patience, do you?"

She shrugged and watched as he cleared the dirt from around the edges of the slab. Once he was able to get his fingers beneath the stone, he pulled it up. With a grunt, he lifted and moved it out of the way.

"More dirt," she said, eyeing what was beneath.

Again, Richard gave her a look before gently scraping the trowel through the dirt. A moment later, he uncovered another object. Carefully, he swept away the last layer of ash and charcoal with his brush. "More light."

Mariah raised her lantern and gasped. There, hidden beneath the slab, beneath scorched black desert sand and thousands of years, the surface of the crystal tablet reflected the light like a shimmering jewel.

Ever so carefully, Richard blew away the remaining dirt and tenderly pried the tablet free with his fingertips. Gripping it firmly, he stood and stared at what he knew was crafted by the hand of God.

Mariah brought her hand to her mouth in wonder.

The lantern light spun an iridescent rainbow of flares off the tablet's surface.

Mesmerized by its splendor, Mariah said, "What a shame that something so beautiful will soon be destroyed." She scanned the strange markings on its surface, knowing that if she could decipher their meaning, they would reveal the greatest secret ever known to mankind.

As if he could read her thoughts, Richard said, "Don't get too caught up in what it might say. It isn't for either of us. Our task is to destroy this before anyone can decipher its message." Cradling the tablet in one arm, he pulled a satellite phone from his jacket and pushed memory dial. A moment later, when Eli Luddington answered, Richard said, "It is ready."

* * *

"That's unusual," Thomas Wyatt said.

Cotten was lost in thought as she stared out the Tahoe's window. Thin wisps of cloud passed across the full moon. She turned to Wyatt. "What?"

"Fog," he said. "Just seems unusual in such a dry place to have ground fog."

In the moonlight, she saw mist moving down the wash toward them. It seemed to undulate in waves, growing within minutes from an almost transparent veil to an impenetrable curtain.

A blade of fear cut through her, gouging the breath from her lungs. "Stop!"

Wyatt slammed on the brakes, sending a cloud of dust and dirt in every direction. Instantly, the mist engulfed the Tahoe, creating a blanket that seemed as solid as the cliffs around them. The only light came from the dim dashboard lamps. Outside, a gray wall pushed on the windows.

"Oh my God!" Cotten said, pressing back into the seat. "This can't be happening!"

"What can't be?" Wyatt said.

"Stop it!" Cotten screamed, her fists clenched, her eyes squeezed tight, her breathing rapid.

The mist had found her.

Then, just as unexpectedly as it had appeared, the fog vanished.

* * *

Mariah and Richard Hapsburg stood at the entrance to the ruins under the desert sky. Mariah watched what seemed to be ground fog form around their feet and swirl about. Soon, it thickened until the ground was lost from view. Then she saw them: tiny pinpoints of light moving down the wash, slipping past the canyon walls and cliffs. Their number grew from a handful to hundreds, then thousands—swirling, twinkling, moving in formation toward Mariah and her husband.

"Richard, what's happening?" she cried. "What are they?"

"Be still," he said. "Don't be afraid."

She watched her husband as he extended his arms and held the crystal tablet out. The mass of fireflies wrapped around his hands, forming a glowing ball that enveloped the tablet. The glow became so bright that it blinded Mariah. She felt the heat generated from the fireflies singe her face. She heard the whirling of their mass as it grew to a roar.

Suddenly, she knew she was in the midst of demons.

* * *

From a quarter of a mile away, atop a narrow ledge, Tempest Star lay on her stomach, watching through high-powered binoculars. "Motherfucker!" she whispered. Turning to the photographer lying next to her, she said, "Did you get all that?"

"You bet your sweet ass," he said, peering through the 500-millimeter lens of the night-vision camera.

THE DESERT HUACA

"CARE TO EXPLAIN WHAT just happened back there?" Thomas Wyatt said as he steered the Chevy Tahoe cautiously along the uneven surface of the wash. It was just after midnight, and the full moon allowed him to maneuver without headlights.

Cotten took a deep breath as she watched the jagged edges of the cliffs move by. "On that night in the Andes, just before everyone died, the dig site was first engulfed by a thick fog. There was always a mountain mist at that altitude, but that night it was unnaturally thick—just like what happened back there."

"But nothing happened back there, Cotten. It was only fog—a natural phenomenon."

"In the desert? Even you said it was strange."

"So there is more humidity tonight than usual. But rare desert ground fog doesn't mean something supernatural happened."

Cotten turned away. "Mr. Wyatt—"

"Thomas."

"Okay, Thomas. I understand that you're just doing your job, trying to make a crazy person like me see things rationally. If what I witnessed that night in Peru qualifies me as crazy, then I am. And you don't need to define 'supernatural' for me. If anyone knows what it means, I do. The least you could do is acknowledge that I have a right to flinch at things that remind me of that night in Peru. Instead, you're trying to make me feel foolish. I don't appreciate that at—"

"Cotten," Wyatt said, "you're way off base. I never said you were crazy, and I am not trying to make you feel foolish. I'm only attempting to take the edge off what was a stressful moment back there. If I gave you any other impression, then I apologize. John Tyler has assured me that—"

Suddenly, Cotten leaned forward. "Is that a light up ahead? Looks like someone with a flashlight?" A hundred yards up the wash, a soft light appeared for a moment, then vanished.

Wyatt pulled the parking-brake handle to stop the SUV without lighting up the taillights. Then he turned off the ignition. "This is as far as we go. Even at our snail's pace, someone could hear the motor a mile away." He grabbed two flashlights from the glove box and the GPS off the dash. "The rest of the way is by shank's mare."

"What?" Cotten said.

"On foot. It's an old expression." He handed her one of the flashlights.

Wyatt reached up and switched off the interior lights so the car would not be illuminated when they opened the doors. Then he eased out of the driver's side. "Keep it quiet," he whispered to Cotten. "And don't turn on your light unless you absolutely have to."

Cotten's flesh grew clammy as she stared into the night. As much as she wanted to find the Hapsburgs and get positive proof that one or more crystal tablets existed, she was afraid. And the most unsettling element was what the tablet would say regarding the daughter of a Fallen Angel. What had made her think the battle ended three years ago when she'd confronted something evil, unspeakable? Did she really believe the Fallen Ones would just give up and fade away? They would never forget it was she who had stopped them from using the traces of DNA in the Grail to clone Christ. She had crushed their plans to bring about an unholy Second Coming. They would never forgive her for that. She should have known when Yachaq referred to her as Mayta, "the only one," that this would go on and on. She *was* the only one. The contract her father had made with God could not be broken. She must accept it. But the chill of the canyon night seeped through her, freezing her courage and filling her with dread.

"You okay?" Wyatt asked her.

"Not really," she said in a whisper.

Wyatt walked around to the passenger side and opened her door. "I'd tell you to stay here while I go on ahead, Cotten, but John said that the answers we seek would be given only to you, not me."

She looked at Wyatt and blinked before sliding out of the seat. He was right. She had no choice.

"We'll work through this together," he said.

Slowly, Wyatt led the way up the dry wash. The surface was covered with loose gravel and sharp-edged rocks. "Careful. Taking a fall around here would not be a good idea," he said. After a few hundred yards, he checked the GPS again, as he had several times since leaving the SUV. "We're close."

Finally, they came to the sprawling base of the landslide debris. In the bright light of the full moon, Cotten saw the outlines of the ancient buildings that had been uncovered by the earthquake. She stood beside Wyatt, silent, listening, watching. All she heard was the soft desert wind snaking along the base of the cliffs.

Wyatt produced a small automatic pistol from under his jacket. "Something's wrong."

"What?"

"It's too quiet. There's no one here."

"Isn't that a good thing?" Cotten asked.

"We should have run into resistance by now. Luddington should have this place locked down. But we just walked right up. Unless . . ."

"Unless they already got what they came for," Cotten said.

"Exactly. We're about to enter the ruins, and there's no one here to stop us. Luddington has obviously called back his guard because they're no longer needed. And tomorrow, you watch, he'll make some big philanthropic announcement that he's going to help finance a university or state team to excavate the site. Suddenly, he's a hero."

"So you figure that if there was a tablet here, they've already recovered it?"

"*If* there was one at all. We don't know that for sure," Wyatt said.

"But isn't the reverse true? If they hadn't found it, they would still be here. It would take weeks to explore the whole site, wouldn't it? Trust me, I know these guys, and they don't give up easy."

"I think you're right," Wyatt said.

Cotten leaned against a large boulder. "Now what? I need to talk to the Hapsburgs. Somehow, some way, I have to find out what the tablet says."

"Do you remember what the markings looked like on the one in Peru?"

Cotten glanced at him, the moonlight creating shadows under his square jaw. "Dots and lines, lots and lots of dots and lines. Like khipu. That's all I can recall."

"Chances are, a tablet found here probably won't have markings that look like khipu anyway. My guess would be petroglyphs. That's what the ancients who lived throughout this region would have understood. But we'll never know standing around. Ready to take a look inside?"

"What for? You and I both know the tablet has already been found."

"We've come this far, and it looks like we've got the place to ourselves for now. Once the excavation team moves in, we won't get another chance."

Reluctantly, Cotten nodded, and she motioned for him to lead on.

After carefully making their way across the debris field, they approached the first of the ancient buildings.

"Incredible," Cotten said, gazing at the stone structures looming out of the darkness in the pale light. "But eerie. This place gives me the creeps."

They walked along a path past thick walls and empty apartments. "Check this out," she said, shining her beam on one of the walls. "Must be three feet thick." She aimed the flashlight at a seam between the stones. "No mortar." Cotten looked at Wyatt. "The bricks are matched together with such precision. Their technology and craftsmanship are amazing."

"We're a pretty pompous civilization," Wyatt said, "thinking we're so advanced. One close look at a place like this and you've got to have a great deal of respect for these people."

"My time in Peru convinced me of that. It's like we are a speck in the universe . . . but somehow still interconnected."

"Humbles you, doesn't it?"

"Very much," she said.

Moving on, they left what Cotten thought to be the main path and explored room after room in the many structures.

"Almost like whoever lived here just up and moved out one day," Wyatt commented.

Cotten shivered, remembering the comments on the same subject from Edelman. "Exactly," she said. "Like the people who inhabited the ruins in Peru. They just disappeared overnight."

A few paces later, they stopped to explore what Cotten guessed was someone's living quarters. As they entered the room through the T-shaped doorway, she saw that broken pottery littered one corner. Suddenly, she felt dizzy—off balance.

"Wait," she said, her voice weak. "I think we must be higher up than I realized. I feel lightheaded."

Wyatt took off his backpack and pulled out a bottle of water. "I don't think the elevation is making you feel that way. At least not altitude sickness. We're only somewhere near six thousand feet." He handed her the bottle. "Take a drink."

Cotten leaned against a stone wall. "Thanks," she said. He was right. It wouldn't be altitude sickness. But something had made her lose her balance.

Wyatt continued to shine his light about.

"Why don't you go on while I sit here and rest a minute," she said. "Just don't be gone long."

Wyatt laughed. "No problem. You take five and I'll nose around."

Cotten sank to the earthen floor, drew up her knees, and rested her head on them. Slowly, the dizziness subsided. She took another drink of water before flipping the flashlight on and panning its beam around her surroundings. Her gaze drifted toward a circular building a few yards away. She stared at it for a moment until curiosity got to her. There was something different about the structure.

"Thomas," she called softly, not wanting to be too loud in case there were any of Luddington's people still nearby. When Wyatt didn't answer, she decided to check out the circular building until he came back.

Cotten made her way over bits of rubble to the tall doorway, using the beam of her flashlight to sweep the path ahead.

Inside, she saw what she guessed was a circle of stones surrounding a fire pit. It appeared that someone had recently dug inside its blackened interior. A flat stone with painted markings on its surface lay beside the hole. An impression left in the bottom of the hole caused her to stiffen. It was the same size and shape as the Peruvian crystal tablet. The tablet had been here.

Suddenly, Cotten felt a rush of warmth like the sunrise in Peru. Then her body seemed to vibrate. She knew then that this was a *huaca*—a holy place. Cotten stepped inside the fire ring and immediately felt all the stress drain from the top of her head and out through the soles of her feet. She visualized herself floating in a sea of light. Clear, perfect, shimmering, liquid light. It seeped inside her through every pore and cell until it filled her and began to spin inside her.

She focused. Intense concentration. The light swept through her center, growing and traveling along every nerve fiber and blood vessel, taking over the tiniest particles of her being.

She was immersed.

One with the light.

One with the universe.

Ancient voices whispered prayers.

Soft footfalls echoed around her.

Distant chants.

Then she felt the intense heat on her face.

VOICES

MARIAH HAPSBURG STOOD UNDER the steaming, pulsating water and relished the way the shower massage made her flesh tingle—or was she still experiencing the rush from the extraordinary event earlier that evening near Chaco Canyon? Whichever it was didn't really matter. The fact was, she felt so alive. So excited. So aroused. She closed her eyes and let the water strike her scalp, flow over her face, and cascade down her body in hot sheets.

Richard had never looked more commanding than when standing at the entrance to the ruins tonight and holding out the tablet like an offering. As if he had the power to appease the beast. He was tall and bold, confident, and almost charismatic. It was clear that he had been born to this, that his legacy was more than generations old. Perhaps tonight was a ritual he had repeated many times. Richard appeared right at home—even comfortable—with the roaring buzz and churning eddy of the insect-like creatures. He showed no sign of cowardice, but rather, the fireflies' mystical presence bolstered his assuredness. He was transformed. Their brilliance illuminated his skin, and for the first time in many years she saw the handsomeness of his face. His face aglow, and the fireflies, so fierce and spellbinding, brought about the most exquisite longing inside her for her husband.

She touched her face, recalling the scars that had disfigured her until her savior, Eli, had arranged to have her put back together. The scars were gone, yet still her face and body would grow old. But Richard would never age. How long before he no longer found her desirable?

"Richard," she whispered, letting his name spool on her breath. He waited for her on the motel room's king-size bed, just on the other side of the bathroom door. Thoughts of him didn't usually awaken her this way, but tonight, amidst the riveting levitation and destruction of the tablet, she had seen him differently. The sheer heat that radiated from the fireflies had brought on a delicious flush throughout her body. The vestiges of that sensation remained with her even now.

She whispered her husband's Fallen Angel name, "Rumjal," leaning back her head and lathering her hair with shampoo. Rivers of foam glided over her shoulders and chest. She followed their trail with her hands, down her neck and across her breasts. Tonight would be different. She wouldn't direct Richard in their lovemaking, nor would she find reason to hasten the act. Tonight she wanted him to take her. And she would revel in the heat of ecstasy.

* * *

The heat on Cotten's face grew in intensity until she recognized what she was experiencing. The fireflies had been there. She sensed them—sensed their diabolical, searing heat. There was even the faint, lingering scent of sulfur. And with that realization, her face finally cooled. But Cotten's mouth became alum dry, and her heart punched her sternum. She knew that absolute, ultimate evil had been in this place.

For an instant, Cotten felt herself distracted by her thoughts, and she began rising up, leaving the depths of the liquid light. She fought to regain her focus. But the light that filled her swirled raggedly as she lost the perfection of the moment.

Concentrate, she thought. *Concentrate on the light.*

She realized her eyes were squeezed tight and her fists were clenched. *Relax*, she told herself, trying to clear away strings of thoughts and tension. *Feel it drain. Let it slip silently out your fingertips, the soles of your feet. Quiet ribbons of tension, dissipating. Thoughts emptying.*

At last, she salvaged the altered state of mind and became filled with the light once again.

A smell—no, a fragrance—entered her nostrils. Pleasing and exotic. A woman's perfume? So refined was her sense of smell that she separated the fragrance into its components—jasmine, lily of the valley, rose, sandalwood, and others that she couldn't identify.

Then, distant conversation echoed as if reverberating through the ancient ruins. She concentrated, listening, fine-tuning her hearing. A man's and a woman's voice. Disjointed phrases and words. A conversation that had taken place inside this structure, but not the voices of the ancients, as she had sensed when she'd first started her journey into the liquid light. These were recent. Fresh.

There's nothing here. Just dirt. The woman's voice.

. . . *holy of holies.* The man.

It is ready.

As the voices drifted off, Cotten smelled the recently disturbed charcoal and soil. A heavy, musky scent wafted in the cold air. Yes, this was the place. The Hapsburgs had been here. They had found the tablet buried in the fire pit, and the demons had destroyed it.

Suddenly, a bright light shone in Cotten's face, and she tried to protect her eyes with her hand.

"Thomas?" she whispered.

"Well, well." It was a woman's voice. "Look who we have here. None other than the world-famous Cotten Stone."

DIGITAL IMAGES

A CAMERA FLASH BLINDED Cotten. She swayed slightly, unsure of her balance. "Who's there?" she said.

"One of your *biggest* fans," the woman said, her words filled with sarcasm.

Another camera flash, and Cotten realized there were at least two other people besides herself in the ancient holy place. She managed to raise her flashlight and aim it at the intruders as she shielded her eyes with her other hand. "I asked who you were. What do you want?"

"Maybe we should get her autograph," a male voice said.

"I don't think it's worth much since her trip to Peru," the woman said.

"Don't move!" Thomas Wyatt's voice boomed through the structure. The hammer click on his automatic pistol sounded sharp and edgy in the stone-walled room. "Slowly place the camera on the ground, along with your lights. Then put your hands behind your heads, both of you." Although Cotten could not see him, she knew his voice came from the direction of the entrance to the room.

Cotten aimed the beam of her light at the face of the woman. She was tall, close to six feet, blond and shapely, in a fleshy, Marilyn Monroe way. Cotten figured her to be in her early forties. Standing next to her was a younger man, maybe in his mid-twenties or not quite, long hair tied in a ponytail, and wire-rimmed glasses. He had what looked like a week-old scruff of a beard.

"You were asked to identify yourselves," Wyatt said, still hidden in the darkness of the room.

"Oh, for God's sakes, you two relax," the woman said. "No one's in danger here." She lifted her arms in a gesture of surrender. "I'm Tempest Star with the *National Courier,* and this is Bennie, my photographer. We're just here covering the story of the earthquake and the Indian ruins. You guys need to lighten up."

"At one o'clock in the morning?" Cotten said. She couldn't believe that Tempest Star—the woman who had plastered her all over the cover of a national tabloid—was standing right in front of her. She really would love to slap her.

"We couldn't get anywhere near the place all day," Star said. "Neither could you, it appears. We're after a scoop."

"Yeah, and boy did we get one," Bennie said, relaxing his arms as well.

"You consider taking my picture a scoop?" Cotten asked.

"No," said Bennie. "Getting a shot of you was a bonus. What we saw here tonight—"

"Shut up!" Star said. "And can you take that light out of my face?" she said to Cotten.

Cotten lowered the beam of her flashlight. "What did you see tonight?"

The photographer glanced sheepishly at Star. "Nothing, really. Just a lot of rocks and dirt." He stooped to pick up his camera. "Oh, and a great shot of Ms. Cotten Stone kicking around some ancient Indian digs."

"So, Stone," Star said, retrieving her flashlight, "what are *you* doing here in the middle of the night? Trying to fabricate another bullshit story to salvage your career?"

Cotten's jaws clamped down. "At least I have a career to salvage. 'Career' is too tasteful a word to include what you do."

Wyatt moved into the light of the flashlights. He motioned toward the digital camera. "Let's have a look at that."

"That's private property," Star said, taking a step forward.

Wyatt aimed the automatic at her. "Now, now. Let's not get technical. You don't want me to ask again."

"I don't know who you are yet," Star said to Wyatt, "but I already know you're a real prick."

"Get the camera, Cotten," Wyatt said.

Cotten took it from Bennie and stepped back beside Wyatt. She studied the controls a moment before turning a knob that caused the LCD on the back to illuminate. As Wyatt watched her, she pressed the backward arrow beside the screen and scrolled through the green night-vision images.

The first showed the most recent picture they had taken, the one of Cotten shielding her eyes. In it, she looked surprised and frightened. Moving in reverse order, the next showed her standing with her eyes closed in the fire ring. Then the pictures changed, first to a man and woman walking with their backs to the camera, leaving the ruins along the dry wash. The next showed them poised at the top of the debris field near the entrance to the ruins. On the next was a massive yellow and white glowing ball. Cotten could just make out the man and woman standing next to it. The man seemed to be reaching into the glowing mass. Next was an image of the man with his arms extended. The night vision was detailed enough to show that he held an object appearing to be the crystal tablet. The woman stared at her feet as thousands of tiny points of light swirled around her legs. The final picture showed the two walking toward the ruins from the crest of the debris field.

"Isn't that the craziest thing you've ever seen?" Bennie said.

"Will you please shut the fuck up!" Star said.

"Maybe we should keep the camera," Cotten said to Wyatt.

"And I'll have you arrested so fast you'll wish you were back at police headquarters in Cusco," Star said. She smiled at Cotten.

Cotten looked to Wyatt for guidance, and he motioned with his head toward the two.

"Do what she says, Cotten," Wyatt said. "You don't need any more negative publicity right now. Getting arrested on your first assignment with the *Gazette* wouldn't look too good."

"The *Gazette*?" Star said. "You're working for the *Galaxy Gazette*?" She laughed out loud. "I knew they were a second-rate rag."

"How about the camera?" Bennie said.

Cotten handed it to him. Then she said to Wyatt, "There's nothing here. Let's go."

"Good idea, sweetheart," Star said. " 'Cause the big news here is that Cotten Stone did her first and last story for the *Gazette* all on one night. And left empty-handed." She laughed again. "I hope you like the pictures we took of you. They'll be on the cover of the *National Courier* in the next edition."

"Let's go," Cotten said to Wyatt, and she walked out of the *kiva*.

She could still hear Star laughing as they made their way back through the winding paths to the entrance of the ruins. When Cotten and Wyatt were at the base of the debris field and moving along the dry wash back to the Tahoe, she said, "Did you see those images?"

"Yes, but I have no idea what I was looking at."

Cotten stopped and looked at Wyatt. "Neither does Tempest Star." She glanced back in the direction of the ruins. "If she did, she would still be throwing up."

UPLOAD

Tempest Star lay naked under the sheets in her room at the Farmington Best Western on Scott Avenue. She couldn't sleep from all the excitement earlier at the ruins. Next to her, Bennie snored lightly. *God, he is good*, she thought, looking over at him. Enough could not be said about the sexual appetite and vigor of young men. But tonight, even after they had sex and he drifted off to sleep, she still couldn't relax.

Something gnawed at her—something that didn't make sense. What she saw tonight was beyond anything she had ever witnessed—or, for that matter, fabricated. Anyone who had observed what occurred at the newly uncovered ruins would have been speechless, shocked, dumbfounded. And yet, Cotten Stone showed no reaction when viewing the pictures on Bennie's camera. Stone's indifference was peculiar, Tempest thought. And that lack of alarm gave it away. No doubt Cotten Stone was hiding something. Stone understood the meaning of the pictures, but she'd kept her cool and calmly walked away.

Tempest recognized the man in the pictures. He was Yale University scientist Richard Hapsburg. She had seen him in an interview after the Peruvian incident, when he commented on the loss of his partner, Dr. Edelman. The woman had to be his wife, Mariah. She was the queen of the society pages with all her New England fundraising events. Mariah Hapsburg was a cash machine for her husband and his far-flung archaeology projects.

Then there was their benefactor, Eli Luddington, who was always in the news with them. What a piece of work he was. Talk about pulling strings and getting things done. As one of the most powerful art and antiquities dealers in the world, he could fill an order for a king's gallery or a president's collection before most people had breakfast.

And finally, the guy with Stone—the mystery man. Good looking, from what Tempest could see. She'd like a shot at him even if he wasn't in the age group she preferred.

Nothing added up, Tempest thought. What was the link between this strange cast of characters and the magic light show out in the desert—balls of fire, waves of swirling insects, and that fog. Where the hell did that come from? Thick fog in the desert, for God's sake. She was going to have to spin some fantastical story out of the raw pictures for her next *National Courier* piece. Usually, it was the other way around. This time she had the real deal in the pics first. Wait until her editor saw them. Normally the art department had to PhotoShop her stuff to make it support the story. Now, she just had to construct some outrageous piece to go with the photos. It would be on the front cover in next week's edition, and—

Suddenly, Tempest heard a soft clicking sound at the door, as if someone was trying to open it. She sat up in the dark room, the sheet falling away from her bare breasts. Shadows moving along the thin light under the door revealed movement on the other side. *Probably a drunk trying to get in the wrong room*, she thought. *He'll realize his mistake in a minute.*

She watched as the shadow stopped. Faint metallic noises came from the door. Somebody was picking the lock?

Tempest heard the lock give with one loud click, and the door opened. Light streamed in, behind it silhouettes of two men rushing toward her.

Bright lights blinded her.

Before Tempest could scream, a strong hand clasped over her mouth.

"What the—," Bennie mumbled as he tried to sit up. A knee pushed on his chest, and he gasped for air.

Tempest stared into the ski-mask-covered face of her assailant before the bright light made her shut her eyes. The tip of a knife pricked the tender skin under her chin.

"Scream and I'll slit your throat," said the man. "Right after I cut lover boy's dick off." He pushed her down on the bed, straddled her, and moved the light beam from her eyes to her breasts.

A gloved hand fondled her, and Tempest grunted a protest.

"Make a sound and you'll wind up flat-chested. You're not gonna scream, are you?" he asked, pushing the tip of the blade against her skin.

Tempest shook her head. Holy shit, he was going to rape her and cut her to shreds. No way was she going to go out without a fight. At his weakest moment, she'd knee him and gouge his eyes with her long acrylic nails. If she was going to die, she'd make him wish he'd picked on somebody else.

"Where's the camera?" the man said, lessening the pressure of the knife.

Tempest swallowed, but it was only air that moved down her throat. Her mouth was desert dry. Her breath came out in a sigh of relief. The fuckers weren't here to rape her. They wanted the goddamn camera.

"Answer the question," the second man said.

"In the bag by the desk," Tempest said.

"See how easy that was?" He got off her and went to the desk. Yanking a large black camera bag from underneath, he unzipped the top and pulled out the digital camera. A moment later, he had the LCD on the back illuminated and was looking at the pictures. "We got it," he said to his accomplice.

"What about their laptop?" the second man said, motioning to the computer on the desk. "They could have transferred the pictures."

"Grab it," he said before turning off the camera's display and removing the memory card. Then he tossed the camera onto the floor and turned to Tempest. "Any of this ever gets mentioned in your paper and we'll be back to finish our little slice-and-dice party."

Within seconds, both men were out the door.

Tempest and Bennie lay in the darkness, breathing hard.

"Bastards," she said. She touched her neck where the knife tip had been. "Shit," Tempest said, reaching to turn on the lamp beside the bed. Her fingertips were slick and shiny red.

Bennie looked at her. "Oh Jesus, Tempest, he cut you." He sat up and scrambled to her side of the bed. "Let me see," he said, wiping the blood from her neck with the sheet.

"I think I'm okay," she said. "Must be just a nick."

Bennie squinted at the wound. "Let's get it washed." He fumbled his way to the other side of the bed and retrieved his glasses from the nightstand. "You think Stone and the *Gazette* had anything to do with this?" he said, walking Tempest to the bathroom.

"I don't think they'd go to this extreme to get the pictures. Assault, breaking and entering. Not worth the jail time." She flipped on the light and examined her throat in the mirror.

Bennie wet a washcloth and gently cleaned the blood away.

"But obviously someone wants them really bad," Tempest said, flinching as the soap Bennie used stung the wound.

He rinsed her throat and dabbed it dry. "Don't think it even needs a stitch," he said.

She slapped his round bare ass. "Thanks, baby." Tempest wrapped a towel around her before walking back into the bedroom. She made sure the door was locked and slid on the chain guard. "Should have done that in the first place," she said.

"I didn't buy into this kind of shit when I took the job," Bennie said, standing by the bed and straightening the sheets. "Should we call the police?"

"Don't be such a pussy. Do you know what this means? We're right in the middle of a huge story. This is front-page stuff." She looked at the camera bag. "Trouble is, they screwed us by taking the memory card *and* the laptop."

"Not quite," Bennie said.

Tempest stood in front of him. "Meaning?"

Bennie smiled at her before pulling her towel off. "Meaning that while you took your shower earlier, I logged in to the production server at work and uploaded the images."

She looked at the young man, and a seductive smile took over her face. Tempest stroked his chest and trailed her fingers down his belly, kneeling between his legs. "Then you deserve a big reward."

CHAUNCEY'S NOTE

COTTEN KICKED OFF HER shoes and sat on the edge of the motel bed while Wyatt sat in the chair opposite her. Beside him, an ice bucket along with two plastic cups and two canned drinks rested on a small table. He had stopped at the ice and vending machine near his room before knocking on Cotten's door. He watched her while she twisted her tea-colored hair into a cord and then clipped it up. In some ways she reminded him of Leah, he thought. Cotten was petite like Leah, and even when trying to be tough and confident, her innocence shone through.

Leah.

The thought of his fiancée wrenched an audible squeak from his throat. After all the chemo and all the misery that accompanied it, in the end, the lymphoma had won. He wondered if he could ever let go of the memory—the pain.

"What are you thinking about so hard?" Cotten asked.

Wyatt blinked. "You remind me of someone I used to know."

"Oh? Someone wonderful and beautiful, I hope."

"As a matter of fact, yes."

Cotten slid the blanket from the foot of the bed and wrapped it around her shoulders. "How can the desert be hot in the daytime and so cold once the sun goes down? I know the scientific explanation, but it just flies in the face of my logic."

Wyatt scooped ice into one of the cups and popped the top on the Diet Coke.

"Hot tea or something stronger would really hit the spot," Cotten said.

"Best we can do," he said, pouring the drink into the cup. He held it out to her. Even her hands reminded him of Leah. Small with long, thin fingers—but minus the engagement ring.

"Thanks," she said. "But if I'm going to drink something cold, I wish it had a kick."

"I'm a Stoli man. What's your poison?" he asked.

"Absolut."

"And I had you pegged for a white zin girl."

Cotten laughed. "You're not the first to misread me."

Wyatt poured his Red Bull into a cup and sipped. "I'll drink anything but gin," he said.

"Too much of it one time and lived to regret it?"

"Actually, I never touched it."

"Then why the aversion?"

"Long story," he answered, shutting down any more questions about gin. No sense in going to that dark place. Wyatt lifted his cup. "Cheers."

"To a totally fucked-up day," Cotten said, leaning forward and touching her cup to his.

"It wasn't a complete loss."

"Easy for you to say. I've got no story, no pictures, nothing to take back. And the worst is, I know what's going to be on the front page of the *National Courier*. My face looking like an idiot, stunned by Star's flash. Want to know the headlines? 'Is Has-Been At It Again?' Tempest Star will use *my* name to draw readers to the *Courier*."

"It's just a stupid tabloid, Cotten. Nobody believes what they read in those rags. They're for entertainment."

Cotten stood. "But they make it into a lot of shopping carts and onto a lot of nightstands. Not good enough to display on the coffee table, but they're bought and they're read. Star is going to take advantage of the situation. She's got all the pictures—shit, you saw them. She'll put her spin on it and make it seem that I was there fabricating a new story like the creation fossil. Star is the one with the documentation. So I go to my boss at the *Gazette* and tell him I have nothing and Star—"

"Look, we'll be back in Fort Lauderdale tomorrow. You've got the whole plane ride to think of something—to put together a story. You're a professional. Tell it like it is—what we did there, what you saw."

"We didn't see anything. We were too late. And I can't mention Star—she's the competition. She has it all, and she is going to bastardize the truth because she doesn't have a clue what she witnessed." She looked at Wyatt. "Do you?"

"Not exactly. Why don't you tell me?"

Cotten sat on the bed again. She looked as if she were about to come undone, Wyatt thought. Her shoulders sagged, and there was a slight flush in her face.

"The Hapsburgs found the tablet. Of that, I'm convinced," she said. "When I was in the round building—the holy place—I sensed their presence, heard their voices. I know they were there." She took a sip of the Diet Coke. "The pictures you saw showed Richard Hapsburg turning over the crystal tablet to the . . . fireflies."

"Fireflies?"

"That glowing ball of light in the picture. I first saw them in Peru. Thomas, I think the fireflies are demons. They took the tablet from Edelman's tent. And tonight they took another tablet from Richard Hapsburg."

Demons, Wyatt thought. Even with the words of the pope, it was so hard to accept. This devil stuff was created by the Church to keep its members in line. That was all. What he saw in those pictures was just some kind of phenomenon—heat lightning, swamp gas, optical illusion—shit! What the hell had he gotten himself into?

"Thomas, I need to find out what was written on those tablets. Not for the news story, but because I need to know what it says. You told me the pope said that the second cleansing would come in my time and that is why there is the rush to find the tablet. I know that the message has something to do with me, because of who I am. And that I'm supposed to be the one leading the second cleansing—Armageddon. How can I do that if I never find out the entire message on the tablets?"

Cotten leaned forward, burying her face in her hands. "God, I hate this. Why does everything have to be so cryptic?" Cotten looked up at the ceiling. "If God wants me to do something, why doesn't He just tell me? I mean, would it kill Him to just get to the point?"

Wyatt looked at her with sympathy, knowing she was in pain. How could he make it easier?

"I'm sorry," she said with a sigh. "I'll just never understand why I was picked. Furmiel or no Furmiel, it seems to me that God had better choices than me. Maybe I think if I complain enough or fail to understand, God will realize that He chose the wrong person and He'll forget about me." She stared at the floor and rubbed her forehead. "I just don't get it."

Wyatt put his drink down and leaned forward, taking one of her hands in his. "Together we'll make sense out of all this. After all, you were chosen because of your legacy, and I was chosen because of mine."

Cotten's head shot up.

"Mine isn't of quite the same caliber as yours, Cotten, but my ancestor, actually my great-great-great-grandfather, was directly linked to one of the crystal tablets—the one they consider to be the last. His name was Chauncey Wyatt, and he was a member of an ancient, secret organization called the *Ombres des Fantômes*—it's French for 'Shadows of Ghosts.'"

"That's just great. Another ancient secret organization. Seems like every time I turn around, I'm running into one."

"Stay with me on this. The Shadows' job was to protect religious relics and documents, including the last crystal tablet. Did you know that at one time the Vatican had a tablet in its possession?"

"No," Cotten said. Her face perked. "Then they know what the message says, right?"

"The tablet was stolen."

"But they have records, and someone would have copied it down. Let's call John. He can find out what it said."

Wyatt gently squeezed her hand. "They deciphered the first part of the message on the tablet, the one predicting the Great Flood and the warning of the second cleansing. But the text of the last portion of the message was nonsensical."

"But the Vatican has a handwritten copy, don't they?"

"All the documents, drawings, and references were taken with the tablet."

Cotten shook her head. "So what are you telling me? And what does that have to do with you and your grandfather?"

"Chauncey was a zealot, not just a member of the Shadows. The *Ombres des Fantômes* were the seed from which the Venatori grew. Chauncey had a falling out with the Shadows but still took to heart his oath to protect the sacred religious relics with his life. He didn't believe that the crystal tablet should belong to the Church, or any religion for that matter. He was convinced that what it revealed was meant for all mankind. And so he stole it."

"That makes no sense. He took the tablet for a noble reason, because it belongs to mankind, but he hid it from the world. The damn thing would have been better off gathering dust in the Vatican archives. At least then we could find it and figure out what it says about me."

"Chauncey left a note in the tablet's place. We think it's a clue to where he hid it."

"What did it say?" Cotten asked.

Wyatt let go of her hand. The words from his grandfather's note were emblazoned in his mind. He'd repeated them at least once every day since his meeting with the pope. Taking a deep breath, he said, "My grandfather's note read, 'The secret does not belong to the Church but to the whole world. To enter the Kingdom of Heaven, you must thread the needle.'"

ICU

THE SLEEK GULFSTREAM G450 streaked across the pristine blue sky high over western Pennsylvania on its way to New Haven Regional Airport. The setting sun cast an orange glow across the farmland below. Mariah Hapsburg watched what she thought was Pittsburgh passing near the horizon. She glanced at Richard sleeping in the seat across the aisle.

What an amazing forty-eight hours she had just experienced. First, watching the excitement Eli expressed upon the news of the earthquake and the uncovering of the ancient ruins. Then the magnificent way in which her husband had found the artifact and taken command of the moment—even his posture was imposing as he offered up the tablet. And the breathtaking sight of the fireflies.

Richard had told her that the first time she encountered them would be astounding. Still, she was not prepared. No one could be prepared for the overwhelming sensation of experiencing the supernatural. The memory made her skin tingle, just as it had in the desert under the full moon.

There was the smell—strong, pungent, intoxicating. And the sound of the swarm. It vibrated through her whole body.

The sheer power that surrounded her—dangerous, forbidden, deadly—was exhilarating. The sight of the demons whirling around her—pulsing, touching.

All of it so incredibly sensual.

And back in the hotel, it was evident the experience had brought on the same kind of arousal in her husband. Richard's lovemaking was fierce and explosive, exactly as she had wanted. Sensing his driving desire for her only heightened her need for him.

Mariah had known the feeling of being desired and coveted all her life. Up until the accident. Everything in her life was divided by the accident. BA and AA—before the accident, and after.

BA was the beautiful life, drenched with money, sex, men wanting her, and women envying her. Then that tragic night. The car spinning, exploding, burning, pain beyond all pain.

She lay in the intensive care unit for weeks, hanging on by the slimmest of threads. When she was finally conscious and lucid, she begged for a mirror. She had touched her face, and she wanted to see it. When the nurses and her visitors wouldn't produce a mirror and encouraged her to wait, that confirmed her fears.

Early one morning, just after the nurse on duty had checked her vitals, Mariah maneuvered out of the bed, trailing her IV line behind her. The bedside table had been deliberately kept out of her reach because of the vanity mirror attached to it. Mariah stretched the arm that was tethered to the IV behind her, but still she couldn't reach the table with her other hand. She extended her leg, and her toes touched the cold metal frame of the table. Careful not to accidentally push it out of her reach, she slowly edged the table toward her, first only with her toes, then finally her foot. It rolled quietly up to her. Mariah took several steps back to relieve the tension on the IV line, pulling the table with her. With both hands, she lifted the hinged section of the table, bringing up the mirror. It only took a quick glance for her to reel and collapse.

She came to on the tile floor, the IV pole across her back. Instantly, she recalled the image in the mirror. Scarred, maimed, disfigured, repulsive.

A flurry of nurses were suddenly at her side, lifting her onto the bed.

"Leave me alone," she cried. "I want to die."

For days, she refused to eat or cooperate with therapists, repeatedly clawing at her face and reopening the wounds. She lay in the hospital bed, praying for God to take her.

With her lack of will, Mariah's recovery took a dive, and her condition became critical again—but she didn't die. Finally giving up on God's help, she offered her pleas elsewhere.

That night, she awoke to find someone holding her hand. Through the bandages and life-support tubes, she stared from a drug-induced haze into the face of an old, gray-haired gentleman—his voice comforting, his manner grandfatherly. In a soft, soothing voice he whispered that if she truly wanted it, he could make her whole again, take away her pain, and give her back her life.

"You can be even more beautiful than before," he promised.

Mariah wept, sobbing as he stroked her hair until she finally fell asleep.

The next morning, she thought it all a dream until she was transported to a private hospital and a team of plastic surgeons arrived at her bedside. They discussed with Mariah how they would reconstruct her face—her body.

"Who is paying for all this?" she asked.

That's when Eli Luddington came into the room. "Your visitor last night is a close friend of mine," he said. "He brought you to my attention. You do want your life back, don't you?"

"But why would you do this?" Mariah asked.

"Because you were in need," he said. "You cried out for help. He answered you, and brought you to me." Eli came to stand close to her bed. "Put your trust in me," he said.

Mariah nodded, and tears of gratefulness welled in her eyes. Eli Luddington was her savior.

Through a series of state-of-the-art procedures performed by the team of surgeons Eli had gathered from around the world, she regained her beauty, strength, and drive. Eli gave her life. And all he asked in return was for her to become a part of Richard's life. Richard was lost, and she was to help him find his way again. Mariah could lead him back into the fold and steady him so he could do his life's work. She would be his strength and his inspiration.

And now, here she was five years later, flying high over the earth, being a part of a miraculous adventure, possessing a beauty few women had, and helping her husband reshape the world. She owed everything to Eli. And she was more than willing to pay.

"Ms. Hapsburg," the female attendant said, bringing Mariah out of her reverie. "There's a call for your husband from Mr. Luddington."

Mariah looked at Richard, sleeping soundly. "No need to wake him. I'll take it."

"Of course," the girl said, gesturing to the handset next to Mariah's armrest.

"Hello, Eli," she said, placing the receiver to her ear.

"Where is Rumjal?"

His voice had the edge of a box knife, and Mariah knew immediately that there was a problem. "He's in the toilet, Eli," she lied. Did he know when she lied?

"Do you have any idea what is plastered across the cover of today's edition of the *National Courier*?"

Mariah felt a film of clammy sweat bead on her skin. Whatever it was couldn't be good. She didn't respond, waiting for Eli.

"The pictures." His words continued to cut through the phone.

"That can't be. Richard's men got the pictures and destroyed them. Unless there were copies or—"

"Mariah, this is no game. As long as we make progress, we'll be left alone. But if we fuck up, we'll get more help than you can possibly imagine."

"Eli—"

"And you don't want the kind of help I'm talking about."

GIN

Cotten climbed the steps to her Fort Lauderdale apartment, Thomas Wyatt carrying her suitcase behind her. "This is home, such as it is," she said, unlocking the door.

Wyatt followed her in and set her bag beside the sofa.

"Sorry about the mildew smell," she said, sliding the laptop case's strap off her shoulder. She set the case on the coffee table. "You can't get away from it when you live so close to the water. Everything has its price. I'll open up and let some breeze blow through."

"I'm sure I'll have to do the same. I'll be staying in the apartment down the street that Monsignor Duchamp had. I want to be nearby."

Cotten smiled at him. "That's nice, Thomas."

"I mean it's my job." He shook his head. "That didn't come out right."

"Don't say any more, you'll just dig a deeper hole." Cotten knelt on the couch, leaned over the back of it, pulled the blinds up, and cranked the window open. “There, that should help. Glad it’s fall and not the middle of the summer, or we’d be sweating right now.”

“So have you decided what you’re going to tell the *Gazette*?”

“Not really. I can give them the truth, but I don’t know how it will play once the *Courier* runs Star’s piece. It’s probably already in the supermarkets.” She backed off the sofa. “Sit down. You’ve got a minute, don’t you?”

“That’s why I’m here,” Wyatt answered.

Cotten plunked down on the other end of the sofa. “I know we’ve gone over the threading-the-needle thing in your grandfather’s note a hundred times before we left and on the plane, but I’m still at a loss.” She curled her legs up beside her. “I just don’t think it has anything to do with making clothing or sewing. We found all the references on the Internet to sewing techniques. None of them led anywhere. Plus, you said your grandfather was a doctor, not a tailor. Maybe it has something to do with a medical technique that was popular during his time. Should we be looking into things like suturing wounds or surgical procedures from the late 1800s?”

Wyatt rubbed his chin. “Not a bad idea. Maybe he was trying to leave a clue to the tablet’s hiding place using medical terminology.”

“Maybe it was hidden in a hospital.”

“Or a medical university. You’re right, though. Medicine and needles do go together. The sewing angle might be too obvious. I’ll run a search on eighteenth-century surgical procedures and see if anything comes up that was called ‘threading the needle.’”

“Why do you think he stole the tablet to begin with?”

“I don’t know. Neither does the pope or John. But judging from the note, he felt strongly enough about sharing what’s on the artifact with the world to take the chance of getting caught. I wish I knew more about him, but it was so many generations ago. I've got a few distant relatives in the UK who might be able to fill in some of the gaps."

"Sounds like a trip to England is in order."

"Maybe."

"Bet you never thought you'd get mixed up in something as screwy as this, did you?"

"No," Wyatt said, followed by a laugh.

"Me neither," Cotten said. "Up until three years ago, I led a pretty dull life. Dull sounds good to me these days."

Wyatt said nothing for a moment, seeming to be deep in thought. "Cotten, can I ask you something?"

"Maybe. Well, I guess you can ask, but whether or not I'll answer . . ."

"Why are you doing this?" He cleared his throat. Cotten could tell he was trying to walk a thin line between not insulting her and attempting to logically answer questions that would dumbfound just about anyone.

"Please don't get me wrong, Cotten. It's just—"

She held her hand up. "I'm not offended, if that's what you think. Thomas, trust me when I say that this has been a mystery to me as well. I never asked for any of it. Three years ago, I was told that I was the only one who could stop the sun, the dawn, from taking place. It was only after John Tyler figured out that I had misunderstood the meaning of the words that the whole thing became clear. *S-u-n* was really *s-o-n*—Son of the Dawn—that's what they called Lucifer in the Bible. And that's about the time all dullness evaporated out of my life. As I understand it, the plan was to clone Christ by using His DNA found in the blood residue inside the Grail. The story goes that Lucifer wanted ultimate revenge against God for casting him and the other Fallen Angels out of Paradise. He was going to create the Antichrist from the DNA in the Grail. When John and I were faced with destroying the clone, we sort of changed roles. John was, and still is, a man of granite faith. Far different from the person I thought I could ever be. I was weak, doubting, unbelieving in anything spiritual or religious—I blamed everything wrong in my life on a lack of God. At the moment of decision in the lab, John realized he couldn't destroy the embryo—the least of his reservations was that it might've actually been Jesus Christ. His faith kept him from committing what he thought was murder, abortion, sacrilege. The scientist in him begged to question if the Second Coming was actually supposed to take place in this manner rather than what we had all been taught in Sunday school."

Cotten stared across the room, the memory so vivid that she shuddered. "I, on the other hand, was simply fighting for my life—our lives. I didn't have the baggage of a priest. After the Grail conspiracy, I was called a hero. I milked it for everything I could, riding high as a famous journalist. That is, until the fossil hoax. I probably deserved that fiasco. I was way too overconfident. It was a setup, you know. But in the end, it didn't matter. Fans are fickle. They love you when you're on top and forget your name when you tumble. I may never be able to recover. But I've done what I have to do to survive. And I'm continuing. Does that kind of answer your question?"

"Much of it, but I have a feeling the well goes deeper. Enough for now. Thanks for opening up to me," Wyatt said.

Cotten looked at him. She'd told him enough to digest for one night. She wondered how deep *his* well was. She didn't know much about him at all. "I feel kind of naked around you, exposed, like you know everything about me and I don't know anything about you."

"Not much to know, really."

"Come on, Thomas, I need some little tidbit. Give me some footing. I feel like a fly under a microscope. The scale isn't balanced. Tell me something about yourself. It'll make us even."

"All right, I was born—"

"No, no. Not the documentary stuff. Spill some dark secret. Level the field for me."

"Like what?"

Cotten thought for a moment. "Okay, here's something. Why no gin? You said you'd drink anything but gin. That might be a good place to start."

Wyatt shifted, as if uneasy. "I don't like the smell of it," he answered, then tugged on his ear.

"Come on," she said. "I don't even care if you tell me the truth. Make something up. Give me something."

Wyatt leaned forward, resting his forearms on his knees. "My mother was an alcoholic, and gin was her choice. I hated the way it reeked on her breath. Even today when I smell it, my stomach rolls over. When my mother drank, she became someone else. She was a morbid and remorseful drunk, so she attempted suicide more times than I can count. Sliced her wrists, overdosed on sleeping pills the incompetent doctor prescribed, drove the car off a dock. My father took the worst of it until he'd had a bellyful. She'd call him at work, crying and saying she was going to kill herself. At first, he'd run home, but that wore thin over time, until finally he got to the point he'd hang up on her and go on with his day as usual. I understand that, but for me as a kid, it wasn't fair. I got left with the responsibility of her care. I can remember so many times waiting outside my elementary school for her to pick me up. When she didn't show, I didn't do what most kids would do. I didn't go to the office. I started walking, hoping no one would notice. Keeping it a secret. Sometimes, what I would walk into at home . . ."

Wyatt took a deep breath, seeming to attempt to recover from the memory. "I hated the drunk person, and the only reason I protected her was so when she sobered up, I could have my mother back. And when she was herself, I wouldn't have ever wanted anyone other than her to be my mother." Wyatt looked down at his hands. "I tried to hide her alcoholism from everyone, because I knew they would think less of her. And my mother, my sober mother, was a remarkable and wonderful woman." He sat back and looked at Cotten. "So now you know why gin makes my skin crawl."

"I'm sorry," Cotten said, more for making him tell the story than expressing sympathy. "I shouldn't have pressed you. I thought it would be some funny college fraternity story. It wasn't right of me."

"It's okay," Wyatt said. "Are we even?"

"Even," she said, almost in a whisper.

The silence that followed was interrupted by the phone. Cotten answered. "Okay, I'll be right down."

"What's up?" Wyatt asked.

"The postman left a package for me at the front office. Be right back."

Cotten hurried down the stairs, wondering if she was more anxious to get the package or to return to Wyatt.

"Funky stamps," the front-desk clerk said, giving Cotten the package.

It was about half the size of a shoebox, wrapped in brown paper and rough twine, and the stamps were foreign—each bore a picture of a llama. The package was from Peru.

"Thanks," Cotten said, taking it from him.

She read the handwriting. It was addressed to Mayta, her Incan name. Attention: Cotten Stone.

Cotten climbed up the steps, tearing open the package on the way.

"A present?" Wyatt asked when she came in.

Cotten opened the box and gasped.

"What is it?"

"Maybe the answer to everything."

SUPERHERO

THOMAS WYATT GOT TO his feet. "So, what is it?"

"A talisman." Cotten held up a bundle of dark gray condor feathers, ringed at the top with smaller white condor neck feathers. A narrow strip of leather coiled around the top of the bundle, binding it to a center stem—a hollow condor bone.

"Unusual gift."

"A reminder," Cotten said. "In Peru, I met a spiritual man who taught me what I guess you would call meditation—but even more than that. I'm still a novice." She handed Wyatt the talisman. "It's to remind me to practice."

"That's the answer to everything?" Wyatt asked.

"Well, my shaman friend thinks so. But I think this is more straightforward," Cotten said, taking the small Elph camera from the package and holding it up. "I had it in Peru."

"Did the Cusco police have it?"

"No," Cotten said. She explained how Yachaq had rescued her and that while in the village she dressed in the native clothing given to her. "I had almost forgotten about it. The camera was in my pants pocket when I fled Edelman's camp. My clothes were left behind in Yachaq's village. He must have found it and traveled to the city to mail it back to me. That had to be a lot of trouble for him." She showed Wyatt the address label she had made and stuck on the back of the camera. "Actually, I got the idea from a travel show on TV. Of course, you have to luck out and have an honest person find it. And I did."

Cotten pushed the power button on the Elph, but as she expected, the battery was dead. "Thank goodness for technology. We'll try plan B." She opened the small door to the bay that held the memory card and ejected it. "I just have to hook up my laptop to the printer."

When everything was connected, Cotten popped the memory card into the slot in the printer, and the pictures began uploading onto the computer.

The thumbnails appeared and lined up on the screen. The money shot at Machu Picchu with Nick and Paul; various pictures of the dig site; Edelman; the mountains; three photos of the tablet; and one of Paul struggling to eat the *cuy*.

Cotten clicked on the first picture of the tablet, enlarging it.

"Shit," she said. "The angle is off a bit. You can't really see all the markings."

Quickly, she clicked on the next picture. "There," she said. "Those are some kind of glyphs." She pointed to the top of the tablet. "That's what Edelman thought was the prediction of the Flood. Her finger slid down the picture so it trailed along the bottom half of the tablet. "You can kind of see the lines and dots, can't you? The khipu-like writing?"

"Sort of," Wyatt said.

"Edelman said that most anthropologists think khipu was a simple accounting method, but there are others who believe it was more than that—a type of three-dimensional language. Kind of like a computer language. So, khipu could be an accounting tool as well as a language."

Cotten chose the last picture and shook her head. Larger fragments of the writing could be seen before the glare took over the image. "It was at night and I had to use the flash," she said. "The tablet reflected a lot of that light right back at the camera."

"At least we can see some of it," Wyatt said.

"But not what I need to see."

"It's better than a stick in the eye," he said.

Cotten looked at Wyatt. "That's a terrible saying."

"Better than nothing, then."

Cotten raked her fingers through her hair and closed the window with the pictures. "So what do we do with this?"

"Print a hard copy first," Wyatt said.

Cotten printed the pictures, then opened her Internet browser, went to Google, and typed in *khipu*. "Maybe we can find one of those experts who believe khipu is a language. Someone must be able to read this."

* * *

Lester Ripple sat at a harvest gold vinyl-topped card table that could barely be seen beneath the sheets of paper that lay helter-skelter on top of it. Just as many were strewn across the floor like rectangular snowdrifts. Every piece had copious amounts of pencil-scribbled equations among sketches of comic-book superheroes.

Ripple's fingers held the pencil so tightly that his nail beds blanched. He mumbled as he tried to keep the pencil up to speed with his brain. Sometimes it just happened like this. He called it brain streaming, like video streaming, but it was all in his head. Getting it out fast enough was the problem.

The point of the pencil was dulling, but he didn't want to stop to sharpen it. In a moment, he would have to give his brain some relief, so he'd sharpen it then. Near the bottom of the paper, Ripple suddenly stopped. The flow of mathematical equations was coming too fast, so fast that they collided in his head. He had to slow down.

Ripple sharpened the point with a plastic handheld sharpener, the kind that had a small razor blade inside. This one was buried inside the rubber head of Batman. The shavings curled out and spilled onto the table. Ripple brushed them together and then piled them up with the shavings from previous sharpenings. That was something else he had to think about. Too much waste. What could be made of pencil shavings—pencil mulch?

Lester Ripple blew the graphite dust off the new point and pushed it against his index finger. Very sharp. He liked that. The sharper the pencil, the more exact his calculations. He tapped the point again with his middle finger—tap, tap, tap. The pencil was ready, but he was not. His head was jumbled, images of numbers and symbols swimming about. He put the pencil lead to the small margin on the side of the paper he had just been working on and began to sketch. "Spider-Man," he said, and smiled. Spider-Man and the likes of him could do anything, especially soothe Ripple's brain.

The phone rang, shocking him so that he snapped the pencil in his hand. Before getting up to answer, he took the longest part of the broken pencil and broke it again so that there were three pieces. That satisfied him and so freed him to go to the telephone on the kitchen wall.

"Ripple here," he said, answering the call. He removed his glasses and rubbed his bad eye. At home, he preferred glasses to the contact lens.

As he listened, he fought back his body's attempt to hyperventilate. He cupped his hand around the receiver and breathed into his palm as he listened. At the end of the call, Ripple said, "Yes. Thursday at eight. Thank you."

Ripple hung up and staggered back to the card table.

He had a job.

BUCKINGHAM

THE BENTLEY ARNAGE LIMOUSINE pulled away from the Newbury Street curb in front of the Chase Gallery. Its four-hundred-horsepower engine slipped the elegant motorcar through downtown Boston with the grace of a ballerina and the authority of a predator.

Mariah Hapsburg sat nervously reading a copy of the *National Courier*. Eli had thrust it into her hand as she entered the limo after the gallery reception. Now he sat opposite her, Richard Hapsburg at his side. They spoke in hushed tones, sometimes falling into a tongue she did not understand. Mariah didn't like it when Eli was upset. And when he referred to Richard as Rumjal, she knew he was upset.

Scanning the front page of the tabloid, she stared at the series of photos showing her and Richard at the New Mexico ruins. As wounding as the pictures were, the captions were worse:

Modern-day tomb raiders carry out mumbo-jumbo in the desert.

Respected Yale scientist Richard Hapsburg performs bizarre ritual trying to communicate with ancient Anasazi.

Socialite wife of Hapsburg takes part in strange clandestine ceremony while state officials are kept away.

Mariah felt a sourness rise in her throat at the ghastly embarrassment the article and pictures were going to cause the university and the resulting damage to Richard's career and hers.

She focused on the last picture in the series:

Disgraced former network correspondent Cotten Stone tries to hide her face. Was she caught trying to report the story or fabricate it? Are she and the Hapsburgs in cahoots?

So that was Cotten Stone, Mariah thought, staring at the photo. She didn't look all that menacing. In fact, she looked a bit . . . meek.

"She isn't very intimidating," Mariah said.

Eli broke off his conversation with Richard to glare at her. "Don't be deceived."

Mariah folded the *National Courier* and placed it on the seat beside her. Cotten Stone ignited a dangerous blaze in Eli, she thought. But how could he be right about this woman? How could one person threaten his power—his plan? Recently, he had deviated from the plan and ordered an escalation of events, remarking that the race to find the last tablet and the secret it held had entered the final stretch.

The Bentley smoothly rounded a curve as the two men in the rear continued their conversation. "In the end, Richard, it comes down to only one thing," Eli said. "The number of souls taken. That is the reason for orchestrating the killings—the suicides. If we can take them this way—take their choice from them—then their souls belong to us for all eternity. That causes Him much pain, the pain He deserves."

Eli's face hardened with his words, sending a shiver through Mariah.

"Unfortunately, this increase in suicides threatens to show our hand," Eli continued. "It has already incited vigorous questioning in the press and among the medical community. But as time grows short, we must take the risk that soon these incidents will be recognized for what they are."

Mariah did not really understand. Eli, Richard—they were part of something she could only partially comprehend. And that kept her out of the inner circle she had been working so hard to penetrate.

"What do you mean?" she asked. "A suicide is a suicide."

Richard smiled patronizingly at her. "Not always," he said. "The ones we speak of are not those suffering souls who are so despondent that ending their lives seems the only answer. Those are not the souls we necessarily take. Some are ours to have, some are not."

"Then what are you talking about?" Mariah asked, more confused.

"Tell her," Eli said.

"The Old Man arranges them," Richard said.

Mariah had heard Eli and Richard mention someone they called the Old Man. In her gut, she knew who that was. He was the one who had come to her hospital bedside. He had brought Eli to her. He already had her soul.

"The Church likes to call them demonic possessions," Eli said. "All that means is that we have taken control and will capture that soul."

Mariah shuddered.

"If Cotten Stone finds the tablet before we do, she will discover the means to stop us," Richard said.

"What does it say? What is the secret?" Mariah asked.

Richard leaned forward and kissed his wife on the lips. The kiss was soft, but it did not feel to Mariah like a kiss of affection. Richard's lips were bitter cold, and he held his mouth to hers for what seemed a long time before he sat back. Even as he sank into the leather, his eyes stayed fixed on hers.

Mariah wiped the frostiness from her lips and turned to gaze out the window.

* * *

The footman inspected the breakfast table—fresh-cut flowers, a choice of cold and hot cereal, and an assortment of fruit. The national newspapers, with the *Racing Post* on top, were neatly stacked beside the two place settings. Folded white linen napkins embroidered with the emblem EIIR, the acronym for Queen Elizabeth II, rested to one side of each plate.

The footman placed the cup and saucer for the Earl Grey tea, being careful to rotate the cup so the handle was adjusted to the perfect angle for an easy grasp. He positioned two small pitchers side by side—one containing maple syrup and the other honey from the royal hives. The silver spoons for the marmalade were not perfectly parallel, so he made the adjustment. The queen preferred light marmalade with her toast, but he often watched her feed most of the toast to her corgis, who would gather at her feet.

This morning, she and the Duke of Edinburgh were late.

Glancing at his watch, the footman left the small breakfast chamber and moved quietly down the hall past the Privy Purse Door toward the page's vestibule. It would take him along the queen's private corridor. From there, he would have a clear view through each door of her apartments.

He had worked in the palace for seven years but rarely ventured down this route out of respect for the privacy of the monarch. Even after seven years, he had only seen a small portion of Buckingham Palace. The tour guide listed seventy-eight bathrooms. He could attest to five.

The footman spotted the corgis asleep in the corridor beside the door to Her Majesty's bedroom. He expected their heads to rise and their ears to pop up at the sound of his footsteps. When they did not, he felt an immediate pang of dread twist in his gut. Something was wrong.

Standing over the dog's bodies, he saw no rise and fall of their chests, no sign of life at all. Glancing up, he realized the door was partially open, and he gave it a gentle push.

It swung silently on well-oiled hinges, opening to reveal the royal bedroom. In an instant, fear rushed through him, and he trembled. Instinctively, he reached for the small communicator on his belt. Raising it to his lips, he pressed the transmit button. Sucking in his breath, he said, "Code red! Code red! Royal apartment one." He gulped down an urge to panic and whispered, "My God. They're all dead."

TWO BEACHES

Prayer is more than meditation. In meditation the source of strength is one's self. When one prays he goes to a source of strength greater than his own.

—CHIANG KAI-SHEK

NAKED AND DRIPPING WET from the shower, Cotten stood in front of the medicine cabinet. The *National Courier's* headlines about the Hapsburgs and her in New Mexico, alongside the front page of Fort Lauderdale's *Sun-Sentinel* detailing the queen's suicide, had sent her reeling. She recognized her symptoms—the trembling and the sensation of not getting enough air into her lungs. She thought perhaps a hot shower would thwart the panic. And it had done a partial job, but she still felt weak.

The medicine-cabinet door squeaked as Cotten opened it. The brown bottle of Ativan stood out on the shelf. She stared at it. If she took the medication, Cotten knew she would be moving a step backward.

But she needed it.

Her hand wrapped around the bottle, and the fingers of her other hand twisted the top. She shook one tablet into her palm and placed the bottle on the sink. Cotten held the pill a few moments longer and then put it in her mouth. She turned on the water and leaned over to cup some in her hand when she saw her distorted reflection in the chrome faucet. She spit the Ativan into the porcelain and rinsed her mouth.

Cotten folded her arms across the edge of the vanity and buried her head in them. After several moments, she rose and stared at herself in the mirror. “No more,” she whispered. Then she took the bottle and emptied its contents into the toilet before flushing.

Yachaq had sent her a reminder—a reminder that she should practice getting in touch with what he called the universal consciousness, and that all answers could be found within herself. Drugs only distanced her from those truths. They set up barriers that the energy of her thoughts could not penetrate. He had been right about so many things; she needed to trust him on this.

Cotten towel-dried her hair and put on her terry-cloth bathrobe before stretching out across her bed. Following Yachaq’s reminder, she started the exercise of finding and emerging into the liquid light. She surprised herself at how much more quickly she was able to suspend her thoughts and become immersed than in previous attempts. Her senses became acute. First, she heard the dripping of the showerhead in the next room, followed by the rustle of the palm fronds outside her apartment window. The passing traffic on the street below was intrusive, and she found that she could filter out those sounds that hindered her immersion into the liquid light.

The smell of the ocean was strong as it entered her nostrils, but the sour stench of decaying seaweed was even stronger. She heard a giggle, recognized a child's voice, and knew the child was blocks away on the beach.

The voices from the apartments and restaurants along the beach-front street were something she tried not to concentrate on, instead pushing them back into the gray edge of the liquid light.

Cotten felt comfortable with her journey into the spiritual place where Yachaq had taught her to go. It felt exhilarating to experience such a heightened state of awareness. She relished it more and more each time she ventured into this world of the senses.

Suddenly, there was something new, something different. In her mind's eye, she had been wandering among the golden palms and sea grape trees along the beach, enjoying the sensation of the warm sand beneath her feet, the tropical breeze that tousled her hair, the salty taste upon her lips. But she realized there were actually two beaches—the one that she walked upon, and another just out of reach. They seemed somewhat similar, and yet there were definite differences.

The palms on her beach were full of fresh coconuts while the palms on the other beach had none. The surf on her beach was rough and breaking, but the surf on the other beach was only gentle ripples.

Even though the other beach was just out of reach, Cotten felt as if she could go there if she simply tried hard enough.

What was happening? Was it real, or just a bit of her imagination? She tried to understand why there were two beaches, and how come she wanted to move from the first to the second.

Suddenly, Cotten crashed back to reality. She felt overwhelmed with disappointment. She opened her eyes and stared at the ceiling. Had she lost the sensation because she tried to overanalyze it? The disappointment was uncomfortable. She wanted to enter the liquid light again and try to roam the beach once more.

Cotten remembered something she had read concerning astronaut Ed Mitchell's spiritual experience on his return during the Apollo 14 mission. That was exactly what had happened to her just before losing the sense of harmony—the sense of freedom to move from one beach to the next.

Cotten sat up—fatigued, drained, and frustrated. Would she ever be any good at this? She was about to get up and head back to the bathroom to dry her hair when the phone rang.

"Hello," she said.

"Hey, kiddo."

"Ted. I've missed you." Cotten sat on the side of the bed. It was good to hear from him.

"What the hell are you doing?" Ted Casselman's voice had a sharpness to it.

Cotten pushed up against the headboard. "What do you mean?"

"I saw Tempest Star's piece."

Cotten slumped. "She's a wacko. The *National Courier* is a piece of shit. You know that."

"Sure I do, and so do you. And you know the *Gazette* is barely a rung above. Star says you're working for her competition. The *Gazette* is just as sleazy. What are you doing to yourself?"

"What do you want me to do, Ted, starve? I haven't found decent work since the creation-fossil debacle. Then I had to deal with the bad publicity from the Peru thing. And the *Gazette* is trying to gain more respectability. They wanted a real story, and they gave me a shot."

She could hear Ted huff in annoyance.

"You know, you really should let me help you sometimes. And by the way, speaking of the creation fossil, I did my homework back then," Ted said. "That Waterman guy, the paleontologist that you said did the validation—he was a fraud."

"Well, gee, Ted, thanks for telling me in such a timely manner."

"My point is that if you'd listen to me, I might save you some heartache. I didn't see any reason to bring this Waterman thing up after the horse was already out of the barn. Didn't want to be an I-told-you-so kind of guy. But maybe now you need to hear it."

This time Cotten breathed out a long sigh. "I know. You're right."

"Listen, I may have a way to get you back at SNN. Right now, you're wasting your talents and digging the hole deeper. I've got stories that are perfect for you—"

"Ted, you're such a good friend. That's the reason I can't take your offer."

"Why not?"

"Because my name would taint SNN and your credibility."

"Bullshit. It's been long enough. The public is forgiving. In no time, the name Cotten Stone will have all the respect it deserves again—*you* deserve again. We can do that for you. I want to help you out of this abyss."

Cotten wiped away the tears that had gathered in her eyes. Ted was one of the kindest men she'd ever known. He'd sure been good to her.

"You're going to hurt my feelings," Ted said. "If you don't take me up on this, I'm going to take it personally."

Cotten struggled for her voice, not wanting it to crack. She cleared her throat. "Let me think about it. I've got to meet Thomas Wyatt for lunch. I'm working on something with him. I'll get back to you later."

"Does this Wyatt guy work for the *Gazette* or have some hare-brained story to tell?"

"No, no, nothing like that. He's a friend of John Tyler's."

"Is he a priest, too?"

"No. I'll explain later. It's a legit story we're working on. It's all tied up with this rash of suicides, among a host of other things. I'll tell you more when I have a good handle on it."

"Good, because I don't get it. I don't understand suicides at any level, much less this weird escalation. Maybe I don't get it because suicide is nothing I would ever consider. Suicide is for cowards."

Cotten's throat tightened as she recalled her father's suicide, and how she had hated him for that for so long. It was bad enough to lose someone she loved, but since it was by his own hand, it was almost intolerable. As a survivor, she had suffered more than just the loss—sickening guilt had crept into the mourning, and she had always questioned herself.

"Ted, I need to go now, but I'll get back to you on your offer. Let the idea stew in my head a day or two."

"I'll be waiting for your call. Take care, little girl."

"Always," Cotten said, then hung up.

* * *

Cotten requested to sit on the patio by the dock so she could look at the water. The day was cool and slightly breezy, perfect for an outdoor lunch. The Southport Raw Bar's motto was "Eat fish live longer, Eat oysters love longer, Eat clams last longer." She got a kick out of that and wanted to remember it to tell Ted.

Cotten picked up the menu and studied it while she waited on Wyatt. Wings sounded good, or maybe just an appetizer of conch fritters and a slice of Key lime pie.

Fifteen minutes after bringing Cotten a glass of water and setting another at Wyatt's place, the waitress returned. "Do you want to order now?"

"No, I'm still waiting on my friend," Cotten said.

"An appetizer or drink?"

Cotten shook her head. "No thanks." She looked down at her watch. Maybe she should have picked him up. He might have gotten lost. He was supposed to rent a car that morning. Maybe that was taking longer than expected.

After another thirty minutes and no Wyatt, Cotten got up from the table and left. She would stop by Wyatt's apartment on the way home and find out what had delayed him.

Standing beside her car, she reached inside her purse for her keys. "Crap," she said, realizing she hadn't turned on her cell phone. Wyatt might have tried to call.

Cotten got in her Toyota, flipped the phone open, and turned it on. No missed calls. No messages. She started the car and headed back toward Wyatt's apartment.

The heavy lunch traffic along the beach caused her to have to wiggle her way to the Sand Dollar Apartments. She remembered the name of the complex and knew where it was, but she couldn't remember Wyatt's apartment number. But he had written it down for her, along with his phone number. She dug through her purse, finally locating the folded paper.

Number 103.

Cotten drove through the parking lot, finding apartment 103 near the south end. She pulled into an empty space and got out. These places looked a lot better than where she lived, she thought. It appeared that the Venatori had a better budget than a freelance reporter. She wondered what the rent was. It had to be twice what she paid.

Standing at the door, Cotten knocked. "Thomas," she called. She knocked harder, and to her surprise, the door cracked open. *He should keep it locked*, she thought.

"Thomas," she called again, easing the door a little wider. Voices came from inside, so she called out again.

When there was no response, Cotten opened the door and entered the apartment. The television was on and tuned to a talk show. That accounted for the voices. The living room was empty. She hit the switch on the remote and turned off the TV.

"Are you here, Thomas?"

The heels of her shoes clacked on the floor tile. The kitchen was empty. The bathroom door was wide open—no one in there.

The apartment had two bedrooms, and the door to one was open a sliver. Cotten pushed on it with her fingertips. The door glided open, and the room came into view.

"Oh sweet Jesus," she said.

SNAKE HANDLER

THOMAS WYATT WAS PROSTRATE on the tile floor, face-down. A small trickle of blood spiderwebbed from under his head and across the tile.

Cotten rushed to him and dropped to her knees at his side. "Thomas," she said, touching his neck. She couldn't find any sign of a pulse—his skin was cool to the touch. She tugged on his shoulder, trying to turn him over, but only twisted his torso at a grotesque angle. It was enough to see his face. His nose was smashed, and blood had dried and caked beneath his nostrils and around a small gash in his forehead.

His eyes were open, but they didn't move.

Cotten scrambled to her feet, grabbed the phone, and dialed 911.

* * *

Cotten took a sip of her Absolut, then put the glass down on the nightstand. She held the phone to her ear, listening to the ring as she lay down on her side. At last she heard him answer.

"John, something awful has happened," she said. "Thomas is dead." She explained how Wyatt hadn't shown for lunch and how she had gone to his apartment and found him on the floor of his bedroom.

"I'm so sorry you had to be the one to find him. Our Washington embassy was notified by your local police. I was informed a short time later. Cotten, we're all shaken by this. We have lost a good and decent man. I called His Holiness with the news and he immediately prayed for the repose of Thomas's soul. Right now, the important thing is, are you all right?"

"Yes . . . no . . . I don't know. It doesn't seem fair. The paramedics said he had a heart attack and collapsed. But he's only in his early forties, John. How can that be?"

"Until the autopsy is performed, we won't know. I've already authorized it. Cotten, do you need me to come there?"

It was all she could do to keep from saying yes. But being close to John while feeling so vulnerable wouldn't be good for her—wouldn't be easy on either of them. "I'm okay, really. It's just so awful. And I don't buy the heart-attack business. It's like when Thornton died after he got too close to uncovering the Grail conspiracy." Cotten remembered the trauma of finding out her ex-lover had collapsed in his hotel shower. He had called her from Rome just the day before, telling her he was on to something and that he feared for his life. "*They* killed Thornton and tried to make it look like natural causes, but we know it wasn't. Now they've come for Thomas. We were meeting for lunch to finalize our options of what to do with the pictures we have of the Peruvian crystal tablet. It's a long story, but I got my camera back, and there were pictures I had taken of the tablet. Thomas was going to call you today and send copies, but—" Cotten swallowed hard. "John, they want to stop us from finding out what it says. They murdered Thomas. They want to get to me, hurt me, make me back off."

"You can't let them do that, especially now that you have photographs of the tablet."

"I don't know what to do next. I don't think Thomas had any family, but I'm not sure."

"No, he doesn't have any immediate family. Cotten, you need to stay calm and clear-headed."

"I will," she said. "The shock of it, you know, it stops you in your tracks."

"What did Thomas think of the pictures? Are they of use? What can you tell from them?"

"Glare has blotted out some parts. The bottom half resembles what khipu looks like. But we can't see all of it. Thomas and I had located some experts. All we had to do was decide where we were going to send the pictures. Now he's dead."

"Let's see what the autopsy shows, a natural death or something suspicious."

"It won't matter. They have the means to make it look like a heart attack. As a matter of fact, I'm sure the autopsy will determine his death was due to some cardiac problem. That's how they work. No signs of foul play—but we recognize it for what it is."

There was a contented silence for a moment, and then Cotten said, "And you know what else? I was just thinking, these two tablets that we know about, the one in Peru and the one in New Mexico, they were both found in places where entire civilizations have disappeared. Just vanished. I wondered if it was a pattern. Has that got something to do with it?"

"Interesting concept. Let me think about that. You might have hit on something."

"I don't have any idea what it would mean, but it seems to be an uncanny coincidence."

"Are you going to be able to sleep?"

"I don't know," she said. She had thought the vodka would help, but she'd lost her desire to drink it. "Will you stay on the phone with me for a while? You don't have to talk. Knowing you're there is enough."

* * *

Richard's face was buried in the crook of Mariah's neck, the scent of her skin, like wheat, wafting into his nose. He loved it when she relinquished herself to him, almost as much as when she made him lie back while she worked her wonders. Either way, she satisfied him beyond belief. There was always this undertone, this hunger for her that lay just beneath the surface.

The lovemaking had sapped all his strength, but Eli wanted them at his place in an hour. By the time they showered, dressed, and drove over there, it would be a good hour.

Mariah's legs were still wrapped around him, though her knees had fallen to the sides and her hips had settled onto the mattress. He started to rise up, and she bit his ear.

"Want to do it again in the shower?" she whispered.

Richard slid down and mouthed her nipple, then took it between his teeth until he felt her twitch. "Always to excess," he said. "Nothing is ever enough for you." He sat up and straddled her and stared down at her face. "You're so beautiful," he said.

She smiled. "And good?"

Richard slapped her thigh. "Worst piece of ass I ever had," he said, climbing off her.

"Have you worked out a plan to deal with Tempest Star?" she asked.

"That's something I'd better get to work on. I'll go over it with Eli," Richard said, strolling nude to the bathroom that adjoined their bedroom. "And Eli wants to talk about the Stone woman." He stood in the archway that opened into their bathroom and turned around to look at her. "You coming?"

* * *

It had taken the full hour for Richard and Mariah to get to Eli Luddington's estate. Mariah took her time washing his back, taking every opportunity to please him. But she had finally been the one to hurry them up so as not to be late.

Just before arriving at Luddington's, Richard said, "Can I ask you a question?"

Mariah nodded, and he said, "Why do you tease Eli? You do everything short of touching his dick."

"Because it makes him happy," she said. "He likes it." Mariah put her hand in her husband's crotch. "And I think you like it, too. You like to watch."

Richard laughed and moved her hand away.

The Escalade pulled through the massive gates and along the half-mile entrance road leading into the Luddington estate. Richard parked, then got out and opened the door for his wife. "Be a good girl for once," he said. "And you're wrong. I don't like to watch."

Mariah batted her eyes, mocking him with a smile.

Richard punched the doorbell. "Be careful with Eli, my dear. Remember, all snake handlers get bit sooner or later."

SEAMSTRESS

THE YOUNG, ATTRACTIVE NEWS anchor at the Satellite News Network Weekend Edition studio desk looked into the camera. A graphic title, "Tragedy in China," appeared over her shoulder. Reading from the TelePrompTer, she said, "The bodies of over two thousand students and faculty were discovered overnight on the campus of Changsha University in Hunan Province, China. First indications are what the government is calling a mass suicide. The students, along with approximately one hundred teachers in this highly respected school of science and technology, were found barricaded in a large assembly hall. Campus authorities revealed that what appears to be the cause of death was the ingesting of a drink similar to popular athletic drinks but laced with cyanide. Details are sketchy at this time, but civil authorities are stating that the region has been thrown into chaos as grieving parents and friends rush to the scene. The military has been ordered into the area to take control of the situation."

The graphic changed to a picture of Jim Jones and the People's Temple.

"The tragedy in China eerily resembles the 1978 mass suicide in Guyana, in which 914 members of the Jonestown People's Temple committed suicide by drinking cyanide-laced Kool-Aid. It is also reminiscent of the 1997 mass suicide of 39 members of the Heaven's Gate cult in California.

"We will bring you further details of this terrible tragedy in China as they come in. But now, in other news . . ."

Lester Ripple chewed another mouthful of his dinner—Orville Redenbacher's Gourmet Popping Corn, lightly salted—and stared at the TV. "Well, that sucks," he said, then licked the salt off three of his fingers. *One, two, three*, he counted to himself. He knew of Changsha University. One of his doctorial classmates was from China and had received her master's from Changsha University. Her name was Gu. She was pretty, he remembered. And brilliant. Brilliant because she agreed with Ripple. Not like the other dickheads who read his thesis. Everyone agrees that there are five seemingly different string theories. That's a no-brainer. That was kind of like asking if a fat dog farts. But so far, no one had bought into his hypothesis that there is a sixth theory, the one he referred to as his thread theory: how endless parallel dimensions, other worlds, exist and are tied or threaded together by a single element that resides inside every human being. Yes, granted, it sounded philosophical, but it was rooted in science and could be proven with mathematics. And that was the amazing beauty of it all. A perfect marriage of two seemingly different schools that together answered the question, "Is there an afterlife?" He pondered the word *afterlife*. That could be a misnomer. After what? He would think about that and give it another name. Maybe *otherlife*, though he didn't think it had the right ring.

He scribbled a note on his napkin to take care of that minor detail, then folded the napkin three times and put it in the shirt pocket that already contained a cereal-box top with an equation written on it and his electric bill, which seemed to have a pattern of numbers running through his account number, the kilowatt hours used, and his meter reading. Things like that didn't just happen for no reason. There are no coincidences. He might play those numbers in the lottery Saturday night.

Ripple smiled at the name he'd chosen for his theory in honor of his grandmother—Ripple's thread theory. She'd spent her life as a seamstress, sewing other people's garments together. As a child, he had watched her for hours as she stitched different pieces of cloth together to form a new and unique piece of clothing. She told him that the cloth was already there, it was just a matter of choosing the right pieces to form the final garment.

His beloved grandmother never knew that as she sewed, she had taught him the secret to the universe. She had expressed it to him in such simple terms one day. Her words were like the clouds parting. Like the earth moving. Like God speaking to him.

"Lester," she had said, "if you want to get anywhere in this life or the next, you have to thread the needle."

LINCHPIN

Eli Luddington led Mariah and Richard into the study. The room was rich with the deep hues of the Brazilian rosewood bookshelves and handmade cabinetry that went from floor to ceiling. Polished brass and silver, beveled glass, Waterford crystal, pure white marble, gold leaf—everything was the finest that money could buy.

"Mariah, you look stunning tonight," Eli said. "Don't you agree, Richard?"

Richard nodded and sat on the leather couch. He patted the space next to him, expecting his wife to join him. But as usual, Mariah had to have her moment patronizing Eli.

It galled Richard to watch his wife glide her hand down Eli's shoulder and arm. But she was never going to change her ways—especially with Eli.

"Oh, Eli, it is always a delight to be in your company," she said.

Eli took her hand in his, lifted it, and kissed her fingertips.

"Mariah," Richard said with a brittle tone to his voice, "we have a lot of business to discuss. I think we should get started if you still want to go to dinner."

Mariah generated an obviously artificial smile and sat.

Eli waved his hand. "Oh, no, Richard. If you have made reservations, I apologize. I've had dinner prepared for the three of us." He glanced at the Roman numeral dial of the antique grandfather clock. "We should be called to dinner in another few minutes."

Eli Luddington grated on Richard. Even when he spoke Eli's common name, it was acidic in his mouth. He wondered how the spoken word could create a displeasing taste. And even more profound was the bitterness in his mouth if he called Eli by his given name—the Great Fallen Belial, from which came the letters *e-l-i* to give him his common name. Perhaps, Richard thought, the name forced him to recall the generations upon generations of the work they had done, and it had finally tapped all of his energy. Whatever the reason, he tired of Eli, of the work, of the mission. And in secret moments alone, the thing he thought about most was how he could ever be free, be done with this. These thoughts were not something he could share, especially not with Eli or Mariah.

Just as Eli predicted, a servant entered the study and announced that the dinner was served.

Eli outstretched his hand, and Mariah stood and took his arm. Richard tagged behind. His eyes fixed on the part of his wife's supple back that the dress she wore left exposed. Like pure sweet honey, he could taste her skin. She would never stay with him if he gave up his power and denounced his birthright. And he did so desire her. She was the only thing that prevented him from walking away from Eli and, ultimately, the Old Man. Somehow, Eli had known it would be that way, and that's why he had first introduced Richard and Mariah. Mariah was the lock Eli held on him. So if not for his wife, it would be over. There was no more thrill in the power, no more excitement over the grandiosity and enormity of the mission that had gone on for eons. None of that enticed him anymore.

Eli escorted Mariah to her seat and then took his at the head of the long, formal seventeenth-century dining table he had imported from Scotland. Mariah was to his right, and Richard sat to his left.

To Richard's surprise, Eli didn't raise his wine glass in a toast. Instead, the first few minutes at the table were uncomfortably silent.

"You do not mind that I serve only the entrée?" Eli said. "We'll skip the appetizer and soup tonight. I wasn't in the mood. I hope that is all right with you both. We'll have the salad and vegetables, of course. I had this urge to go straight to the main course—lamb. It seemed so appropriate."

"Oh, I agree," Mariah said. "And, anyway, I know I should be cutting back on what I eat."

Richard held in a smug smile. She completely missed Eli's point of going straight for the lamb. The symbolism escaped her. An old church prayer rang in his head:

Lamb of God, who taketh away the sins of world,

Have mercy upon us.

The clank of Eli's fork on his plate made Richard look up.

"I can now tell you both that I have bought Tempest Star," Eli said. "We can manipulate her any way we choose. Her only target is going to be Cotten Stone."

"Nicely done, Eli," Richard said. That was one thing off his plate, he thought.

"How did you get her to agree?" Mariah said.

Eli patted Mariah's hand. "I bought her—or maybe it was more like a trade. She wants fame and fortune, and she shall have it. You understand how that works, don't you, Mariah?"

Mariah didn't answer. First, she stared at Eli, and then she looked down at her arugula salad and toyed with it with her fork.

Eli took a sip of his Cabernet Sauvignon. "I didn't toast tonight, as I didn't think this was an occasion to warrant it."

Richard chewed a bite of lamb and wondered if Eli was going to scold him for something or just complain in general. He swallowed and turned to his host. "I would think you would be happy with the Tempest Star victory. Are you dissatisfied, Belial?"

Eli shifted back in his chair and curled his fingers around the stem of the wine glass, clearly reacting to Richard calling him Belial. "Why are you hostile, Richard—Rumjal? Are you suggesting we address ourselves formally, or may we remain on more casual, familiar terms?"

"I was not suggesting anything."

"Then perhaps I detect that you anticipate the pebble that is stuck in my shoe."

Richard rested his fork on the side of his plate. "What is it, Eli? There is always some burr that irritates you."

"I suppose you are correct. But that is the nature of making every effort to keep a plan running smoothly, seamlessly. Any little barb could be a setback."

"Are you not happy with how we handled the Venatori agent? Our contact said everything went off smoothly—no burrs, no barbs."

"Oh, please do accept my accolades for that. I apologize if I have not told you. Excellent work."

"Thank you, Eli. I appreciate it. Cotten Stone should get the message loud and clear. She will remember what happened to Thornton Graham, and she won't miss the parallels. There will be no mistaking who she is dealing with. A shot across the bow, so to speak."

"Why don't you just do away with her? You got rid of the agent, so why not her?" Mariah said.

Richard dabbed his lips with his napkin before looking at Eli for approval. To his wife, he said, "Because she is one of us—at least half of her is. Her father was one of the Fallen. We are capable of doing away with her, but you see, from the beginning it was agreed that we would never harm those who are one of us or our offspring. That is how we have built our numbers. We need a large army. If we cross that line, betray that vow, the agreement would be forever crushed. We can never allow our legion to decrease in number. Better that we either break Cotten Stone or return her to the fold."

"All right," Mariah said, after appearing to digest Richard's words. "I understand that, so that makes me ask another question, Eli. The Venatori agent is dead, and there is no suspicion that it was anything other than a heart attack. Why are you agitated?"

"Because neither of you see the crux, the linchpin. I have no doubt that Cotten Stone will get the warning. She'll make the leap between Thornton Graham and Thomas Wyatt, but she won't heed the warning."

"Why is that?" Richard said.

"Because you have yet to strike her sole weak spot, the chink in Cotten Stone's armor that would bring her to her knees—John Tyler."

THE MEN'S ROOM

"Still want me?" Cotten said over the phone to Ted Casselman.

"Absolutely," Ted said. "Accepting my offer will be the best news I've had all week."

"I've got to clear a few things with you first. Okay?"

"Shoot."

Cotten sank back into the cushions of her couch. "Well, I quit my job. I called the *Galaxy Gazette* and told them I wanted out of my contract. I've already put it in writing, but I haven't mailed it yet."

"It sounds like you've done everything needed," Ted said.

Cotten bit the left side of her lower lip. "Not exactly."

"Just send the letter and leave that bottom-feeder work to Tempest Star over at the *Courier*."

"I wish," Cotten said. "The *Gazette* paid me an advance for doing the story of the ruins in New Mexico. Problem is, I've got no story for them. There's a story there, but it doesn't have an ending yet. That's the piece I want to do for SNN, but I can't get out of my contract unless I pay back the *Gazette*." Cotten's stomach tightened. "And I don't have any money, so . . ."

"I'll take care of it," Ted said.

"No, that's not what I want. Here's the deal. Just hear me out with an open mind."

Cotten spent the next five minutes telling Ted the details concerning the crystal tablets—the one in Peru, the one in New Mexico, and the missing last tablet. She filled him in on the Hapsburgs, Thomas Wyatt and his connection with the Venatori, and his death, which she was convinced was not of natural causes. "This is the story I want to cover for SNN. Ted, this will be even bigger than the Grail conspiracy. With the tablet, I believe we're looking at the handwriting of God, and I'm sure it says He is delivering a message to—"

"Cotten, you don't have to sell me. I trust you, your instincts and your skills. Plus, I know full well that you'll chase down this story whether SNN pays you or not. Am I right?"

Cotten cradled the phone with her shoulder. Her voice came in nearly a whisper. "It's very important to me, Ted."

"What do you owe the *Gazette*? And you don't need to pay me back. The way I see it, SNN is giving an advance and financing one of its top reporters to deliver a prime-time news exposé."

"It's close to two thousand dollars. And I need to take the pictures of the Peruvian tablet to a specialist for translation, which means more travel. Thomas and I did research on khipu experts and found that one of the best in the world is in Chicago. That's where I'll start."

"Not a problem. Lick a stamp and send the letter. You have no business working for a sleazy tabloid. It's going to be good to have you back home at SNN."

"I'm not ready to move to New York yet. I have to get the whole thing about the tablet out of the way first."

"Hey, kiddo. You work from wherever is most convenient for you. We can think about a move later."

"Ted, you are the best. I'm not just saying that."

"Yeah, yeah. You think flattery will get you a raise already."

They both laughed.

"Hey, are you keeping in touch with John Tyler?" Ted asked.

"Yes. I talked to him right after Thomas died, and we talked again yesterday. They've flown Thomas's body to D.C. for a private funeral. He had no relatives, so the embassy staff, along with members of the Venatori, will be attending. John made all the arrangements. We talked for a long time."

"There's something special between the two of you, isn't there? It's a shame he's a priest—an archbishop at that."

"But he *is* a priest. So that's that."

"Uh-huh, like I said, it's a shame." Ted paused a moment, then said, "I won't harass you anymore on that subject. I can tell it's a tender spot."

"Kind of," Cotten said.

"All right, kiddo, lay me out a plan and let me know what's up. I'll get you some money, and when you're ready to make plane reservations, give me a call. I'll book it all through SNN's travel department."

* * *

After arriving in Chicago at O'Hare, Cotten took a shuttle to the Crowne Plaza in Greektown. Her appointment was at three with Dr.

Gary Evans, a professor in the Andean Studies Program at the University of Illinois at Chicago's Department of Anthropology.

At 2:55, she stood in front of his secretary. "I'm Cotten Stone, here to see Dr. Evans." In her right hand, she carried a small zippered leather portfolio.

"Ms. Stone is here," the secretary said into the phone. She listened for a second and hung up. "Dr. Evans is expecting you. Go ahead in."

Cotten rapped lightly on the door and then entered his office.

"Good afternoon," Evans said, rising and extending his hand across his desk. He appeared to be in his mid-sixties, with an oily comb-over and an ill-fitting suit. His glasses were thick, as was his Midwestern accent. The office was small and cramped—books, papers, and folders were stacked in columns lining the walls.

"Thank you for seeing me, Dr. Evans."

"You said you had some khipu," he said, staring curiously at the portfolio. "Please have a seat."

Cotten sat opposite Evans.

"Ever since you called, I've been looking forward to seeing what you found," Evans said. "Especially since you told me I am the first to have the opportunity to examine it."

Cotten moved the portfolio to her lap. "Yes, you are the first."

"How did you come to have the khipu?" Evans asked. "You didn't seem like you wanted to go into details on the phone."

Cotten swallowed hard. "It's much too complicated to explain in a phone call. And I may have misled you. I don't have the actual khipu, I only have pictures."

Cotten unzipped the portfolio and took out three five-by-seven photographs of the tablet, which she had printed at home.

She spread them on Evans's desk. She watched his face—his eyes blinked rapidly and his brows dipped as he scooted the photographs closer to him.

"What is this?" he asked.

"A crystal tablet that was found at a remote dig site in the Peruvian Andes."

Evans reached into his desk drawer and removed a large magnifying glass. Lifting the first of the three photos, he held it at different angles while examining it carefully with the glass. Then he went on to the second and the third.

"What do you think?" Cotten asked. "The bottom part of the tablet looks like a rendering of khipu, doesn't it? The lines are like the rope and the dots are knots. That's what it could be, right?"

"Maybe," Evans said with a shrug. "I don't understand about this tablet. Just what is it? I was expecting you to bring me a sample of real khipu." He glanced up. "I'm not sure what you have here, Ms. Stone, but I don't think I can help you. I'd have to see the khipu itself. The way the textile was spun, the color of the thread, all of that is as important as the knots—or dots, in this case."

"But can't you make something out of it? Can't you at least work with the lines and dots?" She realized she sounded desperate.

"Research takes a lot of time, and I have very little to spare. Can you even verify these photographs or give me some evidence that these are pictures of an actual artifact? It could be just some etchings on glass for all I know."

"But they aren't. I'm telling you it was a crystal tablet recovered from an archaeological dig site in Peru. I took the pictures myself before the tablet was destroyed. Didn't you read about the disaster—Dr. Carl Edelman, the entire camp—"

"The slaughter? Of course I read about it, but I don't recall any mention of a crystal tablet."

"Because it was destroyed. That was why everyone died—because of the tablet. Everyone who saw it had to die."

"You saw it, Ms. Stone, and you didn't die."

Cotten stood and poked her finger repeatedly at the khipu-like drawing on one of the photos. "There is something in that writing, in that khipu, that is so important that—"

"I'm sorry, Ms. Stone."

"Please," she said again. "You came highly recommended. I was counting on—"

Evans gathered the pictures in his hand and held them out to her.

Cotten backed away. "Just look at them again. Please, Dr. Evans. Some moment when you have nothing to do or curiosity gets to you, look at them. My name and phone number are on the back."

Cotten turned and walked out of his office.

* * *

Lester Ripple was early. He was always early. He drove around the block three times before getting out and walking around the building three times. His frigging eyes teared like a baby crying. The frigging cold wind sucked, he thought.

"Third floor," he said aloud, recalling where he'd been told to report. Maybe it was an omen. *Third floor. Third floor. Third floor.*

He checked his watch. Still too early, but he couldn't walk around outside any longer. He knew his cheeks must appear fire-red from the cold, and his frigging eyes—Jesus, his first day on the job and he was a mess. He might get fired even before he started. And he did want the job even though it wasn't in the Physics Department, where he had first applied. They wanted a mathematician in the Anthropology Department. Go figure. Research assistant professor would be his title. Tenure track. That was a good thing. General responsibilities were to develop and conduct a program of funded research, secure grant support, and publish research findings. Now, that last one might have a bug in it, since nobody wanted to publish his thread theory. And that was the key to everything. No way would he back off that. But he wouldn't have the responsibility of teaching classes, and he preferred that option. But anthropology? He was anxious to find out the more specific details of what was expected of him.

Ripple went inside and started up the stairs. Even if he had to kill time, it didn't matter, he would be punctual. There was no tolerance for tardiness.

"Damn, damn, damn," he said, not even halfway up the first flight. His armpits were damp, and a trickle of sweat rolled down his lip. Nerves. That's what it was, he was nervous. The TV ad that professed "Never let them see you sweat" came to mind.

Then, "Oh God," he said, feeling the peristalsis in his bowels. He had to get to a bathroom. He couldn't be sitting across the desk from his new boss and have intestinal cramps—and what if he couldn't hold it, what if he broke out in a sweat and gooseflesh and couldn't hold it?

Ripple rushed up the stairs, finally on the third-floor landing. He fast-walked down the hall, praying for a toilet on this floor. There it was, a brass plate declaring a men's room.

In the stall, sitting on the toilet, he took a blister pack of Imodium from his pocket, peeled it open, and chewed the two double-action tablets. *Saved*, he thought.

Finally, feeling better, he emerged from the stall and washed his hands in the sink. The paper towel dispenser was controlled by a built-in motion detector. How cool was that? He waved his hand in front of it, and out scrolled a paper towel. After drying his hands, he tossed the paper in the trash can.

Something caught his eye. He leaned over the can, deliberating how he could pick it up without getting contaminated. He straightened and waved his hands three times in front of the paper towel dispenser. He tore the paper towel off and put it in the palm of his right hand, using it as a barrier between his skin and the object.

Lester Ripple reached into the trash can and picked out three photographs.

TEMPTATION

IT WAS OVERCAST AS the pope walked alone down the path through the Vatican Gardens. The fleeting warmth of the fall day had faded as evening approached, and he wore a windbreaker over his white cassock. He had spent time in his private chapel grieving the loss of Thomas Wyatt. "In nomine Patris et Filii et Spiritus Sancti," he said, making the sign of the cross and praying that God would welcome the soul of Thomas Wyatt into everlasting peace. The pope held a Bible open to Psalms 23:4 and read aloud, "Even though I walk through the valley of the shadow of death, I will fear no evil—"

"Appropriate choice."

He paused and glanced in the direction of the voice. A man with hair the color of ash, nearly the same color as his silk shirt, sat on a bench beside the path. He turned up the collar of his black topcoat.

"Join me?" the Old Man said, and motioned to the bench beside him.

"What do you want?" the pope said.

"A moment of your time." He smiled, his words taking on a genteel calmness.

The pope hesitated. The Old Man's nonthreatening manner was definitely meant to throw him off-balance. "We have nothing to say to each other."

"Of course we do. In fact, we have more to say than can possibly be discussed here. So, perhaps we should prioritize." He patted the bench beside him. "But first I insist you sit and relax."

The pope slowly sat and closed the Bible on his lap.

"I am amazed," the Old Man said. "You display no alarm at my presence. Commendable."

"Should I?" The pope gestured to the surrounding gardens. "You visit in my province. Perhaps it is you who should exhibit uneasiness."

The Old Man gave him a patronizing wink before saying, "One of your warriors has fallen."

"That is the nature of war."

"Others will follow."

"I asked you what you want," the pope said.

"Ultimately, your surrender."

"Impossible. You reveal your inability to prophesy. Have the eons of humiliation taken their toll and driven you mad?"

"Many have accused me of worse."

"I don't have time for this."

"You must make time. The blood of many will soon be on your hands if you let the daughter of Furmiel gain access to the secret."

"Explain yourself."

"Don't you understand? Can't you begin to imagine how hurt I am? It is not humiliation I feel, but great pain, and a sense of loss—

and rage. If you had Paradise ripped out from under you, you would find a way to even the score. You would be no different from me."

"Perhaps you should have thought of that before you declared yourself on equal terms with the Creator. And no, I am nothing like you."

"I *was* on equal terms with Him. We were all equal. All beautiful. All deserving. He did not like it when I challenged Him. That is what that battle was all about. I and those who joined me were a threat He could not tolerate. And do not kid yourself. You are like me, because in your heart there is hate, mistrust, and darkness. They reside in the hearts of all men."

"You said there would be the blood of many . . ."

"Time is running out. The woman is getting closer to finding the last tablet. I will not let that happen."

"Is that why you took Thomas Wyatt? You are afraid of Cotten Stone?"

"I detest her disruptiveness. If we are rushed into the final days, it will cause us to show ourselves. This in itself will turn many against us."

"Once again, what do you want?"

"Your intervention."

"If I do, will it save the lives of those you speak of?"

"Why don't you do what's best for all and convince her to stop, turn around, give up. She will only face more pain if she continues. She will wind up hurting the one person she loves the most."

"And if I do as you ask, what will I gain in return?"

"Power beyond all power."

"I already have power."

"Riches that exceed those of any king who ever lived."

The pope made a sweeping motion toward the papal palace. "Look around you. What do you call this?"

"You have a small mind. You don't envision what I can give. It is beyond your scope of understanding."

"I have never professed to be anything other than a simple man."

"Then I will give you the wisdom and intellect to propel you beyond the realm of the greatest thinkers of our time, or any time in history."

"Do you know the secret? The one she seeks?"

"Yes."

"Tell me, and I will do as you ask."

The Old Man laughed out loud.

"Why is that funny?"

"I am no fool."

"You know what I think?" the pope said.

"Enlighten me."

"I think you're desperate. But you must know there is no temptation to which I will succumb."

"I won't make this offer again."

"And I believe Cotten Stone is about to strike a crippling blow that will hurt you."

"Look at your hands. Do you see the blood? Can you live with that?"

The pope stood, turning his back on the Old Man. "Begone from me, Satan," he said. When he glanced around to repeat his command, the bench was empty.

THE HULK

Lester Ripple took everything off the card table in front of the television and stacked it in three piles in the hallway that led to the single bedroom. He needed a clear space to work. Clear space, clear mind.

He sat in the Samsonite chair and spread the three photographs on the vinyl-topped table in front of him. Beside them he set a lighted magnifying glass.

Ever since finding the pictures in the men's room, he could hardly wait until he got home. On the first day of work, he certainly didn't want anyone seeing him pilfering from the bathroom trash can. But the quick glimpse of the photos had immediately snatched his attention. Dr. Evans must have believed him to be a muddle-headed fool as his concentration and focus during the all-day orientation diverted to thoughts of the pictures. All Ripple could think about was taking another look. He remembered that a portion of what appeared to be etchings on something like a block of glass was covered with glyphs or pictographs, but the bottom portion was what flabbergasted him.

Was it truly what it appeared to be?

At the end of the day, he bumbled his way down the halls and out of the university building with the three photographs snugly stashed in his briefcase. Now, safe in his apartment, he could take his time examining them.

Ripple leaned over the first photo and held the magnifying glass above it. He peered through the lens, running his finger along the rows of lines and dots. He felt the trigger in his brain fire, and then the rapid succession of thoughts.

Numbers. Mathematical expressions. Numbers, symbols, and words? Expressions and equations. Pieces. Fragments. Yes, numbers, and symbols, and words. All running together, his brain processing them like a supercomputer.

Suddenly, Ripple sat back and turned off the magnifier. He was out of breath, as if he had run up several flights of stairs.

The Hulk. That was it. He would sketch the Incredible Hulk in green marker and wait for everything to catch up in his brain.

Lester Ripple grabbed the latest edition of *The International Journal of Theoretical Physics* off the end of the sofa, then took a fine-line permanent green marker from a 7-Eleven cup on the counter and returned to the card table. It had taken a whole year to save for the subscription, costing him over $1,800. But it did serve dual purposes. He read the journal, and he doodled and drew in it.

Lester picked a page in the journal that didn't have any of his previous sketchings and began to draw. In the margin, the Hulk took form, his face a grimace, as if he strained to lift an impossible weight.

Quickly, Lester felt better, the clutter in his brain organizing, sorting, and methodically storing the information in a meaningful structure. He hummed "You've Lost That Lovin' Feelin'." Tom Cruise and his flyboy buddies singing it in *Top Gun* was one of his all-time favorite scenes. Maybe he would watch the movie again tonight. It was one of the most played in his DVD collection.

Ripple only drew the Hulk's head, face, and left side of his body, but that was enough. If need be, he'd stop again and draw the right side.

He returned to the examination of the photographs and then began jotting notes on a piece of scrap paper that had fallen to the floor when he cleared the table. Soon he found there wasn't enough room on the paper for all of his postulations and calculations.

Ripple trekked to the kitchen. A stack of yellow legal pads filled the cabinet beneath the silverware drawer. He used a lot of yellow pads.

There was also a plastic bin of sharpened number 2 Ticonderoga pencils and his Batman pencil sharpener. He took three pads and three pencils along with his sharpener back to the table.

Three hours after beginning his study, Lester Ripple stood and paced around the table.

Who could have written this? Who had duplicated his thread theory? Yes, it was more expanded than his, written in a combination of encoded words and quantum mechanics equations. Some parts appeared as direct sentences, but then mixed in were complex equations all written in a three-dimensional binary code. The hardest part of deciphering it was to know when the code was language and when it was mathematical equations. The parts blotted out by the glare left questions, and he so wanted to decode the last lines, but it was impossible, as the flash had obliterated them. But he was sure whatever was written there further corroborated his theory.

And so here was his thread theory, scribed on a mysterious block of glass, proving that there were many worlds, parallel worlds all generated by the energy of thought, all existing at the same time. The thread theory held that every thought is mirrored in the world in which we live—and, for that matter, throughout the entire universe. All possibilities have already been created. All outcomes already exist. In these photographs, someone besides Ripple had professed the connectedness or threading together of all matter, energy, soul, and spirit. Identical to his theory, it explained the bridge between the rules of the quantum world with its wave-particle duality and the rules of classical physics. He had answered the question, "If electrons can be in two places at once, why can't you?" The answer was simple when the mind was allowed to view the concept of reality with different eyes.

Ripple sat again, taking another look at the photographs and his notes. Then he turned over the first photograph and read again the name and phone number written on the back.

In a strong, bold voice, he said, "Ms. Cotten Stone, this is Dr. Lester Ripple from the University of Illinois at Chicago, Department of Anthropology." He practiced the introduction two more times as he walked to the kitchen wall phone.

* * *

"Evans wouldn't even look at them, Ted," Cotten said on her cell phone as she inserted the keycard into the lock of her Crowne Plaza room. "I left the pictures with him, but I don't think he's going to give them another second of his time. I'm sorry for costing you more money."

"Hey, dead ends happen," Ted Casselman said. "You know that's the nature of our business. Who else did you and Wyatt have on your list of experts?"

"Evans was the most promising." Cotten put the empty portfolio down on the foot of the bed. "It's probably a waste of time and money for me to fly all over the country trying to get somebody else to examine the photos." Cotten plopped down on the bedspread. "Besides, I want to go to Thomas's funeral. I feel the need to be there."

"It won't change anything."

"I know, but it's the right thing to do. We had really started to get to know each other. I'm sure he would have come to say a last goodbye to me if it were the other way around. As soon as that is over, then I'll be back and on the story again. But for now, I have to put this behind me."

"Do you need help making arrangements? Hotels?"

"Ted, you're worse than a real father. I'm a big girl. I know how to get around."

"Just looking out for you, kiddo."

"Talk to you soon," she said before shutting the cell phone.

What a waste of time, coming here, she thought as she kicked off her shoes and lay back. No doubt she would get the same reaction from the other khipu experts. What she needed now was a huge break.

Her cell phone rang. Cotten flipped it open and looked at the caller ID, expecting it to be Ted calling her back. But it was from area code 312—Chicago.

CHRISTOPHER COLUMBUS

Cotten searched the patrons in Starbucks for someone wearing a baseball cap with Wile E. Coyote embroidered on it. Lester Ripple had said that would be how she could recognize him. That should make for an easy ID, she thought. But as she scanned the room, no Wile E. Coyote hats stood out.

A heavy tap on her shoulder made her turn.

"Ms. Stone? I'm Lester Ripple from the University of Illinois at Chicago, Department of Anthropology, Andean Studies Program." It sounded rehearsed. Lester snorted, wrinkling up his nose, then offered his hand. He was short and chunky with blond hair sprouting beneath the cartoon cap, probably thirty years old, and had watering eyes. He held a battered briefcase at his side.

"Nice to meet you, Lester," Cotten said, shaking his hand. "I'm sorry that I couldn't quite follow what you were telling me on the phone."

Lester's head bobbed in a series of nods. "I—I have a spot over there." Ripple turned and led the way. "Excuse me," he said, bumping into virtually everyone along the way. "Excuse me, excuse me."

He personified the cliché of the bull in a china shop, she thought as she followed. Even his shirttail hung out on one side, and he had missed a couple of belt loops in the back of his trousers. A classic nerd.

"Here," he said, pulling out a chair for her.

A sheet of paper that had been on the seat floated to the ground. Cotten saw the word *saved* written on it, underlined three times. Another paper, also with the word *saved,* lay in the middle of the circular table with a cup of untouched coffee holding it down.

"I've been here for a while," Lester said. "I didn't want anyone to get our table while I used the restroom." He picked up the paper from the floor. Sitting across from Cotten, he said, "Okay, you've heard about Christopher Columbus, right?" He rolled his eyes. "Sure, everybody knows about Columbus. But did you know the mind can only see what it believes is possible?"

Ripple stared at her, obviously waiting for a response.

Cotten shook her head. "I'm sorry, but I'm not following."

Ripple pressed the heels of his hands to his eyes. "I know, I know. I'm having a problem."

Maybe she shouldn't have agreed to meet with this guy. He was more than weird—definitely messed up.

"Okay, here I go," he said. "I study quantum physics, which means I study the world on the quantum level—smaller than the atom. Down there, in that world, all the rules of this world don't apply. And vice versa. In the quantum world, we find something called quantum superposition, which means that it's possible for particles to be in two or more places and states at the same time. Because, for instance, atoms are not things, only tendencies. Quantum physics only calculates possibilities, and all possibilities exist. It's not until consciousness chooses one possibility that it becomes reality." He started to scribble on a napkin. "Look."

Cotten looked at what Ripple was writing. It appeared to be math equations—brackets, numbers, symbols—but it could have just as easily been the doodling of a nutcase. "Mr. Ripple, you're—"

"Lester. Call me Lester."

"Lester, you're going to have to talk to me in plain English if you want me to understand."

"Do you want coffee, latte, mocha something?" Ripple asked.

"No thanks. Maybe later."

"I don't drink it either, but I bought some so I could save our table. It's decaf just in case I have to take a sip." Ripple wadded up the napkin, removed his cap, then vigorously rubbed the top of his head, making clumps of his hair stand out at odd angles.

He was beyond peculiar, Cotten thought. But there was some essence of sincerity and brilliance nearly eclipsed by his bizarreness.

He dragged another napkin in front of him and tediously drew the outline of a cube, then pushed it in front of her. "Stare at it. Tell me what your point of view is when looking at it. Are you looking from the top down or from the bottom up, or from the side?"

"From the top," she said, glancing at Ripple.

"No, no, no. Don't look at me, look at the cube," he said, sounding short of breath.

Although her patience was wearing thin, Cotten stared at the drawing. Then, without warning, her perspective changed. She looked up and smiled. "Now I see it from the side," she said.

"There you go."

"It's just an optical illusion," Cotten said.

"Yes!" Ripple clapped his palms on the table. "I didn't do anything to change the drawing—all the possibilities already existed. It was your consciousness that defined the reality of the perspective—of what you saw. That's what the world really is. Possibilities, or as you said, illusion. Reality is illusion. Illusion is reality, but only when you perceive it and become a participant."

Cotten sat back in the chair. She had a small inkling of what he meant, even if it was foggy.

"I know this is hard for you to embrace and believe. So, back to Columbus. The story goes that when Columbus's ships approached the islands in the Caribbean, the natives who lived there could not see them. Why? Because they could not imagine them, had no conception of a hundred-ton, three-masted ship. Their shaman looked at the sea and saw the ripples produced by the bow of the ships, so he knew there was something there. But his mind could not see the ships. After much practice of looking at the horizon, the ships finally took form. He could see them. And once the shaman described them to the others and they concentrated, they too could see."

"That's not a true story," Cotten said.

Ripple shrugged. "All quantum physicists understand these principles, but there is a small hole in what they can explain. I told you that in the quantum world atoms can exist in more than one place at once. And there is plenty of documentation. That's not a Columbus story. But there is the breakdown between the quantum world and what we see with the naked eye. Why can't this table be in two or three or a thousand places at once, like particles are able to in the quantum world?"

Ripple wiped his head again.

"I have no idea," Cotten said, becoming more fascinated by the moment.

"I have discovered the answer. It's part of my thread theory." Ripple took a brown envelope from his briefcase. He opened the clasp and removed the three photographs. "And that is what is written on the object in these pictures you claim you took. All my equations and explanations are here in this code." He pointed at one of the pictures. "You said they came from an archaeological dig in Peru. How could that be?"

"I don't know how it could be, but that's where the tablet was found. I was there when they excavated it." Cotten paused, then folded her hands in her lap. "All that you've told me sounds very interesting, Lester, but I'm not sure I believe that is what is on the tablet. I have reason to believe the inscription is much more than some kind of New Age physics."

Ripple's face scrunched up, and his right eye teared profusely. "But that *is* what is written on it. It's written in a three-dimensional binary code. Very sophisticated. Some of it is equations and some of it is language."

"Then tell me what the language part says."

"Sure," Ripple answered. "It says that all possibilities already exist and stuff like that."

"That's it?"

"Mostly. I can't see the last couple of lines because of the glare from the camera flash."

Another waste of time, Cotten thought. "I'm sure you'll get someone in the scientific community to hear you out," she said.

Ripple wiped a hand over the top of his head. "Can I keep the pictures?" he asked.

"Sure. I have copies. Thanks for your time, Lester. I'm going to have to run. I've got to check out of my hotel and grab a flight to Washington."

"Oh, government work, I suppose," he said, a frown of disappointment gripping every inch of his face.

"A funeral," she said.

"I'm sorry."

Cotten stood to leave.

"What is it that you want the writing to say?" Ripple asked.

"I wanted it to tell me how to stop Armageddon."

SIG-SAUER

Richard Hapsburg steered the rented Buick LaCrosse along Massachusetts Avenue, approaching Observatory Circle. He was three cars behind his target—the passenger in the rear seat of a gray Volvo S80. Richard was already aggravated because he had missed an earlier opportunity to take a shot—hesitating and then losing the few seconds his target was exposed. If he screwed this up, Eli would have his testicles in a vise.

The SIG-Sauer P226 sat on the passenger seat beside him. Richard was no sharpshooter, but he had been given the task against his will. He had suggested to Eli that an assassin be hired, but the idea was rejected. Clearly, Eli wanted no outsiders, no possible leaks. And Richard was certain that Eli was testing him yet again.

Richard continued following the Volvo on 14th Street and US-1. He couldn't pull up next to the S80 and fire while they were moving. How could he drive, and aim, and shoot with any accuracy?

Richard wasn't worried about someone getting the license plate number and then tracking the rental back to him. He had presented false identification when he got the car, and he had rigged a dummy license plate over the official one. Getting caught wasn't going to be a problem, but getting in a good kill shot was.

All the way along I-395 and George Washington Parkway, Richard thought through his plan. There was one more opportunity—Reagan Airport.

He sped up, passing two cars until he was right behind the Volvo. He could see the target's head through the back window. Only a few feet separated the two vehicles.

The Volvo pulled curbside where arriving passengers waited for shuttles and hailed cabs. Richard pulled in right behind. He lowered the LaCrosse's window and propped the semiautomatic in the opening underneath a copy of *Sports Illustrated*.

The driver got out and walked around the car. He opened the S80's back door.

As the target emerged, Richard pulled the trigger.

* * *

Cotten Stone made her way through the crowded arrivals along the concourse at Ronald Reagan Washington National Airport. Her carryall at her side, she was bone-tired from the flight and disheartened about her Chicago trip—her meeting with Dr. Evans and the strange but intriguing Lester Ripple. The ache of Thomas's death lingered in her gut as she prepared to attend his funeral. She knew better than anyone that the Fallen Ones were sending her a message to back off, give up. But she had no intention of doing so. Thomas would not have allowed it. And she would not let his death be in vain.

Cotten had made a reservation at the Georgetown Inn. As soon as the funeral was over, she would get in touch with Ted and get on track. There was no way she could let him down. He took a huge risk bringing her back to SNN. Both of their careers were on the line.

As the crowds thinned at the end of the concourse, Cotten paused and looked for Monsignor Duchamp, who had promised to pick her up. Suddenly, she stopped as her eyes fell upon a tall man standing a few yards in front of her. He wore jeans, a black turtleneck sweater, and a heavy suede jacket. His smile radiated through the crowd. In an instant, she recognized those eyes.

"John!" she whispered, and ran to him. Dropping her bags and throwing her arms around his neck, she held him tightly. "I can't believe you're here."

John Tyler hugged her as the other arriving passengers made their way around them.

Cotten pulled back. "Sorry. Somebody might get the wrong impression—me throwing myself at an archbishop." She looked up at the ceiling. "Why do I do this?"

John wrapped his arms around her again and whispered, "Hello, Cotten Stone."

"Hello, John Tyler," Cotten said. They stood locked in the embrace for a moment. How at home she was with her head on his shoulder—with him so close. The faintest hint of his aftershave mixed with his skin brought a flood of memories.

Finally, Cotten let go and backed away. She wiped away the tears. "I'm so glad you're here."

"Me, too," he said, grabbing her suitcase and laptop. "Let's go. I have a car waiting." He led the way toward the exit doors.

Outside, John motioned to a gunmetal gray Volvo S80 parked at the curb. As they approached, Cotten recognized the man standing beside the car.

"Hello, Ms. Stone," Monsignor Philip Duchamp said, holding the door open.

"It's a long way from New Mexico, Monsignor," Cotten said. "Good to see you again." She slid into the back seat.

"Same here," Duchamp said. "Excellency." He nodded to John, who slipped in beside Cotten.

A moment later, the S80 pulled away into traffic.

* * *

Richard drove into the shopping mall and parked the LaCrosse in the middle of the packed lot. His heart still pumped almost viciously, pummeling his chest from the inside. He'd missed Tyler but had no idea where the stray bullet had ended up. He hadn't seen anyone fall. He had fired, but the suppressor on the gun and the noise at the terminal completely muffled the sound of the shot. Nobody had even flinched. He'd thrown the gun and sports magazine on the seat and hit the gas, racing out of the airport terminal.

But he had missed.

Eli would not be pleased.

Richard got out of the car and removed the dummy plate, tossing it in a refuse can nearby. When he got back into the vehicle, he reclined the seat and turned on the radio. After tuning in a classical station, he adjusted the volume and then leaned back in the seat, closing his eyes. He wasn't cut out for this.

Richard Hapsburg had had enough.

POWER GRID

LESTER RIPPLE BALLED UP all the sheets of yellow notepad paper arranged helter-skelter on the top of the card table. "Useless," he muttered, throwing the wad on the floor.

He didn't get it. Just flat didn't understand what Cotten Stone meant about how she was going to stop Armageddon. What on earth could she have possibly thought was on that tablet, or whatever it was? The code inscribed there was his theory to the finest detail, and then some. What did it have to do with her? She was a ditzy network reporter, for heaven's sake.

Lester looked down at the photographs and wiped his nose with his forearm. The drippage didn't require a tissue; he didn't have a cold or infection. The snot was clear. Just allergies. No different from rubbing away eye boogers.

He held the magnifier over the part of each photo where the glare-obscured text was hidden. "Armageddon," he said. Did she really mean the last big war, or was she referring to some personal battle? He should have made her explain more.

"I can put this together," he said. "I can figure this out."

Lester Ripple took in a huge breath through his nose and blew it out. He wanted to let his mind rest. His most incredible enlightenments came at those times—times when he opened himself to the universe and let all that energy flow into him. That was how he first discovered the basis of his thread theory. He would make his mind pure and receptive. But first, as his grandmother had taught him, he must thank the Creator for giving him the wisdom he sought. If, instead, he prayed for wisdom, then that would empower his brain to admit that he didn't have it to begin with. What always worked was thanking the Creator for already possessing what he had.

Live as if it were true, and it will be, his grandmother would say. See what you want, and it will come to you.

Lester knew the answers were all in his head. The secret was how he envisioned them. Like with the drawing of the cube he had shown Cotten Stone. All that mattered was his point of view.

When the light flooded inside him, Lester Ripple sensed peace. The race in which his brain was always engaged had slowed and drifted away. Good. This was very good. How could he explain this experience to anyone? It was as though he existed on a power grid that connected everything in the universe and maybe beyond.

* * *

Cotten stared out the window as the Volvo headed toward the Georgetown Inn.

"You're barely going to have time to freshen up before the funeral." John said. "You must be exhausted."

"Mentally. Physically. You name it. But in a couple of hours it will be over, and I'll go back to the hotel and rest."

John took Cotten's hand. "You're a tough lady. Trust me when I tell you that God will never put more on your plate than you can handle."

Cotten leaned against John and rested her head on his shoulder. "I don't know what I would do without you," she said.

They rode in silence for a while before John spoke. "I've been thinking. Chauncey Wyatt, Thomas's grandfather, was responsible for the theft of the tablet from the Vatican back in the 1800s. We know the note he left was some kind of clue to where he hid the relic."

Cotten lifted her head. "He told me about his grandfather and the note, but we couldn't make any sense of it. We talked about going to the UK and tracking down some distant relatives."

"I was thinking along those same lines," John said. "I've had the London branch of the Venatori do some digging. They turned up a great-aunt."

"Then that's where we need to go right after—"

Duchamp suddenly slammed on the brakes, throwing Cotten and John forward. The Volvo screeched to a halt, but not before a loud thud and smack of something large flying across the hood and into the windshield.

"What the hell was that?" Cotten said, staring through the bloodied glass.

SEDUCTION

COTTEN SAT ON THE side of the road in the grass as the police directed traffic around the accident scene. She assumed they had all been here for such a long time because there were fatalities. Duchamp was noticeably shaken, and Cotten wished she could make him feel better. He had jumped from the car immediately after stopping, and John and Cotten followed. The image still clung inside Cotten's head.

The mangled and bloody body of a woman lay sprawled on the pavement. And as if that were not enough, her infant son was only a heap of flesh a few feet away—both dead.

Yellow tarps covered their bodies now, for which Cotten was thankful. The faces of the mother and child were vivid in her mind. Cotten stared at her hands. Though she had wiped them on her skirt and again on the grass, ruddy stains still remained. Her blouse had wet, red blossoms in the front, and a smear of blood streaked her forehead. The baby had not died instantly, as the mother had, and Cotten had tried to stop the bleeding from the infant's head, but she couldn't save the child.

She had to stop thinking about it. But she could hear Duchamp still speaking with one of the officers.

"I don't know where she came from. I never saw her," he said, repeating himself over and over to anyone who would listen.

Cotten watched as John put his hand on Duchamp's shoulder and led him to the side of the road where she sat. Cotten stood.

"I think the police have everything they need for their investigation," John said.

Duchamp's face was pale—no color in his lips or cheeks.

"It wasn't your fault," Cotten said.

Duchamp shook his head. "Maybe if I had been paying more attention . . . if I had only seen her . . . swerved in time to miss—"

"Stop torturing yourself," John said. "This accident is another of the suicides. The woman jumped in front of the car. There's no other explanation. One of the officers said they found her vehicle parked in the emergency lane down the road. Keys, purse, diaper bag, all left inside. She wasn't going to return. This was a deliberate act."

"But, John, the baby," Cotten said. "Why did she have to kill the baby, too?"

"That's all part of *their* strategy. The more horrific, the better," John said. "And don't think we weren't targeted. They are trying to bring it home to you. Like with Wyatt."

Cotten threaded her hair behind her ears. "We have to stop this. We have to find the last tablet."

* * *

"I'm not coming back," Richard said into his cell phone.

Mariah threw her purse on the bed. She was ready to go to Eli's for dinner, and now Richard was pulling some sort of stunt.

"What are you talking about? Didn't you take care of Tyler?"

"I tried, but it didn't work out. I can't do this any longer. The fire has gone out inside."

Mariah paced around the bed with the cordless. "Richard, you listen to me. You are tired and upset. You can't make decisions in that condition. You aren't thinking straight. Get on the next plane and come home. I'll talk to Eli. He'll arrange for some other way to finish Tyler."

There was silence on the line. Mariah bit her bottom lip hard enough to draw blood. If Richard went down, she'd go down with him, and she was not going to allow that. She had come too far to turn back.

"Are you still there?" Richard asked.

"Yes."

"I love you, Mariah. Come with me. We'll be together—go somewhere, anywhere in the world—away from Eli. Maybe we'll start a family, if you want."

"Richard, what's the matter with you? Do you hear yourself? You don't sound like the same man who was in New Mexico. You sound pathetic."

"New Mexico was my last hurrah. That type of power has lost its hold on me. I reap nothing from it. There's no excitement. And I've lost faith in—"

"Bullshit. You were born to this. It's in your blood. We will all stand together and win. You can't just decide that you don't want to play anymore. It doesn't work like that."

"It worked for Furmiel, Cotten Stone's father."

"And look what happened to him. He became so despondent he killed himself."

"Mariah, will you come to me?"

She hung up the phone without answering. She had thirty-five minutes to get to Eli Luddington's, and now she had to change clothes. The pants outfit was gorgeous, but she needed to wear a dress tonight.

* * *

"He fucked it up," Eli said to Mariah, sitting at the head of the dinner table, she to the right of him. They dined alone.

Mariah reeled. If Eli had talked to Richard, she was doomed. "You spoke to Richard?"

"He doesn't answer his cell."

A short reprieve, she thought. If she could keep them from talking long enough, and prevent Eli from boiling over, she might be able to bring her husband home. "Maybe his phone battery is dead. That happens," she said.

"Richard has a charger for the car *and* his regular charger. He's avoiding me."

Mariah put down her soup spoon. "I'm sure he will call soon. He's been under a lot of stress lately. Let me talk to him. Give him some space, Eli. Trust me with Richard, like you always do. Remember, that's my job."

"Your husband is not happy."

Mariah cringed. Her vow to Eli, the only one she had ever had to make in exchange for what she thought of as her *rebirth*, was to keep Richard loyal and solidly enmeshed in the mission.

"I've done all I can. Richard is just the brooding type."

"Have you kept him satisfied at home?"

"What do you mean?" she asked.

"Is the sex good?"

Mariah pushed her soup bowl away. "Everything is fine. You know how Richard feels about me. And he's very jealous of you." *Step one.* "And he should be. You are such a powerful and handsome man. What woman wouldn't be attracted to you?"

The hard, angry lines in Eli's face softened. "I like it when you flatter me."

Mariah reached for his hand and stroked it. "It's not flattery, and you know that."

Eli sipped his wine. "Let us hope Richard calls soon and has a reasonable explanation and good news."

Mariah's appetite dwindled. Eli was serving six courses, and if she appeared worried, he would pick up on it.

"Richard isn't as strong as you. He has weaknesses."

"That's precisely what brought you into the picture."

"I could never admire Richard the way I admire you." She lowered her eyes, pretending to be embarrassed by the confession she was about to make. "If it were not for Richard . . ." She looked at Eli, forcing her eyes to tear. "Only because you want me with Richard do I stay with him. You understand who it is I really desire, don't you?"

Eli swallowed the rest of his wine. "You have never said anything like this before."

"I thought it inappropriate. But I've shown you a thousand times in the way I touch you and allow you to touch me. Have you never noticed how I respond to you? Could you be that blind? Even Richard sees."

Eli poured another glass of wine and sat back, seeming to study her.

Mariah's stomach clenched so tightly that it pained her. Hopefully he didn't see through her. *Step two.* Mariah slipped her hand under the table until it came to rest on his thigh. She tested the situation first, not moving. When he showed no signs of objection, she faintly stroked his leg.

Smiling, she said, "We could have the best of both worlds. Richard doesn't have to know. I can still keep my promise to you—serve you in more than one way."

Eli just kept looking at her. She could see he was weighing what she said. That was a good sign. One of the knots in Mariah's stomach loosened.

"And isn't that why you asked me here for dinner while Richard is away? Because you want to be with me like I want to be with you?"

Mariah withdrew her hand, stood, and went to Eli, standing close beside him. "Finish your wine," she said, moving his free hand beneath her dress so it cupped her crotch. "And when you have taken the last sip, I want you to come upstairs and taste me. Then whisper in my ear how I compare."

Mariah stepped back, unzipping the back of her dress so one shoulder fell away, exposing her back and a side glance of a bare breast. *Step three.* As she left the room, the dress fell to the floor.

VIOLET

"THE VENATORI MUST HAVE a hefty budget to put us up in suites at the Cadogan," Cotten said to John when he came to her room after settling in. "This has to cost a fortune."

She and John had arrived in London three days after Thomas Wyatt's funeral.

"You like the room?"

Cotten spun in a circle. "What's not to like? This is definitely up-town. But I don't know why they would spend this on me. And I don't mean to hurt your feelings, but why spend it on you and not one of the Venatori big guns?"

John's eyes arrested hers. "They did."

"What do you mean?" She paused as she realized what he had said. "Okay, you've got that long title—the something-something that's got to do with sacred archaeology, but not the something-something of the Venatori."

"Your innocence has always been such a part of your charm," he said with a smile. "The prelate of the Pontifical Commission for Sacred Archaeology was my position. Now it's more like my cover."

"Cover?" She took a step back. "You make it sound like some covert—"

"It has to be that way. It's no secret that the Venatori exists, but no one can track the hierarchy. That makes it difficult for there to ever be a clear target at the top. I report only to the pope. I have no rank or title."

"Did Thomas know?"

"No. Field agents don't know my position, although Thomas might have suspected, based upon my close relationship with the Holy Father. Though we spoke often, Thomas actually reported to someone else, who reported to someone else."

"Sounds like the CIA," she said. "So when you got promoted—I suppose that's the right word—to archbishop, you became the head of the Venatori?"

"Yes, that's the simplest explanation. The Venatori has a global, well-known identification among security agencies, but no one outside the organization really understands how deep it runs. That is strictly my domain, along with the pontiff's." John motioned to chairs at one of the numerous oak tables placed around the elegant hotel suite. When they were both seated, he said, "We will find a way to stop these suicides, Cotten, and to solve the mystery of the tablet. The sole goal of the Venatori is to defeat our enemy—your enemy."

"Everything is coming too fast. There are a million questions. Is what's going on around us the beginning of Armageddon? What am I supposed to stop? I'm not sure what I am expected to do."

"The best place to start is at the beginning. In this case, it is Thomas's grandfather, Chauncey Wyatt." John removed a paper from his jacket pocket and unfolded it. "We've already begun our quest by coming to London. I made a list of things on the plane while you slept. First of all, the Venatori has discovered that Thomas did have a distant relative. Her name is Violet Crutchfield. She lives in the countryside outside of London. She will be our first stop.

"Second, we've come up with a couple of things concerning the note Chauncey Wyatt left behind after the theft of the tablet—particularly his reference to threading a needle. There is a biblical reference in Matthew's gospel about it being easier for a camel to go through the eye of a needle than for a rich man to enter into the kingdom of God. And there is the old story about there being a gate in Jerusalem called the Eye of the Needle because a camel couldn't pass through it without stooping and having all its baggage removed first. It is believed that the parallel is that you can only come to God on your knees and without your baggage. Unfortunately, there's no archaeological or documented record of such a gate. But if we don't find something here, we might have to consider taking our search in that direction."

Cotten nodded as she pictured flying to the Holy Land and trying to find a mythical gate into the city.

"Here's another one for you to think about," John said. "There is something called threading the needle that has to do with our vision and depth perception—the reason God gave us two eyes instead of one."

Cotten grinned at him. "Is this going to be a science experiment, Mr. Wizard?"

"Actually, yes." John stood. "First, we need to find a piece of string."

"I packed a sewing kit. Will that help?"

"Perfect. See if you have a spool of thread."

Cotten searched in her suitcase, coming up with a small plastic box. "How's this?" she asked, removing a miniature spool of black thread.

"Excellent." John took it and held the end of the thread under his chin. He then unwound enough to hold the spool at arm's length and broke it off. Handing the spool to Cotten, he said, "Now you do the same."

Cotten looked at him curiously. "All right." She repeated what John had done.

"Look straight ahead," he said. "How many strings do you see?"

"Two."

"But you know there is only one, right? Now close your left eye. How many strings?"

"One."

"Switch eyes."

"Still one."

"That's because we all have two eyes, and that gives us depth perception. Look again with both eyes and focus on a single spot on the string."

Cotten obeyed. "The strings come together and make a single thread," she said.

"That's your point of focus and what is referred to as threading the needle."

Cotten had a flash of déjà vu as she remembered viewing the line drawing of the cube shown to her by Ripple at the Chicago Starbucks.

"John," she whispered, returning to the chair and sitting, "I think I'm starting to understand a bit of what's going on here. Do you believe we can be in two places at once, like the thread, just depending on where you focus, where you choose to be?" The thought filled her mind. "When I was in Peru, I was taught a kind of meditation technique, which I'm still trying to master."

John took his seat across the table. "This was something the shaman taught you? The man you told me about?"

Cotten was still putting random pieces of thought together. "The last time I practiced what Yachaq called liquid light, I felt as if I were in two places—I saw myself standing on two beaches. And I believed I could move from one to the other." Cotten shoved her fingers through her hair. "And then in Chicago, I met a strange little man who saw the pictures of the tablet that I took to the University of Illinois. He's a physicist, and he told me the writing on the tablet had to do with quantum mechanics. He said what was inscribed in binary code on the tablet was identical to a theory he had developed. He referred to it as a thread theory, and he tried to get me to understand how particles can exist in more than one place at a time in the quantum world. He said he had proven how the same was true in the world around us. Lester Ripple said all possibilities and outcomes already exist—much the same as what Yachaq professed to me in Peru. The concept is that there are many paths or threads. Where you focus is where you choose to live your life. Am I making sense?"

"Very much. It's what we call free will."

* * *

The next morning, after breakfast, Cotten and John boarded the train for the one-hour ride to Hanborough Station, near Oxford.

After arriving, they took the fifteen-minute walk from the station to the farmhouse belonging to Violet Crutchfield, Thomas Wyatt's great-aunt.

"Winston Churchill rests in peace near here," John said as they walked past a sign to Bladon Church. "Here's a piece of trivia. They used to bury suicides in the public highway with a stake driven through them."

"That's awful," Cotten said, looking back over her shoulder at the sign.

"Then, in the early 1800s, some came to think it was barbaric, and a law was passed that allowed suicides to be buried in the usual churchyard, but—"

"There's always a *but*."

"But . . . they could only be buried between the hours of nine p.m. and midnight, and of course without the rites of the Church."

Cotten said, "But that was the Church of England, not the Catholic Church. Suicides can't be buried in Catholic cemeteries, right?"

"That's true," John said.

"Look." Cotten pointed to a two-story stone building across a field. A sign by a gate read *Crutchfield*. "That must be it."

"Must be," John said.

Two chimneys poked out from the roof of the rambling structure, which was surrounded by overgrown gardens mixed with as many wildflowers as weeds and shrubs. Smoke spiraled out of one chimney. "Somebody is home," Cotten said.

They walked up the flagstone walk and stood in front of the weathered wooden door. John rapped with the tarnished brass knocker. "Hello," he called out.

They waited a few minutes before knocking again. A moment later, the door opened with a groan.

"Good day," John said.

Standing in the doorway was a frail, elderly woman, slightly bent with age. Her hair was so thin her pink scalp showed through.

"Mrs. Crutchfield?" Cotten asked. "Violet?"

The woman's eyes stared at John through her smudged bifocals. "Is this your woman?" she asked.

"I beg your pardon?" John said.

She moved to the side and waved her cane, gesturing for them to enter. "Go into the parlor where it is warm," she said. "Do you want me to get pneumonia?"

Cotten glanced at John as they stepped into the old house.

"Now, sit there and warm yourselves." The woman tapped the back of a settee facing the fireplace.

Cotten and John waited for her to settle into a rocker before they took a seat.

The parlor was an antique dealer's dream come true. The room was filled with dark furniture, many pieces draped with throw blankets. Atop every table were vases, teapots, statuettes, framed photographs, and lamps. A tapestry hung off the side of an antique upright piano.

"Are you Violet Crutchfield?" John asked.

The woman appeared startled. "Of course I am. What is the matter with you, Alistair? Have you gone balmy?" She nodded toward Cotten. "The boiling pot is in the scullery."

"Scullery?" Cotten said.

"Get the boiling pot and set it on the stove. I only need the linens laundered today. Get on with it."

Cotten glanced at John.

"Mrs. Crutchfield, I'm not Alistair. My name is John Tyler, and this is Cotten Stone."

For a few moments Violet rocked with her eyes closed. Then she looked at Cotten and said, "Cotten. Hmmph. What kind of name is that for a pretty girl?"

"We've come to ask a couple of questions," John said.

"You need to bring in more wood," Violet said. "I need it stacked there." She pointed her cane like a weapon toward the hearth. "And you've been neglecting the garden." She grew quiet for a minute. As if she had just seen them for the first time, she said, "Who did you say you were?"

"John Tyler," he said.

Violet rocked. "Would you be so kind to put another log on for me, John Tyler? These old bones chill easily."

"I'd be happy to." He went to the stone fireplace. It appeared to serve as the only heat in the farmhouse. With the fire tongs he lifted a split oak log.

Suddenly, John stopped cold. He slowly added the log to the fire while he gazed at the cast-iron fireback that protected the firebrick and radiated the heat into the room.

Dead center of the fireback was the seal of the Venatori.

THE LIST

THERE WAS A BRIEF knock on the farmhouse door before Cotten and John heard the tumble of a lock followed by the painful moan of the door opening.

"Hello, Mrs. Crutchfield. It's Dorothy. I've just let myself in."

A middle-aged woman came into the parlor and set her tote bag on the floor before unwrapping the scarf around her neck.

"We have company?" Dorothy said, looking at Cotten and John.

Violet Crutchfield stared at her two guests. The confused expression made Cotten believe the old woman didn't remember talking to them.

"Hello," Cotten said, standing to introduce herself. John also rose and followed with his introduction.

"Nice to meet you," Dorothy said. "I'm Mrs. Crutchfield's housekeeper. It was my mother's job before me." She turned her attention to the old woman and spoke loudly. "And how are we today, Mrs. Crutchfield?"

"Chilly. The air is so damp," Violet said. "Would you put another log on, dear?"

Dorothy looked at the fire. "In a bit. The fire needs to burn down to some hot coals. This will keep you toasty." She grabbed a throw blanket off the nearest chair and put it over Violet's legs. Then she said, "Are you friends of Mrs. Crutchfield?"

"Sorry," Cotten said, "we should have explained. I'm a news reporter. We're doing a historical piece on British physicians and medicine of the 1800s. One of Mrs. Crutchfield's relatives was a London doctor—Chauncey Wyatt. We are hoping to find some background on Dr. Wyatt—you know, old notes, diaries, photos, the kinds of things that would give us a look into the way the medical doctors lived and practiced during that time period, and the obstacles they faced."

"Really?" Dorothy said. "Well, our Mrs. Crutchfield's maiden name is Wyatt. She married Neville Crutchfield."

"She lives alone?" Cotten asked.

Dorothy kept her back to Violet so she wouldn't hear. "Oh yes, ever since Mr. Crutchfield perished thirty-three years ago. Barren, she was. No children to look after her. She has outlived her siblings as well. But most of the time she doesn't remember much. She does well, though, to be ninety-four."

Violet rocked forward. "Who are your friends, Dorothy? Don't be rude. You need to introduce them."

"You see what I mean." Dorothy arched her brows, then faced Violet. "They have come to see you about your family. A Dr. Chauncey Wyatt. Do you recognize the name?"

A broad smile graced Violet's face as if memories burst through a dam. "I have a tintype of him somewhere. In the attic, probably.

This was his house when he retired." Violet laughed. "That was before I was born, of course. He died here."

"She is probably square with that," Dorothy said quietly. "She sometimes has remarkable recall of things in the past. And I know for a fact the house has been in the family for generations."

"Do you think she has that tintype or anything else that was Dr. Wyatt's?" John asked.

"There is an attic full of old stuff. She won't let anyone clean it out. Says it would be like erasing her family, like dusting a shelf."

"Poof," Violet said, seeming to overhear. "They would just disappear, as if they never lived."

* * *

The attic was drafty and dusty. Cotten sneezed and turned up her collar. The heat from the fireplace below didn't penetrate here. "If I were a ghost hunter, this is the first place I'd investigate," she said.

"It does have a spooky quality about it," Dorothy said. "I don't think I would want to clean it out even if Mrs. Crutchfield asked." Dorothy put her hands on her hips. "Sorry the lighting is so poor. You have a look about. I'll be down in the kitchen, preparing Mrs. Crutchfield's lunch. Can I expect you to join us?"

"Thank you," Cotten said, "but we have very little time."

"Did you see the fireback?" John asked when the housekeeper left. "It has the seal of the Venatori. I'll put money on that it belonged to Chauncey Wyatt."

Cotten said, "I'll have to take a closer look before we leave."

"Look at this place," John said, scanning the contents of the attic. "How many generations' stuff is up here?"

"More than we have time to examine."

They spent the next hour scouring through boxes and file cabinets, desks and shelves. There were a number of chests and boxes with contents referring to the Wyatt name, but nothing for Chauncey. Finally, Cotten opened a dusty leather and wood chest. Right on top was a logbook with Chauncey Wyatt's name on the cover. "Pay dirt," Cotten said. She flipped through her find. "It's Chauncey's records of patients and appointments." She stopped on a page. "Here's a patient being treated with catarrh. Any idea what that is?"

"No," John said as he abandoned his search and joined her. "Let's see what else is in the chest." He lifted a wooden music box with a brass crank and porcelain knob. He tried it, but the crank was frozen.

Cotten found a pair of candlesticks and a silver tray about five inches square with ball feet and a twisted silver handle. "What is this?" she asked, holding it up. In the center of the tray were the initials CHW in high relief.

"I think it's a calling-card receiver," John said. "Whenever anyone came to visit, they left their calling card in one of these in the parlor. I wonder what Chauncey's middle name was." He cleared a place on the floor, took everything out of the chest, and arranged the items so they could see each one.

"What was important about this newspaper article?" Cotten said, picking up a yellowed article. Trying to see in the poor light of the bare overhead bulb, she read as she sat on a rickety, spindle-backed chair. "John, listen to this. This says that rumor has it that two of London's finest physicians have been working feverishly on a project to cure asthma. But it is believed that these two gentlemen are also undertaking an even more spectacular project."

"What was the project?" John asked.

"It refers to an interview with Dr. Erasmus Wilson, a fellow Freemason, that yielded they were working together on something that would make all Londoners proud, and they would be announcing it soon."

John took a small spiral notebook from his jacket. "Erasmus Wilson," he said as he wrote down the name. "All right, what else have we got?"

Cotten said, "Looks like only old junk except for the scrapbook, a box of pictures, and maybe this." She picked up the brittle sheet of paper. Across the top in a sweeping handwritten script was the title *FINAL CONTENTS*. Below the title was written a list starting with four copies of the Bible. The words *English*, *French*, *Latin*, and *Italian* appeared beside the notation. Also on the list was a copy of Joseph Whitaker's Almanac for the year 1878; a picture of Queen Victoria and a cutout of a cartoon from *Punch* magazine showing the queen exchanging humorous gifts with Prime Minister Benjamin Disraeli; a sliding scale of weights and measures; a railway guide; four hand-carved tobacco pipes—two briarwood and two scrimshaw; the London city directory; a street map; and a copy of the *Daily Telegraph*.

"What on earth kind of list is that?" John said. "Anything come to mind?"

"No, but there's a note written at the bottom."

John motioned for her to read it aloud.

"'The secret is protected by the word of God.'"

SUICIDE

"Ted, come quick!"

Ted Casselman looked up from his desk at the woman standing in the doorway to his office. The expression of fear on her face was unmistakable.

"What is it?" he asked.

"In the men's room," she said. "One of our techs just shot himself."

"Are you serious?" he said, moving quickly around his desk to follow her. He was on her heels as they sprinted down the hallway of the Satellite News Network's video-editing department.

A uniformed SNN security officer blocked the doorway. Seeing the news director, he said, "In here, Mr. Casselman."

Ted slipped past the officer and entered the men's room. In a far corner, a young man lay collapsed on the floor, the tile wall behind him smeared in red. An automatic pistol rested in his lifeless hand.

Ted rushed to the body and felt the man's neck for a pulse. The head wound was massive, and he was not surprised to find no sign of life.

"Were the police called?" he said to the security officer.

"Already done, sir. They're on their way."

Ted backed away, leaning against the nearby row of sinks. He shook his head. "What's going on?" he whispered to himself. Just that morning, his next-door neighbor had died of an apparent prescription-drug overdose. Driving to the train station, he had come upon two horrific traffic accidents, both of which appeared to involve single cars. One had rammed a light pole head-on, and the other a tree. Each had multiple fatalities. At the train station, a woman had thrown herself onto the tracks in front of an approaching commuter and was killed instantly. During his subway ride into Manhattan, there was an apparent murder-suicide two cars ahead of him. Now this—someone on the SNN staff.

Ted stepped into the hallway outside the men's room. A dozen people crowded around. Some were crying. Everyone looked totally distraught. He would have to get some crisis counseling scheduled right away. "Everyone, please go back to your desks. There's been a tragic accident here, but there's nothing any of us can do. We need to try to continue our normal routines as best we can."

"There's news of suicides taking place throughout the city," a young staff member said.

"Yes," Casselman said, "I've heard the same reports. I don't know how much validity there is to the stories, but it certainly explains my ride in this morning. Why don't you stay on top of it and get something to me for the noon news. In the meantime, let's all try to get through this together."

Ted made his way to his office. He could hear the whispers of concern and sobs of sorrow as he passed each cubicle. What was all this about? Had the whole world gone nuts? He rubbed the center of his chest, where pressure built inside.

Ted opened a desk drawer and pulled out a small container of aspirin. Popping one of the pills in his mouth, he washed it down with the cold coffee from a Dunkin' Donuts cup. He was already on an aspirin a day, along with cholesterol-lowering medication. His doctor had advised taking an additional pill any time he felt the pressure in his chest.

There was a commotion in the hall outside his office, and Ted saw SNN security leading the police and EMTs toward the men's room. He thought about getting up and following them but knew that he could do nothing for the dead tech. Considering the way his chest felt, he thought he should avoid the additional stress.

His assistant, a young journalism intern from New York University, walked into his office. "Mr. Casselman, one of the producers said you would want to see this." She placed a newspaper on his desk before leaving, closing the door behind her.

Ted stared at the front of the *National Courier*. A picture of Cotten Stone embracing John Tyler glared back at him. The caption read, "Cotten Stone, embattled reporter, gets religion from Archbishop John Tyler." Farther down the page was a picture of Cotten sitting on the side of the road, her face in her hands as John consoled her. The caption under this photo read, "Stone and Tyler get into an accident while rushing to their hotel together."

Ted picked up the paper and scanned the article. "What a crock of shit," he said. "Cotten is going to freak out when she sees this."

As he laid the paper back on his desk and picked up the phone to call Cotten, Ted saw more police officers move past his office. After a moment of waiting for the call to move through international routing, he heard her voice.

"Hey, kiddo," he said. "I hate to call you with bad news, but—"

HIT-AND-RUN

"SORRY FOR SLEEPING ALL the way back," Cotten said as she and John got off the Underground at the Warren Street Station, the last leg of their trip from Hanborough. "I just couldn't keep my eyes open another minute."

"That's what shoulders are made for," John said.

"I can't believe Dorothy let us borrow the scrapbook and all the other stuff. We'll be able to take a closer look at everything back at the hotel. I just wish I had a clue as to what Chauncey's list was all about."

John waved for a taxi, but with no luck, they kept walking toward the Cadogan.

Cotten's cell phone rang. She took it from her bag and glimpsed at the caller ID. "It's Ted." She flipped open the phone as John stepped off the sidewalk to hail another cab.

Just as he did, a black BMW pulled away from the curb half a block down on the opposite side of the street and sped toward them.

"Hey, kiddo," Ted said. "I hate to call you with bad news, but—"

The approaching BMW swerved, crossed two lanes of traffic, and headed straight at John.

He jumped back, but it was too late.

The impact lifted John up and threw him toward Cotten. She heard the sickening thud and the gunning of the engine as the car sped away.

"John!" Cotten screamed as he crashed to the sidewalk. She fell to her knees. He was face-down, eyes closed. Quickly she hit the end button on her cell phone and dialed 999 for police and an ambulance.

"I don't know," she said after being asked her location. "Help us," she said, thrusting the cell to a man leaning over John's body. "Tell them where we are. Please."

The stranger took the phone and gave the location to the emergency operator.

John didn't move.

Cotten stretched out on the pavement next to him, resting her cheek on the cement so she could see his face. A crowd had encircled them, their voices muffled. But bits of their conversations leaked through.

"Is he dead?" someone asked.

A child's voice rang out. "Oh, look, Mum, there's blood."

Cotten blocked out the onlookers' voices, building a tight, safe cocoon around just the two of them, insulating them from the world. She stared at John's face, willing his eyes to open so she could see them again—deep blue like no other eyes in the world. "John," Cotten whispered, putting her hand on the back of his head, as though it might comfort him. "Come back to me."

* * *

Ted heard Cotten scream John's name, then the call ended abruptly. He sat stunned, staring at the receiver as if it were the first time he had ever seen a telephone. He started to press redial, but before he could, his office door opened again.

"The cops want to talk to you," the young intern said.

"Be right there," he said, hanging up the phone.

Suddenly, Ted felt nervous and uneasy. He massaged the back of his neck and rolled his head from side to side. Something was wrong. His stomach soured, and the bitterness rose to his mouth. He felt unsteady, as if he might pass out. *What is the damn thermostat set at?* he wondered. He was freezing. Ted leaned back in the chair and closed his eyes. This would pass in a minute or two. He'd just rest for a little bit, and then he'd be fine. He felt the pressure building in his chest.

In a few minutes, Ted opened his eyes. He rose, went to the two windows looking out into the hall, and twisted the long plastic rods to close the miniblinds. Returning to his desk, he sat and slid open the bottom drawer. From a small space behind the files, he pulled out a handgun and held it in his lap.

NIGHT VISITOR

"In a stunning announcement today, the Vatican declared that the Catholic Church believes the widespread wave of suicides throughout the world is being caused by demonic possessions," the SNN reporter said. Over the reporter's shoulder, a picture appeared of the pope standing in front of a bank of microphones and reading a statement. The room he was in was crowded with reporters and dignitaries of the Church and various foreign governments.

"The pope has called upon all Catholic priests to commence performing the ancient ritual of exorcism on anyone showing signs of possible possession and suicidal tendencies. As widespread panic takes hold of many communities and cities across the United States, Europe, and other parts of the world, thousands flock to churches, temples, mosques, and other houses of worship, hoping to find answers to the mind-numbing rash of self-induced killings."

* * *

The pope slumped in the chair beside his bed. The commotion of the news coverage had finally died away. He was alone, unable to push from his mind the madness that seeped into every corner of the world around him.

He felt old and weak. For the first time in his papacy, he wondered if he could go on. The weight was so heavy on his shoulders—and his mind. Everything around him was crumbling. The bleakness drifting over the world was becoming unbearable. What was he to do?

"Perplexing, isn't it?"

The pope looked up to see who had spoken.

The Old Man sat on the couch on the opposite side of the bedroom, his form partially hidden in the shadows.

"What do you want?" the pope asked.

"Things are turning dark. Perhaps now would be a good time to reconsider my offer and do as I have asked. After all, saving yourself should be your first priority."

"You have not won."

"Oh, but I am so very close."

"You will be defeated in the end. We will drive you out. I have over four hundred thousand priests throughout the world and have ordered them to immediately start performing exorcisms."

The Old Man laughed. "You are wasting your time. My hosts outnumber you a million to one. I like to think of it that way—being hosted. And who will minister to the Buddhists and Muslims, the Hindus and Jews? They're all dying by their own hands as we speak. Dear old friend, this goes beyond you and your Church. My legions can get to thousands of souls at a time, of all denominations and beliefs, unlike your trivial priest army. You are but a mere speck upon the face of the earth."

The pope's eyes narrowed, and there was hate in his heart, something he had never experienced before. "But we still have one weapon against you." He glared at the Old Man. "Cotten Stone."

YOO-HOO

LESTER RIPPLE OPENED HIS eyes and stared up at the ceiling of his bedroom. He had glued small, glow-in-the-dark plastic stars and planets across the ceiling, and in the darkness of the room, they always gave him the sensation of floating through the solar system. As he stared at the soft, cream-colored celestial bodies, he realized that of all his immersions onto the power grid, the one he had just experienced had been the most fulfilling and stimulating.

It was not unusual for Lester to visualize the many threads leading to different paths. He had even crossed over to different ones now and again just to feel the surge of energy it brought. But tonight, the energy had been almost intoxicating. Excitement flowed through him as he realized that he was not the only person in the world who knew the secret to quantum threading. Someone had known before him, and inscribed it thousands of years ago upon the surface of the relic in Cotten Stone's photographs.

But what was hidden by the glare of the camera flash? What was it that she seemed so desperate to learn? And what did it have to do with the concept of stopping Armageddon?

Suddenly, Lester had a thought. Each of the photos had been taken from a slightly different angle. A small portion of the inscription hidden by the glare was revealed in each. But together, the whole statement could not be read. Perhaps a bit of electronic enhancement could bring out enough to help him find the answer she needed.

Lester got up and went into his kitchen. He flipped on the light and opened the refrigerator. Grabbing a can of Yoo-hoo, he shook it vigorously and then popped the top. Downing the chocolate drink in several long gulps, he moved to the card table and glared once again at the three photos. *Time for a bit of magic*, he thought.

He picked up the pictures and went to his PC, which was set up on a desk beside his TV. Next to the PC was the flatbed scanner that he sometimes used to scan the covers of his favorite comics. He powered up the PC and blew his nose on a paper napkin while waiting for the computer to boot. After it was up and running, he launched Adobe PhotoShop. Placing the first photo on the scanner, he instructed PhotoShop to scan and import the image. Once completed, he repeated the same procedure for the remaining two photographs.

Lester slid his chair closer to the monitor and studied the digital version of picture number one. He clicked on the enlarge command three times. One, two, three. Zooming into the area of the tablet that was obstructed by the glare, he tried to make out the hidden khipu. No luck.

Next, he clicked on the image menu and used the mode command to convert the scan from color to grayscale. Suddenly, the portion of the image hidden by the glare revealed a tiny bit of the khipu previously obscured. The first piece of the line was not an equation, but language, of that he was sure. He scribbled what he could read on a yellow pad and then clicked on the levels control. Adjusting the light, dark and midtone curves, he was able to retrieve a few more pieces of the binary code. After making a note of what was revealed, he clicked on the second digital image and zoomed in on the glare portion.

In this photo, the tablet was at a slightly different angle. Even without processing, he saw a tiny bit of the lines not clear in the first photo. Going through the same steps of conversion to grayscale and levels adjustment, he was able to make a few more notes.

Lester blew his nose again before starting to work on the third photo. This one revealed the largest portion of the code. Performing the enhancement procedure once more, he was able to make out just a bit more of the message. He noted what it said, then picked up the yellow pad and photographs and went back to the card table. Dropping the photos onto its surface, he sat and pondered his notes. Being so used to thinking in terms of physics and quantum mechanics theories, he had to work hard at understanding the simple language revealed by the code.

After rearranging the bits and pieces of his notes, the message materialized.

Lester Ripple giggled, proud of himself that he could solve the puzzle. After all, he was a problem solver. He rose and again went to the refrigerator, drawing out the last can of Yoo-hoo.

He raised it in a toast. "So you want to stop Armageddon?" he said. "Well, Ms. Stone, you're in for a big surprise."

GENE POOL

Eli Luddington sat in the wingback chair and dialed the cordless phone. Tempest Star answered.

"I think we need a change in game plan," he said, sipping a Rémy Martin Louis XIII.

"Why? I got you the front-page picture of Stone hanging all over that priest. It's at every shopping-market checkout counter. Do you know how many people read it? Even if they don't buy it, they read the caption while they stand in line. Both Stone and Tyler are dead in the water."

"Well, one of them is out of commission."

Mariah came into the room wearing Eli's robe. She sat at his feet, her back against his shins.

Eli put the phone on speaker and placed it on the table beside him. He opened his knees so she could lean back while he played with her hair.

"What do you mean?" Star asked.

"It seems Archbishop Tyler was struck down by a hit-and-run in London."

"How unfortunate."

"It might reel in a token of sympathy. And now I am thinking that is a good thing. I know that Cotten Stone is getting close to finding the tablet. We have hampered her, made extravagant efforts to discredit her—and your coverage was definitely brilliant—but in the end, we must face the fact that she will find the relic. We have done about all we can to delay that. If we keep a close watch on her, we may be able to steal it away, as we have the others. But I'm starting to wonder if we may want a change of tactics. This time, we need to be there when she finds it. As a matter of fact, we should let her find it."

Mariah gently arched her neck, laying her head between Eli's legs. "Come on," she whispered, turning around and kneeling. "I lit candles all around the spa." She took one of his hands and pulled him forward.

Eli resisted, and Mariah sighed. She slipped her hand inside the robe, teasingly caressing her own breast. Her other hand stroked her belly, and then moved inside her thigh.

Eli's voice sounded ragged as he watched Mariah and spoke to Star. "We have to give Stone her head, like you would a horse. Give her enough rope for her to climb to the top, so we can push her off the cliff. And we need to make sure the world is watching. We'll show her up close and personal how much blood will be on her hands. The world will see her fail, and all that will be left to do is harvest their souls."

Mariah got to her feet, letting the robe fall open. She leaned over to whisper in his ear, "I'm going to have to start without you." Then she headed out of the room.

"Listen, Tempest, something has come up that requires my attention. I'll get back to you later."

"I hope so, because I'm not sure I follow what you want me to do."

Eli hung up. He smiled to himself. Mariah Hapsburg thought she was manipulating him. What she didn't understand was that her devious plan was all in his favor. She thought she could lure Richard home with a child. Of course, Richard would think the unborn was his. And there was another thing Mariah didn't know. Her husband had already come to Eli, his tail between his legs. As always. And Eli had given Richard one more assignment—one last task, then he would be done with Rumjal. For Eli had already begun the process of filling Richard's place in the ranks with someone much stronger. Someone who had Eli's genes.

WAITING ROOM

COTTEN SAT IN THE waiting room on the surgical floor of the hospital. Nearby, next to the door, stood a Venatori agent.

"Would you like some coffee?" a nurse asked.

"No thanks."

"Is there any news about my son?" a woman sitting in a beige upholstered chair asked the nurse.

"The doctor will come out to see you as soon as the surgery is over," the nurse said.

"Can you check?" the woman asked, her bottom lip and her voice trembling. "Please."

"Of course," the nurse said.

The woman took a tissue from the box on the floor beside her as the nurse left. She appeared so bedraggled and distraught—her hair hung in strings, some falling in front of her red, swollen eyes.

"Your son is in surgery?" Cotten asked.

The woman nodded. "He's only ten."

"I'm sorry," Cotten said. "I hope he is going to be okay."

"He broke his neck," the woman said. "He jumped from a tree. No reason. Just jumped. He couldn't have meant to hurt himself . . . could he? I mean, all these suicides. Something awful is happening. Did you hear what the pope called it? Demonic possessions. Can you believe that?"

Cotten said, "Downstairs in the emergency room, that's all anyone was talking about."

A man in scrubs and a blue mask dangling below his chin came into the room. "Who is here with Archbishop Tyler?"

"I am," Cotten said, getting to her feet.

The doctor extended his hand. "I do have good news. The archbishop has suffered some head trauma, a concussion, but no fracture to the skull. We'll keep a watch on that situation—make certain there's no bleeding, et cetera. And he had a compound fracture of the left radius."

"Compound?"

"The broken end of the bone came through the skin. These types of breaks are susceptible to infection, because the bone isn't protected by soft tissue or skin. We had to go in and clean the injury site and stabilize the fracture. If infection sets in, that is a whole new set of problems, and it can be difficult for the bone to heal."

"But he's going to be all right?" Cotten asked.

"He will be here for several days so we can monitor him. We'll keep him on an IV to make certain he stays well hydrated, and we will give him some big doses of antibiotics. But yes, he's going to be very sore, but he should mend just fine. I've prescribed a painkiller if needed. He has several bruised ribs and other contusions."

"Thank you," she said.

"I'll be checking on him later. Hope this hasn't ruined your holiday."

Cotten wasn't sure how to respond. "Actually, it was a business trip." What else could she call it? "When can I see him?" she asked.

"He's in recovery now. He should be up in his room in an hour or so."

"Thank you so much."

When the doctor walked away, Cotten looked back at the woman whose son was in surgery. "I hope you'll have good news, too. I'm sure you will."

Cotten left the waiting room and made her way out to the parking lot, where she could get a stronger signal on her cell phone. Flipping it open, she scrolled to Ted Casselman's name in her contacts list and pressed talk.

TWO LONDONS

Heaven means to be one with God.
—CONFUCIUS

As DUSK FELL OVER the city, Cotten put her cell phone to her ear and listened to Ted Casselman's SNN office phone ring. It was chilly outside of the hospital lobby, so she turned her back to the wind. Maybe Ted was at lunch, she thought, glancing at her watch to compute the time difference.

Just as she expected his voice mail to pick up, a strange voice answered.

"Ted Casselman's office."

"Hello. This is Cotten Stone. Is Ted in?"

"Oh, hello, Ms. Stone. No, he, um . . . no, he isn't." The young woman stumbled and stuttered.

"Who is this?" Cotten asked.

"I'm Mr. Casselman's assistant. Mr. Casselman is, um . . . I'm sorry, it's just so awful."

"What's wrong?" Cotten asked, feeling the first twinge of fear creeping into her gut. "Has something happened?"

"Yes," the young woman said, her voice breaking.

Cotten held her breath.

"A suicide this morning. Right here at SNN. We're all devastated."

Cotten spun around, and the frigid air bit her cheeks and stung her eyes. "Ted?" she whispered.

"Oh no, Mr. Casselman's fine. He's down the hall speaking to a detective. But I know he wanted to talk—wait, here he comes now."

Cotten finally took a breath. In the instant that she thought Ted had died, an invisible knot had tightened around her throat.

"Cotten, I've been trying to get in touch with you," Ted said.

"I'm sorry about hanging up on you like that. John was struck by a hit-and-run this afternoon just as I answered your call. He's pretty banged up, but he's going to be okay. I know it wasn't just any hit-and-run, though. This was deliberate. Like Thornton. Like Wyatt. They want to get to me."

"I am so sorry, Cotten. Is there anything I can do for John? For you? Everything seems to be spinning out of control."

"I don't think so." Cotten tugged her collar more snugly around her neck. "Your assistant said there was a suicide at SNN. What happened?"

"A young tech shot himself in the men's room."

"You're right, the world is out of control," Cotten said. "So, as if I need more bad news, what bad news were you calling me about earlier?"

"It doesn't seem important now, in the scheme of things." Ted sighed. "Tempest Star put your picture on the front page of the *National Courier*. You with John, in the airport, hugging. It's not the pictures so much, but the captions. And there's another picture, with you on the side of the road crying and John consoling you. She's tried to paint a portrait of you two having an affair."

Cotten shook her head. "Amazing. I guess they got to her, too. They're covering every angle, Ted. Scare me, make me feel guilty, cause me grief, slander me. You name it. All the stops are out."

"Cotten, I have to tell you something, but I want to ask you a question first. Do you agree with what they are saying about all these suicides? Are they what the Vatican is calling demonic possessions?"

Cotten put the phone to her other ear and walked, head down. "Demons, possessions . . . I don't know. But what I do know is, it is a concerted effort to create mayhem and panic and to claim souls. It is *their* work, Ted. Of that I am sure. I'm—"

"Cotten, today, not too long after the body of the tech was found, I had something happen to me. It was as if someone entered my thoughts. Not like what insane people say are voices in their heads telling them to do something. These were *my* thoughts. It's hard to explain. I went so far as to take a gun out of my desk and consider using it on myself."

"Oh God, Ted."

"It was so bizarre. At first I felt sick, kind of dizzy and disjointed, not really connected to myself—or anything else, for that matter. I thought it might have to do with my heart condition. I became so overwhelmed with the feeling of despair washing over me that I actually started to cry. The world was all askew, and there seemed to be no hope for the future. I blamed myself for the tech's suicide. Why hadn't I seen the warning signs? I kept thinking how I am responsible for the staff and it was inexcusable that I hadn't recognized this kid's despondency. There was a price I had to pay. I wondered how I would ever face his family and friends—my family and friends—after such negligence. I was buried in shame, disgrace, dishonor, blame, hopelessness, and remorse. I was thinking there was no way I could be redeemed. And Cotten, I realized that I didn't even know the dead man's name. What did that say about Ted Casselman? Existing in this life one more moment would be a disgrace.

"Then something pulled me out of it. I don't know what it was, but the words I said to you once came back to me. That suicide was not something I would ever consider. Suicide was for cowards. I realized then that I had to fight these thoughts that were filling my head—that they belonged to someone or some*thing* else, not me. My mind became a battlefield as I fought off the thing in my head. And I did fight. But it wasn't easy."

"Ted, not that you aren't strong or that you didn't struggle, but you have to understand, if you didn't pull the trigger it's because they let go of you so that you could tell me what it was like. They want me to know how easy they can take control of anyone—and give back a life if it serves their purpose. They want me to understand that they can get to you, to John. Next time, they won't let go—you won't come back."

Ted took a moment before responding. "That's even more reason why I want to put you on the air and do a special report to expose these suicides for what they are. Let everyone know how easily this can happen to anyone. Use it against the evil that's causing all this. You're the best one to do it. You know firsthand what we're up against."

"But I don't have anything to offer. Do you know how this sounds to most folks? Devils and demons—that's the stuff horror films and conspiracy novels are made of. I can't just get on television and spook the shit out of everyone." Cotten hesitated. There was more than that. All afternoon she had thought about the attempt on John's life. And now Ted's near-suicide. "I don't know if I want to go ahead with any of this. Because of me, you and John are at risk. If I give up, back away, then maybe all the suicides will stop, and you and John will be safe. I couldn't go on if you or John—"

"It's never going to stop unless we do something—*you* do something. You know that. If you don't stand in their way, they will win. You are the only one. And we don't have time to wait." Ted's voice was sharp. "What happened to me today is happening to hundreds or thousands of innocent people every day. Something—I don't care what you call it—took over the very way I think, Cotten. You have to do something about it right now. If it saves one life, it's worth it. I'll make all the arrangements. Can you get back to New York in two days?"

Cotten felt numb. Ted was right—she had to stop this nightmare. But the cost might be more than she could bear. "I don't think I can leave London so fast. John and I need to be here, at least for a little while longer. Plus, they say he needs to stay in the hospital a couple of days."

"Then we'll do it from our London studios. Start putting together your report. I'll get back to you with details."

"I'll do my best," Cotten said.

"Cotten?"

"Yes, Ted?"

"I'm finally starting to understand."

* * *

“I’ll wait outside,” the Venatori agent said as Cotten entered John’s room. After checking on him, she went and stared out the hospital room’s window south from Hampstead down over central London. It was midnight as the wind blew, and low clouds rolled past the window. She watched the city with St. Paul’s Cathedral, Big Ben, and the spires of Westminster in the distance.

Cotten struggled to understand what was happening around her. Right down to those she knew and loved. Was the reference to the daughter of an angel just a meaningless, cryptic verse from thousands of years ago, or was it talking about her? What if Edelman had guessed wrong when he interpreted the obscure glyphs? Would a broadcast help save lives or only create more deaths?

She glanced at John, sleeping soundly. She’d do anything to protect him. And they knew it. The Fallen Ones had tried once again to take him from her. First, attempting to disgrace them both in the eyes of the Church and the world with Tempest Star’s tabloid pictures. Then they tried to kill him to send her a message.

Cotten sat beside John’s bed, reached out, and touched his face, staring at him. They wanted her to be afraid to lose him. As she watched John, hearing his easy breathing, she realized that maybe she had it backward. Why did they want her so afraid? The revelation came instantly. It meant that she had the ability to stop them. They feared her. They were the ones who were terrified. She had to be very close to discovering what they wanted kept hidden away forever. The secret of stopping them, stopping Armageddon. This new line of thought strengthened her.

Earlier, the staff had brought in a cot, and Cotten decided it was time to try to rest. Lying down, she closed her eyes and slowed her breathing, clearing her mind. She was exhausted, but not sleepy. Instead, she would turn to the liquid light. Recalling all that Yachaq had taught her, she began to immerse herself. Maybe within the light, she could find direction.

Cotten allowed the light to come and pour inside her. It flowed in from every surface of her body. She welcomed it into the center of her being, where it spun into pure light. She felt the intensity as she envisioned its force spinning inside her core.

Do not let go of the light, she remembered Yachaq saying with his soothing voice. *Set your mind free so it moves effortlessly, not stopping on any thought, traveling through space and time in absolute stillness. Exist only in this perfect moment.*

Cotten blocked out all thoughts, concentrating only on the pureness of the light.

She heard the wind outside the window and the hum of the elevator down the hall. There were whispers from the nurse's station as two people discussed the latest news of the mass suicides. Nervous clinking of glass and pans came from the cafeteria somewhere in the hospital. Down on the street, a woman asked a cabbie to take her out of the city. There was fear in her voice.

Then Cotten heard the rush of blood flowing into warm water as a woman somewhere nearby sat in a tub and slit her wrists, and the crash of the chair as it was kicked out from beneath the man who had just hung himself from a steam pipe in a building's basement a block away. The rope from which his body swung creaked under his weight.

People were dying everywhere. The sounds of their deaths grew like the squeal of feedback from a sound system turned up too loud.

Cotten shook with fear, her body turning cold and sweaty. She felt as if she were coming apart, being pulled in a thousand directions by those who begged for her help. Their cries filled the darkness of the room, her mind, trying to extinguish the liquid light.

She pushed hard to keep the light in sight and not lose the vision Yachaq had taught her. The answer must lie within the light. There was no other place to look.

If Ripple and Yachaq were right, that all possibilities and outcomes already exist, then she would choose to exist in a different world—a better world.

With concentration, she cut off the sounds and the thoughts that accompanied them, moving out and away, becoming light herself, light that vibrated with the rest of the universe. Connecting with all energy.

Suddenly, she saw a tree-filled park outside the hospital, just beyond the electric sliding doors at the front entrance. Unlike the interior of the hospital lobby, the park was bright, cheerful, and full of people coming and going. There were no calls for help, no moans of pain, no screams of death. It was noon on a bright day.

As the doors slid open with a whoosh, she walked onto the grass. The air was brisk but held the warmth of midday. She looked around at the people along the sidewalks. There was no evidence of urgency or worry, sadness or emergency. A few smiled or nodded as they passed.

Like the two beaches she had seen from within the liquid light in her Florida apartment, Cotten knew she was seeing two Londons. One was a dark place being eaten alive by evil and death, and then there was this one, a place filled with life, hope, and promise.

She knew that the liquid light allowed her to view a different path, another life that existed—another possibility. She had seen *and* taken it, had chosen to witness this beautiful, peaceful world and participate in it. She had moved from one of Lester Ripple's threads to another, from one of Yachaq's forest paths to a different one.

In so many ways, Yachaq and Ripple had taught her the very same thing: all possibilities exist at the same time. We choose which path to take.

Cotten stood on the grass and breathed in the fresh air. She wanted to simply walk across the open field into a life filled with peace and contentment.

But she suddenly realized there was one problem from which she could not walk away. No one here needed her help. She could not turn her back on those who did.

Slowly, she turned and stepped back through the sliding doors.

QUANTUM LEVEL

THE HOSPITAL ROOM WAS quiet except for the occasional whoosh of the automatic blood pressure apparatus as it pumped up and then deflated on John's arm.

Cotten pulled the chair closer to the bed, just beyond the end of the guardrail. She rested her head on the cool sheets. The liquid light had drained every ounce of energy from her. Practice, Yachaq had told her. It would get easier. Cotten closed her eyes and slept.

* * *

When the nurse came in to check on John, the door cracked open, and the light from the hall spilled in, waking Cotten.

"How is he doing?" she asked when the nurse had completed her tasks.

"Everything looks good." The nurse paused for a moment, then asked, "He's very special to you, isn't he?"

"In so many ways," Cotten said with no hesitation.

When the nurse left, Cotten sat back in the chair and glanced down at her watch. It was midnight—six p.m. in Chicago. Lester Ripple's phone number was stored in her cell phone. She hadn't paid enough attention to what the strange little man had tried to tell her in Starbucks, but now it was becoming evident that Ripple was explaining what could very well be liquid light.

Cotten stood by the window and opened her cell. She checked and found that she had a decent signal. After scrolling to Ripple's number, she pushed the talk button. It was Saturday, so hopefully he was home and not at the university.

"Ripple here," he answered after the third ring.

It sounded as though his mouth was full. "Hello, Lester. This is Cotten Stone. We met a few days ago—the photographs? Am I interrupting your dinner?"

"Yes, yes, yes. No. I mean yes, I remember you, but no, I was just snacking. Oh my."

Cotten could picture him fumbling with a paper plate covered with something not necessarily in the government's nutrition pyramid. "I need a favor. Can you explain again about your theory, your thread theory? But remember, I'm kind of a blank slate, so keep it as simple as you can."

Cotten heard Lester gulp down a drink and then snort.

"It is very hard to understand, and almost impossible to explain. See, the rules change at the particle level. Particles don't behave the same way as larger objects. That's the first thing you have to accept. The laws that govern our everyday life don't apply in the quantum world." Ripple's words came faster and faster as he spoke.

"Okay, Lester, I think I follow you."

"Have you ever thrown a stone in a pond of water and seen the ripples spread out? Light travels like that—well, sort of—in ripples, in waves. Hmm. Hmm. Hmm. The easiest way for you to understand is to imagine throwing two rocks in the water at exactly the same time but in different places. The ripples spread out until they finally bump into each other. Then they either cancel or amplify each other. Got it?"

"Got it," Cotten said.

"I'm skipping all the heavy science stuff, so you'll have to trust me. I'm kind of taking some license so you can understand."

"All right."

"Pretend you have a machine gun and a wall in front of you with two holes, and then a second wall behind the first that will detect where every bullet hits. If you fired a few rounds through those holes, then checked the second wall, what kind of pattern do you think you would see? Where did most of the bullets hit?"

"I guess they would be clustered in two spots lined up behind the holes they went through."

"Yes, yes, yes," Lester said, sounding thrilled that she had come to the right conclusion.

"But ripples or waves wouldn't do that, would they? If light waves went through the holes, like ripples on the water, they would move forward, spread out, and interfere with each other. So if we could see where they would land on the second wall, we'd see a wave pattern, an interference pattern, not two clusters like the bullets. Right?"

"I think I'm following so far."

Lester cleared his throat. "This is good. You are going to like what's coming. Bye-bye, rules. So, you know that light travels in waves and what its pattern would look like if light passed through two holes, or slits, in a wall. But if we fired individual photons, one at a time, we wouldn't expect to see the wave pattern, we'd expect to see the bullet pattern."

"That makes sense," Cotten said, rubbing her forehead. But she still couldn't tell where Lester Ripple was going with this.

"Aha. We'd expect that a single photon would go through one hole or the other, just like a bullet. It couldn't go through two holes at one time. But guess what? Whackety, whackety, whackety. If we check the detector wall after millions of photons have been fired individually, we don't get two clusters like bullets, we get a wave or interference pattern. It's like a single photon went through both holes at the same time. Each photon was in two places at once. Are you starting to see?"

Cotten felt a hitch in her breath. Two places at once. She understood that for sure. Two Londons. Two beaches. "Yes," Cotten said. "I think I do see."

"There's more. What if we could arrange some kind of apparatus that would record which hole a photon went through? Guess what? When we do that, the photon behaves like bullets. They only go through one hole, never both at once, and their pattern on the detector wall is a cluster pattern. It's like if they know you are watching, they do what you expect—only go through one hole. It won't go through both holes if it's being observed. Everyone is puzzled how that happens on the quantum level and not in our everyday, biggie-size world. But I've discovered how big things can behave like particles in the quantum. I can prove that large objects, like bowling balls, chairs, even people, can move to other threads, that you can move—you can choose which hole you want to go through, which world you wish to exist in. And I don't mean just move your consciousness, I'm talking about *you*. All of you."

"Hang on, Lester." Cotten was breathing hard as she leaned against the glass of the window. Ripple had the scientific explanation, and she had the spiritual one. *So what is reality? Where does it exist? The only place it can—in your mind, where you create, observe, and participate in your own reality. The observation part Ripple was explaining was consciousness. It all comes down to free will, just like John said.* When John awoke, she was going to have to tell him all this. This was the secret on the tablet, she was certain. That's why part of the message on the tablet was in language and the other was equations. Physics equations. Ripple's thread theory. An old biblical quote she'd heard in her early Sunday school days resonated in her head: *The Kingdom of God is within you.*

"Ms. Stone, are you there?" Ripple asked.

"Yes," Cotten said faintly.

"There is something else you should know."

"What is that, Lester?"

"I figured out what was on the part of the tablet hidden by the glare."

Cotten held her breath.

"You wanted it to say how to stop Armageddon. You got it wrong. It says Armageddon has to happen."

CABINET CARD

On the day John was discharged—his arm still in a cast and sling—Cotten sat across from him at the oak table in her room at the Cadogan Hotel. Between them on the table were spread the items from Violet's attic.

"You sure you're up to this?" she asked.

"Never better," he said with a weak smile. "And it's not like we've got all the time in the world."

"If you get tired, just say so, okay?"

He nodded. "Yes, Doctor Stone."

She picked up Chauncey's note and read the last notation at the bottom: "The secret is protected by the word of God." Looking up, she said, "Maybe it's a clue to where he hid the tablet, or maybe the purpose of all these objects on the list. There doesn't seem to be a connection between any of these things. Maybe he had some kind of fetish, and this was his to-do list of objects to add to his collection. We really need to see what was going on in London in 1878."

"But like you said, there's no thread or theme to the list," John said. "If it were all Bibles or briarwood pipes, it would make more sense." He glanced at the list again before opening the moldy scrapbook. "This thing is about to crumble into a million pieces."

Cotten watched him gently pull back the cover. The old binding crackled as it opened for what was probably the first time in over a hundred years. She went and stood beside John, watching over his shoulder as he carefully turned one page, then the next. Notes, letters, newspaper clippings, and drawings covered the pages. Most of the sketches were in ink and depicted various parts of the anatomy, including internal organs. There were also illustrations of insects, flowers, and small animals.

"Quite an artist," she said.

"Looks like his interests were wide—botany and medical," John said. "But what was he up to in 1878? Why did he need all those things on his list?"

"Here's an article about Chauncey and his buddy Erasmus Wilson. Remember the other article we found in the attic?" It was folded in half, and Cotten helped John spread the crumbling newsprint open to read the body of the text.

John read aloud, "London dermatologist Dr. Erasmus Wilson and pulmonary specialist Dr. Chauncey Wyatt have developed a new medication they claim will reduce the symptoms of asthma, the debilitating disease that actually affects them both."

"So Chauncey was a doctor and a scientist," Cotten said.

"And a philanthropist. Remember the mystery project also mentioned in the other article? This must be what they were referring to. Says here that he and Wilson donated over twenty thousand pounds to bring an ancient Egyptian obelisk from Alexandria to London."

"Nice to have money," Cotten said. She reached for a small metal box bound by a piece of twine and untied the knot. Opening it, she carefully removed a handful of cabinet cards—paper photographs mounted on heavy card stock. On the front of each card, the photographer had his professional information along with some decorative work in the margins. Each displayed a faded sepia image of a moment in time over 130 years ago.

The first photo showed a distinguished gentleman with a long, dark beard and wire-rimmed glasses posing on the steps of a large building. Cotten turned it over. In a handwritten script similar to the list from the attic was written *Westminster Hospital, 1875.* "This must be Chauncey," she said. After examining it, she passed it to John.

The next showed the same man standing over what Cotten guessed were about a dozen bodies lying on the ground, each covered with a sheet. On the back was written *Cholera Epidemic.*

The following card showed the man in front of another large building. At his side stood a Russian wolfhound. On the back was inscribed *Christ's Hospital, Newgate with Rex.*

The last of the photographs was a tintype showing the man standing in the middle of a large group of formally dressed men and women—top hats, tails, and long flowing dresses. A white horse took up one side of the picture. Sitting atop it was a woman Cotten recognized as Alexandrine Victoria, the queen of England.

"Impressive," Cotten said. It appeared to be some sort of ceremony. Behind the group was an enormous stone monument. "This must be the Egyptian obelisk Chauncey and Wilson financed," Cotten said. "Looks like this is a picture of when they dedicated it. Must have been a big deal. Queen Victoria showed up."

Cotten was about to hand the picture to John when she realized she hadn't yet examined the back for any notation. There was a note glued to the back. As her eyes focused on the now-familiar sweeping script, she gasped.

John looked up from the album. "What is it?"

She stared at him through wide eyes. "Remember what Chauncey's note said? The one he left behind at the Vatican?"

"Yes. 'To enter the Kingdom of Heaven you must thread the needle.'"

"John, this is a picture of Chauncey Wyatt at the dedication of Cleopatra's Needle, 1878."

LOST CIVILIZATIONS

God has no religion.

—MOHANDAS GANDHI

"IT'S IN A TIME capsule," Cotten said, scrolling down the webpage on the screen of her laptop. "Chauncey must have hidden the tablet in the capsule with the other items on his list."

She had performed a Google search for Cleopatra's Needle and discovered that it was erected in 1878 on the bank of the River Thames. A time capsule had been sealed inside the monument's base containing items collected by the project's sponsors, London physicians Erasmus Wilson and Chauncey Wyatt.

"The contents of the capsule match Chauncey's list almost item for item," John said, reading off the screen as he stood behind Cotten.

"There's no mention of the tablet," Cotten said, "but then there wouldn't be. Chauncey stole the tablet. His note said that to enter the Kingdom of Heaven you have to thread the needle. He left clear clues. That's got to be where it is."

"I think we've nailed it," John said.

Cotten steepled her fingers at her lips. "Do you think we've been wrong all this time, thinking we were supposed to stop Armageddon? Is Lester Ripple right about what the tablet says, that Armageddon must happen? Is that part of the secret?"

"I've thought a lot about that," John answered. "I think Ripple is right. You can't wipe out the Apocalypse. For God to save the world from Satan's legions there must be one final battle, and He will win. When the disciples asked Jesus to teach them how to pray, He taught them the Lord's Prayer. Part of it says, 'Thy kingdom come. Thy will be done, on earth as it is in heaven.' Before God's heavenly kingdom can come to earth, first evil has to be eradicated. There is no evil in heaven."

"And what about the ability for each of us to create our world, or to exist in two places? Like my two Londons, there could be millions of Londons, but the one I want for my reality is the London at peace. For that to happen, I have to actually live the life of peace in God's image for it to become my reality."

"Cotten, I believe that this is bigger than just one religion's viewpoint. This concept of living the life you want is the basis of spirituality. Unfortunately, religions, including mine, tend to separate everyone into groups. But the concept of spirituality is a belief system and a way of life that anyone, anywhere can live."

Cotten nodded.

"Scripture teaches us that there will be a final battle some call Armageddon. And just before that event, there will be what are referred to as trying times. God doesn't want us to have to live through all the misery—the misery directly caused by Satan. And it doesn't matter what you call God—Allah, Shang Ti, Krishna, Theos, the Light, Om, the Creator, or whatever. He wants us to know that He has provided so we can, by choice, by the free will He gave us, choose another path, another life. He told Noah how to escape the Flood. Why would He not tell us how to escape the End of Days?"

"Then that explains what happened to the people who lived in the lost city in Peru, or the ones in the New Mexico ruins, and all those ancient civilizations that received a tablet and then seemed to vanish overnight. They interpreted the secret and moved on."

"Why not? What other explanation is there?"

"Then when we find the tablet, it will say that we can do the same by believing it, willing it, existing in it. Reality is what we choose it to be. The same as Ripple's quantum thread theory. This is what we have to share with the world. This is what Chauncey meant by it belonging to the whole world."

John took one of Cotten's hands. "Yes, and led by the daughter of an angel."

* * *

A crisp wind blew down the River Thames, bringing with it the distant sound of sirens echoing throughout the city as emergency vehicles responded to the ever-increasing suicides. Cotten tucked her hands into her overcoat as she stood next to John on the Victoria Embankment. They both stared up at the Egyptian obelisk known as Cleopatra's Needle.

The platform on which the monument rested was located along the riverbank between the Westminster and Waterloo bridges. It was late afternoon, and a handful of Londoners wandered along the Embankment sidewalks.

"There are two obelisks, you know," John said, holding open the Fodor's London guidebook. "One here, and its twin in Central Park in New York. Let's hope we've got the right one."

"This is the only one connected to Chauncey Wyatt—it has to be the one."

Cotten walked around the monument. Each of the four sides of its base was adorned with a large bronze plaque. The surface of the obelisk displayed carved hieroglyphics, and the bottom was wrapped in a collar of winged Egyptian gods. Cotten read each plaque; together they told the history of the monument from when it and its twin were first quarried by the pharaoh Thothmes III around 1500 BC. Both obelisks were moved two centuries later to stand in front of the Caesarium Temple in Alexandria. Cleopatra's Needle was brought to London by Wilson and Wyatt and presented to the British nation in 1878 while the twin, sponsored by another group, went to New York.

Completing her journey around the base, back to her starting point, Cotten said, "Learn anything more in your travel guide?"

"I think you'll find this interesting," John said. "One of the reasons this obelisk is preserved so well is that it stayed buried under the desert sand for over six hundred years after it was toppled by an earthquake. As a matter of fact, because of that, it was referred to as . . ."

"As what?" Cotten said, staring at John.

"You're not going to believe this."

"I'm ready," she said, half-expecting a goofy answer.

"It was called 'the fallen one.'"

Taking that as an omen, Cotten circled the obelisk, dragging her fingers along the pedestal as she stared up at the needle. An expression of wonder came over her face. "This is it," she said. Then, with a look of satisfaction, Cotten pulled the cell phone from her pocket, scrolled through the names, and pressed talk. A moment later, she said, "Ted, I think we've found it. Are you ready to do this?"

THE BROADCAST

"We haven't gotten permission to open the time capsule yet," Cotten said into her phone. "We need to hold off on the broadcast until we get our hands on the tablet. And the network isn't going to approve what I have to say without it."

"All SNN needs to know is that you're doing a report on the suicides."

Cotten sighed. "Ted, you could be out on your ear if you do this. Let's just wait until we have the artifact."

"We can't," Ted said. "There's not a second to waste. The rate of suicides is escalating constantly."

"The authorities only need another day or two to clear up the red tape for us to open the base of the monument and remove the capsule."

"People need some thin fiber to hold on to, Cotten. You can give them that. Tell them what is happening so they understand—and give them hope. We'll cover the removal of the capsule when the time comes—a live remote, right on location at Cleopatra's Needle."

"But what if the tablet is not there?"

"You know it will be. It has to be."

"Ted, you're the one who's been warning me all along the way to—"

"It's different now. The creation fossil was a setup to ruin you. This is different. God has led you to it. You're the one, kiddo. The only one."

* * *

Cotten waited for her cue from the floor manager. In a moment, she would be live on SNN. Ted had managed to pull it all together in just two days. Cotten looked around the studio, watching the dozens of crew members working out the last-minute glitches before going to air. John sat in a chair in the shadows beyond the cameras, two Venatori agents at his side. He gave her a thumbs-up.

The floor manager held up five fingers, then counted down and pointed to Cotten.

"Welcome to a special report on the increasing rate of suicides throughout the world. I'm Cotten Stone, reporting for the Satellite News Network."

"Cue graphics," the UK director said in the control room overlooking the sound stage. Beside him, the technical director punched up the graphics feed on the on-air digital video switcher.

Over Cotten's shoulder on the monitor, the words "Global Crisis: Suicides" appeared in a red font that looked a lot like blood.

"We're broadcasting from the SNN studios in London, where just today the wife of the prime minister took her own life with an overdose of painkillers."

"Ready PM's wife," the director said. "Go." He pointed to the number three preview monitor.

A recent picture of the prime minister's wife waving to onlookers at a school-dedication ceremony appeared behind Cotten, dissolving to a grainy still shot of a hearse parked in front of Number 10 Downing Street.

"Tonight, we're going to bring you an in-depth report on the unprecedented escalation in suicides occurring throughout the UK, the United States, and virtually every other nation on the globe."

"Chyron, ready stats?" The director snapped his fingers. "Go." The operator of the chyron character generator started the playback of a series of electronic charts representing the rise in global suicide rates.

"Despite a denial from the International Psychiatric Foundation and other medical organizations that there is any correlation between the increase in suicide rates and a possible link to demonic possession, we are faced with the fact that the numbers don't lie." Cotten paused while a series of statistics broken down by countries scrolled on the screen.

"The Vatican announced that it has empowered all its priests throughout the world to begin the difficult task of performing exorcisms on persons displaying suicidal tendencies. The announcement came from the pontiff himself in a news conference from the Vatican State Palace, where there is grave concern that we, as a civilization, are in dire peril from the influence of evil throughout the world."

"B roll, ready?" With a snap of his fingers, the director pointed at the on-air monitor. "Go."

A collage of footage showing emergency personnel attending the victims in various foreign countries appeared, replacing Cotten.

"It seems," she said, "that this alarming phenomenon does not show prejudice or discrimination. The victims of the widespread suicides vary from the ultra rich and famous, like the queen and her immediate family here in the UK, to homeless persons living in the shadows of our great cities."

"Cue C roll—homeless in Moscow." The director motioned to the bank of preview monitors, and the technical director readied his finger over the button. "Now."

In a room a few doors down from the control room, an electronic relay clicked, and the images played back live to air.

"Something evil is moving across our land, our cities, our world. It is taking our loved ones and friends away from us. Stealing their lives and their souls." Cotten paused.

"I've come here tonight to tell you about what I believe is a message from our Creator, a message written by the hand of Almighty God. And I hope that I will be able to give you cause for optimism that the dark days we are living in will soon change."

"What the fuck?" the director said. "What is she doing?"

Across the Atlantic in the New York SNN master control center, the VP of broadcasting said, "Casselman, what the shit is going on?"

Ted Casselman watched the massive bank of monitors as he felt the pressure building in his chest. If this didn't ignite a full-scale heart attack, nothing would. "I don't know, sir," he said. "I'm sure she'll get back on script." He wished he had the nitro pills that he'd left back in his briefcase.

Cotten continued. "I've chosen this moment to tell all watching that there may be an answer to what is occurring around us. I believe that secretly hidden away somewhere in this city is the last of twelve crystal tablets. Each was given to great spiritual leaders of the world many thousands of years ago."

"Mother of God," the technical director whispered into the intercom system.

"What in the hell is she talking about?" the New York VP said, staring at the TelePrompTer feed.

Cotten looked directly into the camera lens. "The purpose of each tablet was to deliver a message from the Creator that not only predicted the first universal cleansing of the earth in the time of Noah, but also contained an additional message meant for a world far into the future. The future is here. And so is the End of Days. Armageddon is upon us. We can't stop it, for if we do, then they will win. The evil that is sweeping across our world must be wiped away by the hand of God. The last battle has to take place for good to triumph over evil. It is the evil ones who want to stop Armageddon, because that is the only way they will triumph. And I believe that written on the last tablet is the secret to surviving the final battle, the second cleansing, just like Noah survived the Flood."

"That's it," the UK director said. "Get ready to cut away. Cue commercial block number one."

"Get the fucking bitch off!" the New York VP yelled. "Go to a commercial!"

"Wait!" Ted Casselman stared at the wall of monitors.

"What do you mean, wait?" the VP said. "She's in la-la land with this Armageddon bullshit. I told you that putting her back on the air would be a major mistake. Now do you believe me?"

Cotten hurried. She knew they were about to cut her off and she had to finish before they did. "Each tablet revealed a means, a secret, to see and choose a path in life that will take us to a better world. A choice that precedes a cleansing just like the one our ancestors experienced, the Flood that swept away the evil of their world. I believe that we, too, can escape the last cleansing, escape the horrors of the final days that will rid the world of evil. The crystal tablet will tell us how to do that."

"Look!" Casselman said, pointing to the network feeds.

The VP followed Ted's eyes and glanced at the rows of monitors displaying other international programming. "My God, what's happening?"

CNN, BBC, NBC, ABC, CBS, and Fox, along with networks in China, Brazil, India, South Africa, and a dozen others were systematically switching over to the live SNN broadcast. Even Al-Jazeera was displaying Cotten Stone with closed-captioning in Arabic along the bottom of the screen.

"They're all taking our feed," Ted said.

"The message was understood by the mighty civilizations of Atlantis, the Druids who built Stonehenge, the people who built the moais of Easter Island, the southern Maya civilization, the Mali of western Africa, the Anasazi—all vanished overnight without a trace. They vanished because they heeded the message on their tablets and chose a path to a new life. One that we can choose as well. All we need to do is believe. It doesn't matter if you are Hindu, Jewish, Buddhist, Christian, Muslim. We can no longer box ourselves into cells of organized religious groups that turn their focus on the messenger rather than the message. We are all connected to each other and every living thing. We are one and must stand up to the evil around us."

The New York VP slumped in his chair as he watched the international news organizations switch to his network. He whispered, "I've never seen anything like this."

The London director said into his headphone mic, "The whole world is watching us. Don't anybody touch a fucking thing or I'll personally rip your heart out."

TWO EMBANKMENTS

The Kingdom of God is within you.

—LUKE 17:21

THE RESPONSE TO THE SNN broadcast had been phenomenal, and with the news that there would be a live broadcast at the obelisk, thousands had flocked to London.

To avoid traffic jams, and for added security, Cotten would arrive by boat: a small riverboat used for tour groups had been rented and secretly hidden away until the last moment. As darkness fell, a car driven by a Venatori agent arrived at the back entrance of the Cadogan Hotel and whisked Cotten and John through side streets to a dock a half mile from the monument. When the SNN crew radioed that they were in place, Cotten and John boarded the boat for the short ride to the monument.

As they rounded the bend in the River Thames and passed under the Waterloo Bridge, Cotten gasped. There before her was the obelisk, ablaze from a wall of media floodlights. It reminded her of a space shuttle illuminated just before a night launch. Cleopatra's

Needle was pointing like an arrow straight to the heavens. That was more than appropriate, she thought.

But what caused Cotten to catch her breath were the masses of people gathered along the Victoria Embankment. John had warned that once the word got out, she could expect a crowd of curiosity seekers. But before her, in a wall of faces and bodies that seemed to stretch endlessly in all directions, were thousands of people. Savoy Place, Strand, Fleet Street, Whitehall—all a sea of bodies packed tightly together. As she looked over her shoulder at the Waterloo, she realized that traffic had been replaced with people leaning over the bridge's railings to catch a glimpse of her. Even farther down the river, the Westminster Bridge was packed, bringing city traffic to a halt. Across the water from the Needle, the Jubilee Gardens and the banks of the Thames in both directions were covered by throngs of observers, as were the rooftops and windows of the buildings lining the streets beyond the Embankment—all awaiting Cotten Stone.

As the boat approached the steps that led from the river up the embankment to Cleopatra's Needle, a bank of camera lights swung toward Cotten, and a deafening roar filled the air.

Police constables had kept the concrete steps at the water's edge clear for her and had roped off a small area surrounding the obelisk. With John grasping her arm to help her balance, Cotten climbed the damp steps to the landing at the base of the Needle.

A flash from above made Cotten look up. Tempest Star and Bennie had crossed the ropes to get a close shot of her. A constable responded, ushering them away.

Stepping on the landing, a reporter thrust a microphone in her hand. She was pleased to see that it displayed a Satellite News Network logo around its neck.

Cotten held the mic close to her lips and said, "Hello."

What happened next sent a shudder through her. Her voice filled the air from every direction, echoing along the river and across the city. It appeared that almost everyone present had a portable radio or cell phone that was receiving the media simulcast of the event.

Cotten sucked in her breath in amazement as she heard the sound come back at her from thousands of tiny speakers lining the streets, sidewalks, and pathways of the London riverfront.

As the cheers of the crowd died down, Cotten said, "I can't believe there are so many of you." This caused the crowd to again swell up in applause. But she knew it was not applause of joy, but more of apprehension. Most were here out of desperation. The weight of responsibility upon her was immense as she heard scattered pleas for help and prayers for mercy.

"I understand why you came here tonight, and why so many more are listening and watching in other places. I hope that tonight we can end the pain, the darkness, the evil that moves among us."

The cheers rose again as Cotten's voice reverberated along the parks and paths of the Embankment.

A flutter of panic shot electricity down her arms. What if the tablet wasn't inside the time capsule? What would happen to all these people?

* * *

Eli Luddington watched the SNN broadcast on the large plasma display in his library office. Beside him, Mariah stood with her hand on his shoulder. She felt so fulfilled, so complete. Eli had informed her that she would soon see the signs of new life within her.

She had been chosen by him to continue his legacy with a child who would follow in his footsteps. Even now, it grew inside her. She was privileged and blessed, he said. Few received the honor of being the vessel for the next generation of the great Nephilim. For her, it no longer mattered if Richard returned or not. She had changed her mind. Her plan was eclipsed by Eli's great vision. She touched her abdomen. This was Eli's child, and with that came the windfall of miraculous benefits.

"This will be so fitting an end to the thorn in our side," Eli said as the cameras zoomed in for a close-up of Cotten Stone greeting the crowd with the priest at her side. "She will watch as the one who matters the most to her falls even as she goes down in disgrace. The blood of millions will be on her tonight, but the blood of John Tyler will stain her hands forever."

He smiled at Mariah. "Revenge has the sweetest taste."

* * *

The thunder of applause shook the foundation of the platform beneath Cleopatra's Needle. As it died away, Cotten nodded to the pair of London city engineers who had come with them on the riverboat. The men proceeded up the steep tier of steps and stood in front of one of the four large plaques mounted on the base of the obelisk. Using large wrenches, they loosened the bronze bolts holding the four corners of the plaque and slid it away.

The removal of the plaque exposed a square cavity. A dozen video news reporters moved in. With great care, the two engineers removed a wooden chest.

* * *

Richard Hapsburg maneuvered his way through the crowd until he was a few yards from the Needle. He saw Cotten Stone standing beside John Tyler and watching the engineers remove the time capsule. A twinge of shame chilled him. He had gone back to Eli, asking for another chance. Though he wanted to, he couldn't muster the same kind of courage that Cotten's father, Furmiel, had. Richard felt the weight of the SIG-Sauer in his jacket pocket. He avoided the perimeter of the floodlights, slipping forward until he was by the river's edge and there was nothing between him and John Tyler.

* * *

Cotten watched the engineers gingerly hold the chest between them as they made their way down the steps. She wondered what Chauncey Wyatt would think if he were present to witness the completion of his secret task. Tonight, in this spot along the River Thames, the mission of the Shadows of Ghosts would finally end. Chauncey could rest in peace, she thought.

They set the chest at her feet, and Cotten waited while John made the sign of the cross and blessed it. Cotten felt her heart flow over with excitement as she realized she was fulfilling her destiny this night on the banks of the historic river. She glanced around, trying to take in the magical event. As her eyes fell on the distant bend in the river, all her excitement vanished, replaced with dread and fear. In the distance, a mist appeared over the water, moving toward the Needle.

"Oh my God," she said, before realizing the microphone was still at her lips.

John turned to her. "What?"

Cotten looked in the opposite direction along the Embankment and saw the mist rolling across the water. It came from both directions toward them.

* * *

Richard reached inside his jacket and gripped the pistol. It felt cold and heavy. He remembered how awkward it was in his hand when he had fired from the car in D.C. This should be easier tonight. He'd finally conceded and accepted his life as it was. Oh, he'd been weak over the last several days, thinking he might beg God's forgiveness. Like Furmiel. Richard had come just short of getting on his knees before coming to his senses. After all, why would he be shown mercy?

* * *

"Open the chest!" Cotten screamed.

"What is it, Cotten?" John said.

"They're coming." She pointed toward the river. "We have no time."

John glanced down the river.

"It's only river fog," one of the engineers said. "Nothing to be concerned with, missy. Happens all the time."

"Just open the chest!" she cried, her voice breaking.

One of the engineers broke the latch, and with a rusty squeak, the man raised the lid.

Cotten crouched and rummaged through the contents. Papers, maps, books, documents, tobacco pipes, pictures. "Dear God, where is it?" *It's not here*, she thought. *What if I was wrong and the world is watching?*

Cotten glanced back at the river, hoping the mist would have dissipated. But it had grown fiercer, blocking out the sight of the bridges. She could no longer see the opposite bank of the river. Looking in each direction along the Embankment, she watched the crowds of onlookers vanish into the thickening mist. She would not be able to save anyone. Even if she found the tablet and it confirmed everything she believed it would, there would be no time. How could she teach all these people about the liquid light in a matter of seconds?

* * *

Lester Ripple lay on his bed, staring up at the plastic glow-in-the-dark stars. He closed his eyes and thought of Cotten Stone, wondering what she was doing tonight. Did she really understand what he had tried to teach her? In her own way, she seemed to be more in touch with the power grid than even he was. There was something about her. Something different. Maybe someday they could meet again at Starbucks and have a latte. She seemed to be intrigued by all the science. She had a problem, and he helped solve it. The least she could do was have a latte with him, even if he didn't drink coffee. After all, he was a problem solver. Solve, solve, solve.

* * *

She dragged out books, including four Bibles. Chauncey had written in his note that the tablet was protected by the word of God. Cotten started to reach into the chest again, but then she suddenly returned to the Bibles. That was it! The secret was protected by the word of God. The Bible!

"Which one, which one," she said, opening the first one, then tossing it aside. She gripped the largest—a leather-bound Bible—and yanked it away from the other time capsule items. It was heavy, too heavy. Cotten pulled the book into the brilliance of the camera lights.

It was then that she heard the crowd start to react to the mist. Clutching the large volume to her chest, she looked along the Embankment and saw what she feared the most—what she had prayed would not come.

Like twinkling stars in the twilight of night, the fireflies came.

First a few, then hundreds. Soon the Embankment became ablaze in their glow.

They emerged from the mist and swirled around the tip of the Needle, fanning out across the Embankment and the river, rushing toward the throngs of people.

Panic swept the crowd.

Somehow Cotten also knew they were swarming not just along the banks of the river, but also across the towns and cities where millions listened and watched.

* * *

Richard clutched the gun in his pocket. He felt the dampness of the mist as it rolled off the water. He heard the buzz of his brothers approaching. What if this Stone woman was right? What if this was the beginning of the end for him and his kind? He was tired. Exhausted. Maybe he would actually welcome the end. He had no zeal anymore. Mariah had left him. Eli had no respect for him.

Richard lifted the automatic and aimed at the priest. It was going to be a clean shot, no obstacles to block it. His finger tightened on the trigger. "Squeeze," he whispered.

But he couldn't.

For the first time, he realized the enormity of the transgression he had made eons ago. And maybe now he understood the meaning of eternal damnation.

Richard turned back to the river and, with a flick of his wrist, tossed the gun into the dark, swirling waters of the Thames. He fell to his knees.

* * *

Cotten ripped apart the strands of twine holding the Bible together. The book fell open. There, hidden in a cut-out, was the crystal tablet.

She grasped it in both hands and stood.

The sound of the swarm increased to a roar. Like a blast furnace, the heat from the demons scorched her skin. The scent of sulfur filled her nostrils. She heard the screams of the people succumbing to the onslaught.

"Oh God, help me." Her words echoed across the Embankment and along the river at her back. "Help me to see, to hear."

She knew that there was little time left before the demons swept up the souls of all present. The believers had come to see the tablet, to witness the handwriting of God. As she held it in her hand, she looked at the inscription. The words were written in Enochian—the tongue of the angels, the language of heaven.

The language of her heritage.

Scanning the words, her gaze fell upon the reference to the final cleansing.

"Cotten?" John said.

Quickly she translated in her head. "Ripple was right." She turned to John. "It says that Armageddon has to happen." As she read on, she realized that Edelman had misinterpreted the ancient glyphs on the Peruvian tablet. In Enochian, it became so clear to her. And at the bottom of the tablet, the portion that no one understood, were brackets and symbols and numbers—Lester Ripple's thread theory, his scientific proof that *the Kingdom of God is within you*. Suddenly, it all made sense. But she had no time to explain to those gathered before her or the millions watching around the world.

Cotten looked up. "John, it doesn't say the second cleansing will be led by the daughter of an angel. It says that the daughter of an angel will lead them away."

She realized that even Chauncey had gotten it wrong. The message on the tablet wasn't meant for the world, it was meant for her. The last secret was not just a reference about her, it was a message from God *to* her.

Suddenly, she knew she had the power to defeat the demons. It had been there all along.

She understood.

She wasn't going to teach everyone liquid light. She had to create the reality—her consciousness would exist in the new world and her consciousness would have all these people there. It would be by their free will which world they chose as their reality.

She would lead them away from the pain, the suffering, the darkness.

Cotten grasped the tablet firmly and held it higher. The mass of people reacted with a plea for help.

The blinding light of the fireflies reflected off the surface of the crystal and shone back across the Embankment in rainbow spears. The reflection pushed against the brilliance of the fireflies with a powerful force that seemed to halt their advance for an instant.

In that second, Cotten became totally immersed in the liquid light. She blocked out the roar and the crippling heat of the demons. Her senses became acutely aware of what lay before her, and she suddenly envisioned two Embankments. The first was amassed with thousands of souls reaching out to her in desperation, holding on to their last moment of life. The second was a scene of tranquility and calm as fall-colored leaves fluttered in the crisp breeze. The massive crowds were there as well, but each face bore an expression of content, happiness, and peace. Ripples on the river sparkled in bright sunlight like diamonds under a blue sky. The air was fresh and sweet. The city glistened. This was the reality she chose for herself, and she would put them all—all those who would come—in her reality.

She must lead the way and take those who believed with her. Knowing this was the moment—there would be no other—she gripped the crystal tablet and stepped onto the second Embankment.

ALLIGATOR LAKE

There are two ways to live your life. One is as though nothing is a miracle. The other is as though everything is a miracle.

—ALBERT EINSTEIN

COTTEN LOOKED OUT THE window across the water. Being at Thomas Wyatt's cottage brought her much peace. The ever-changing surface of the lake, almost like a living creature, mesmerized her. Everything about it calmed her soul.

The perfect place to make the biggest decision of her life.

She walked out onto the porch and took a sip of the warm tea from the heavy mug she held. Winter had invaded the remote North Florida woods with invigorating cold air. Cotten didn't mind. The crispness of the cold felt good—clean and fresh.

She heard the sound of tires crunching along the gravel entrance road as a car approached through the pine forest. Cotten wandered to the end of the porch and watched the Mercedes sedan pull up beneath one of the many giant oaks scattered across the fifty acres of backwoods. Monsignor Philip Duchamp opened the driver's door and got out. He gave her a friendly wave before pulling the handle of the side door.

John Tyler emerged from the car and waved to her as well. "Is this the place?" he asked as they approached the porch.

"This is it," Cotten said, smiling. She wrapped her arms around him as he stood on the porch. Before stepping back, she kissed him lightly on the cheek. "So now it's Your Eminence, Cardinal John Tyler." She gave a bow and smiled broadly.

"Just clawing my way up the corporate ladder," John said.

"And Monsignor," Cotten said. "As ever, it's good to see you." She motioned to the door. "Gentlemen, glad you could make it. What can I get you two? Hot chocolate or green tea?"

"Hot chocolate would be great," Duchamp said.

"The same," John said as he and the monsignor chose two chairs around the dinette set.

Duchamp picked up a newspaper from the table and read the headline: "International Peace Accords Signed." He smiled before continuing aloud. "Treaties are being drafted and confirmed around the globe as world leaders choose new paths to peace." He looked at Cotten and then John. "Who would have thought this day would come?"

"If anyone ever doubted miracles," John said, "there's the proof."

Cotten set two steaming mugs of hot chocolate on the table and took a seat opposite the two men.

"I am still amazed at what happened, Cotten," Duchamp said.

She sipped her green tea before speaking. "I never realized that I had been in training since the day I arrived in Peru until the moment I stood on the Victoria Embankment. In that instant, Yachaq's words came back to me. He told me that just as there are many paths in the forest leading to different destinations, all the paths of life lie before us each day, each minute—we simply choose which to follow. He taught me to see with new eyes. Standing at the base of Cleopatra's Needle, I knew what I had to do. I had to choose a new path for all those who were ready. I chose for them to be a part of my reality in this place."

"Sort of like changing lanes on the expressway," Duchamp said, "and having everyone behind you shift into your lane, too?"

"Exactly," Cotten said with a nod. "Now everyone has a fresh chance to choose new directions in life, but without the immediate threat of the evil that was devouring innocent souls right before our eyes."

"It doesn't mean there's always going to be clear sailing ahead. Evil still exists," John said. "But whether we call it the power of intention, the law of attraction, liquid light, whatever—all we have to understand is that all possibilities already exist, and everyone has the ability to do what Cotten did. Make good choices, walk the right paths, and the final reward will be the Kingdom of Heaven."

Duchamp placed the paper on the table. "I suppose the big question is, what happens next?"

"And that's why we're here today," John said.

"What do you mean?" Duchamp asked.

"In the world we left, Satan and his army have found a strong foothold," John said. "There are still so many who were left behind who deserve to be spared."

"And we have a limited amount of time to do so," Cotten said. "God's message declared that there will be a final cleansing to wash away evil forever."

John rested his mug on the arm of the chair. "The secret must be offered to those left behind before the End of Days occurs."

Suddenly, Duchamp seemed to understand as he looked at Cotten. "So, do you stay here, where peace could last a thousand years, or return to help those who face an impending End of Days?" He hesitated, drumming his fingertips on the table in apparent thought.

Cotten said, "John, would you like to take a walk?"

"I would love to." He rose and looked at the monsignor. "We might be a while."

With a knowing glance, Duchamp picked up the newspaper. "Take all the time you need, Your Eminence."

Cotten and John went out onto the porch and down to the dock extending over the lake in front of the cottage. They walked to the end and stood in silence, gazing toward the far shore. The black water lapped against the pilings, and a breeze stirred the surface just enough so that a small skiff tied to the end piling bobbed gently.

"I've decided to go back," Cotten said.

"I knew you would. And I'm going with you."

"No," she said, turning to John and touching his face with her palm. "You should stay here. I *must* go, but you don't have to. There are so many here who need your faith, your guidance, your wisdom. You can teach them."

"I realize that, Cotten, but you're not the only one God speaks to. I get a message or two from him now and then. The people in this world already understand. Look at the headlines in today's paper," John said. "And Duchamp can take care of the needs here."

"I know he can. It's just that if anything should happen to you because of me . . ."

The wind blew Cotten's hair in her face. John brushed it back and threaded it behind her ear. "Do you really want to return without me?" he asked, taking her hand.

She smiled. "No."

"Then it's settled."

She lowered her eyes and stared down at the water. She had something else to say to him, but didn't know if she had the courage. *Just do it, Cotten,* she thought. *Just look up and say it.*

But she didn't have to look up on her own. John put his hand under her chin and lifted her head. "What's wrong?" he asked.

Cotten opened her mouth but couldn't force the words.

John cocked his head as if to ask again what was wrong.

"John," she started, then paused before speaking again. "When you had the accident in London, I was afraid that I would lose you forever, and I felt sick and angry with myself."

"It wasn't your fault."

"Well, I'll always feel it was my fault, but that's not what I'm talking about. There was another reason I felt that way. Because of something I hadn't done . . . hadn't said." She wavered, then finally spoke. "I want you to know that I love you."

He took her in his arms. "I know. I've always known. And you know that I love you, too."

They held each other for a long time before finally stepping apart and again looking toward the distant horizon.

"So, shall we?" Cotten asked.

"We shall," John said.

She closed her eyes and began their immersion into the liquid light.

* * *

Inside the cabin, Monsignor Philip Duchamp glanced up from the newspaper. The evening brought a gathering darkness across the lake, the growing shadows masking the far shore. He could barely make out the skiff lazily swaying on its tether at the end of the empty pier. Duchamp stared for a moment at the serenity of the scene before returning to his reading.

Read on for an excerpt from the next
Cotten Stone Mystery by Lynn Sholes & Joe Moore

Indigo Ruby

COMING SOON FROM MIDNIGHT INK

THREAT LEVEL

THE MOON SHONE DOWN on the stone courtyard like a pale spotlight over the opening of a drama. It cast a powder blue hue across the cold marble sanctuary.

Candles flickered in the night air, their flames protected by high, ivy-covered walls. Their light cast a warm glow upon the circle carved in the smooth stone floor.

Rizben Mace stood in the middle of the circle, the five points of the pentagram shooting out from his bare feet like blades of an ancient weapon. Underneath his black robe, he was naked. The rustle of the cool satin against his skin aroused him.

Two dozen figures, torches in hand and cloaked in black like Mace, ringed the courtyard. Kneeling before him were six robed children, their faces hidden beneath their hoods.

Holding a gold cup of wine in one hand and a jewel-encrusted dagger in the other, Mace said, "I call upon Samael, the Guardian of the Gate."

In unison, the children intoned, "Samael."

A finger of high vapor clouds drifted across the moon.

"I call upon Azazel, the Guardian of the Flame," Mace said, "the Spark in the Eye of the Great Darkness."

Again, the small voices spoke, "Azazel."

The torches seemed to brighten.

"I call upon the Light of the Air, the Son of the Dawn."

"Son of the Dawn," the children repeated.

A hot breath of wind swooped down and swirled around the perimeter of the courtyard, causing the robes of each shadowy figure to furl about their forms.

Mace held the dagger and the golden cup in outstretched hands. The flames reflected off the polished metal, causing it to appear as if fire burned from within. "In the name of your mighty sword and the flowing life blood that gives you the power to conquer, enter into the minds, hearts, and souls of these young warriors and fill them with your terrible and crushing strength."

Mace lifted his arms high, and the children stood, forming a single line. Each in turn kissed the blade of the dagger and took a sip from the chalice. When all had done so, they returned to their places and pulled back their hoods to reveal their young faces.

Mace opened his arms in a sweeping gesture. "Oh great Son of the Dawn, behold, the new soldiers of your vanquishing army."

* * *

Rizben Mace stepped out of the temple lodge and down the three levels of narrow steps onto the sidewalk. It was always such a jarring transition, he thought, going from the medieval courtyard hidden deep in the heart of the building out into the harsh glare of the Washington, D.C., streetlights. And from his ceremonial robes back into a suit.

Mace reached in his pocket and took his cell phone off vibrate. The text message he had received earlier during the ceremony had forced him to rush through the ancient ritual.

Standing on the sidewalk, he glanced to his right at the Sphinx-like granite lion guarding the entrance. It had a woman's head with a cobra entwining its neck. Its matching sister stood guard to his left. His limousine waited at curbside, where a Secret Service agent held the door open. A black Suburban with a forest of rooftop antennae sat poised like a timber wolf in front of the limo. Two police cruisers, one at the front of the small caravan and one at the rear, were at the ready, their blue and red strobes casting a hypnotic glow on the tall bronze temple entrance behind him.

Mace slipped into the back of the limo, and the heavy, armored door shut with a bank-vault thud. Immediately, the caravan pulled away—sirens screaming, engines racing. The acceleration pushed him into the plush leather seat as he glanced at his watch. A few minutes past 11:00 p.m.

"What do we have, Dan?" Mace asked his advisor.

"About an hour ago," Dan Turner said, "we received word of a significant increase in cyber intrusions on a global scale. The Internet is down in parts of Asia and Africa, and it's spreading across Europe. Three-quarters of our worldwide monitoring stations are experiencing simultaneous attacks, and over four hundred thousand servers have been infected and shut down."

"Is it just the Internet?"

"So far."

"What are the source addresses?" Mace asked.

"Mostly from China. A few in Malaysia."

"Random targets, or a focused assault?"

Turner looked at his notes. "It looks random. But it's huge."

"Has anyone told the boss?" Mace asked.

"Not yet."

"Make the call, Dan." Mace rubbed his face. He could still smell the smoke from the torches and taste the faint sweetness of the wine on his lips. "I'm going to recommend raising the threat level to orange for specific infrastructure. No reason to get the general public in an uproar."

"I agree, sir," Turner said. He picked up one of several phones from the communications console and pushed a speed-dial number. In a moment he said, "The secretary of Homeland Security is calling for the president."

Lynn Sholes (Florida) leads fiction workshops and trains educators in teaching writing. This is her eighth novel.

Joe Moore (Florida) has worked in television for twenty-five years and won two regional Emmy awards.